# heliopolis

Also by James Scudamore

The Amnesia Clinic

# heliopolis

## James Scudamore

HARVILL SECKER LONDON

Published by Harvill Secker 2009

4 6 8 10 9 7 5 3

First published in Great Britain in 2009 by
HARVILL SECKER
Random House, 20 Vauxhall Bridge Road
London SW1V 2SA

www.rbooks.co.uk

Addresses for companies within The Random House Group Limited
can be found at: www.randomhouse.co.uk/offices.htm

The Random House Group Limited Reg. No. 954009

A CIP catalogue record for this book
is available from the British Library

ISBN 9781846551888

The Random House Group Limited supports The Forest Stewardship
Council (FSC), the leading international forest certification organisation. All our titles
that are printed on Greenpeace approved FSC certified paper carry the FSC logo.
Our paper procurement policy can be found at www.rbooks.co.uk/environment

**Mixed Sources**
Product group from well-managed
forests and other controlled sources
www.fsc.org  Cert no. TT-COC-2139
© 1996 Forest Stewardship Council

FSC

Set in Dante MT by Palimpsest Book Production Limited,
Grangemouth, Stirlingshire

Printed in Great Britain by
Clays Ltd, St Ives plc

To Rose

'Rio is a beauty. But São Paulo – São Paulo is a *city*.'
— Marlene Dietrich

# Orange Juice

It's early, not yet seven a.m., and once again I'm waking up beside my adoptive sister.

This has got to stop. She's a married woman.

The air-conditioning is on high, and my head feels like it's immersed in freezing water, even though Melissa's body is cleaving to mine wherever it can, making me hot and clammy beneath the covers. I sit up, and reach for the remote control that operates the blinds. They track smoothly upwards and the city, bile yellow, pours in from every direction.

Melissa's penthouse is at the head of a long avenue that bisects the Garden District straight through to the smog-cloaked towers of downtown. From up here you look down on the treetops and the green parakeets that flit between them. At night gridlocked traffic lights up the avenue in glittering ribbons of red and white. During big football matches, when a goal is scored, the fireworks burst silently beneath you.

I stretch and lie back to think of more ways in which I could mark Ernesto's territory, to see if he'd latch on to the fact that I'm sleeping with his wife. You'd think he'd have noticed something by now: whenever these stopovers take place I find myself brushing his body hairs from the bed before I get in it, so I must be leaving a few of my own, and I make a habit of draining every half-glass of water he leaves on the bedside table. But he hasn't. So I'm taking bigger risks. I sit in his dressing gown reading his diary on the computer when Melissa's in the shower, and altering it here and there if I feel I've been unfairly represented. I drink his wine. I eat his leftovers. I use his toothbrush. I've even written him messages on the bathroom mirror with my finger in the hope that they might shimmer into view next time he has a shave. But so far, he hasn't a clue. He's too busy out saving the rest of the world to notice that he's losing his wife.

I'm thinking these ignoble thoughts about Ernesto, touching the back of his wife's neck and trying to make her move so her nipple will brush against my chest, when the sound of a helicopter directly overhead deals a defibrillator jolt to my heart.

Melissa's father, Zé Fischer Carnicelli, hasn't been down to street level in the city for over fifteen years. He lives in a gated community of 30,000 inhabitants, way out of town, and is flown from there to his downtown office every morning in a helicopter that has the word *Predator* painted graffiti-style over its nose, along with gnashing teeth and a pair of evil yellow eyes. He's approaching retirement, but he still keeps regular office hours. A chauffeur drives him between his house and the heliport, then back again in the evening. During the day, he might hop to another high-rise to meet someone for lunch, or to attend an afternoon meeting, but he never touches the pavement. It's not just a question of safety: if he went by car he could get snared in a traffic jam lasting hours. Nobody who's anybody gets driven to work in the city these days.

On his way, he's delighted to pick up Melissa and deposit her at her office. He doesn't see as much of his daughter as he'd like now that she is married, and this way he gets to spend the first few minutes of his day with her as they speed over the boiling, stationary traffic. Because Melissa's penthouse is directly under the helipad, he doesn't even need to phone ahead: she sees the helicopter coming and hears it rumbling on the roof, which gives her just enough time to take a slurp of coffee, grab her keys, and rush upstairs to kiss her Papai good morning.

Being found in bed with Melissa by her father is a far more terrifying prospect than getting caught by her husband. If Zé walked in now, my life would end – it's that simple.

'Relax. It's not him.' Melissa stirs, and detaches her lips from the hollow beneath my jaw. 'It's too early, you know that.' She squirms gorgeously on my leg, naked and hot.

'Ernesto?'

'When did Ernesto ever fly? Don't move.' Her hand strays into my hair, placating me as gently as possible so she doesn't have to wake up.

She's right about the helicopter. The sound of blades beating overhead soon recedes. I lie still for a further half-hour, pretending that more sleep might be within reach, before accepting the inevitable.

'I'll squeeze some juice,' I say, sitting up. The sticky noise of her body separating itself from mine banishes the night with all the finality of a plunge into cold water. It's like ripping off a Band-Aid: for better or worse, the wound is exposed. Once again, we face the facts.

In the hallway, the naked form creeping across the mirror startles me, and for an instant I am Ernesto, stumbling on this burglar in his bed. I stand up straight, to assess what he would face if he walked in now.

I'm a shade or two lighter than my mother, which implies that my biological father was lighter still. Because I'm cashew to her caramel, it's likely his skin was even less toasted: milk and honey, almond cream. Where that leaves me, I don't know: probably, to employ an expression still in common

3

usage in spite of the racial democracy we are said to enjoy, with 'one foot in the kitchen'. That said, my prosperity of recent years helps: 'money makes you whiter', as they say. Colour isn't immutable: it's just a matter of context.

Either way, things don't look as good as they once did. Baldness is carving twin channels towards the back of my head, like a boat's wake. My skin is pitted and flawed like tired fruit, and my cheekbones look swollen, almost bruised. Otherwise, I'm like a sylph: I might not be here at all. If you took a swing at the place where you thought my belly was, you'd probably miss it. My metabolism is a super-tuned engine, always processing, churning with hot acid. It's why, in spite of my appetite, I am always underweight. It's why my clothes hang well. It's why I can't sit still. It's why people always think I'm nervous, and why nobody ever properly relaxes in my presence.

The sylph in the mirror sighs. Ernesto. She married Ernesto the gentle giant – five years on, I can still hardly believe it. I wonder if there's something about his bulk she finds reassuring. His weight, pinning her down. Perhaps it reminds her of being kidnapped, provides an element of Stockholm Syndrome that splashes Tabasco on all that marital meat and potatoes.

How did I become this interloper, this bed-hopping marriage wrecker? I smile like a villain to make myself feel better, and say, 'Ludo dos Santos, pleased to meet you.'

I halve oranges at the granite island in the middle of the kitchen and squeeze them as quickly as I can, adding an extra spoonful of pulp from the juicer to my glass to bulk it out. I'm padding back across the polished penthouse floor with two tumblers of frothy yellow when I feel the throb of another approaching helicopter. I see the flickering bug as it picks out this building and rears up over it. And now it is time to panic, because no matter how unlikely it is that he'll come down to the apartment, this one is carrying Melissa's father.

Who is also, of course, my father.

My full name is Ludwig Aparecido dos Santos. People assume my mother was a music lover, but I'm told that 'Ludwig' was a bar in the city years ago, whose name was written above the door in a curly silver script that pleased her. As for the rest, the name 'Aparecido' refers to my mother's some-time contention that instead of having a real father I 'slipped down a rainbow', while 'dos Santos' was the name given to orphans during the infancy of the country, because they were deemed to be in the care of the saints.

The point is that it's my real name, not an adopted one. Zé, Melissa's father, took me aside not long after the process was finalised and explained why he wasn't giving me his:

'It would give you more problems than advantages. And we can't afford to take chances after what happened to Melissa.'

As he is chief executive of the MaxiMarket supermarket chain, and also enjoyed a brief stint as Minister for Agriculture before a change of government sent him back to commerce, he and his family have always been prime targets for kidnappers. Melissa was ten when she was taken, and she only escaped because she had the presence of mind to fake an epileptic seizure. Her kidnappers were so spooked by it that they threw her out of a moving car and were never heard from again.

'She's a little shaken,' I heard Zé saying into the phone that weekend. 'It's most unfortunate. But we still have her.'

*Unfortunate.* I doubt he'd pay any attention at all if someone grabbed me.

Melissa's kidnapping occurred because she wandered off into the streets after school when the chauffeur was late picking her up, but it wasn't her fault – in this city, you're only marginally safer in a vehicle. They changed the traffic laws not long ago to prevent carjacking: red no longer means 'stop'. Now, it means 'proceed with caution'.

Unlike Melissa, I do not live in the clouds. Nor do I inhabit a fortress, like her father. I have a studio apartment in a reasonable area – one of three candy-bar blocks in beige, pink and white, clustered around a communal pool. My apartment is on the first floor of the white one, nestled in its base: it's like living in a cave at the foot of a cliff. My sole concession to deterrence is the balcony wall, into which I have embedded shards of bottle glass in blue, green and red, but these are obscured by the dense foliage of the plants I grow to remind me of the farm where I grew up.

Zé lectures me on the subject. 'You're naïve, Ludo. The minute we adopted you, you became different. One day it will happen – someone will target you – and there will be no use regretting it after the fact.'

He may have a point, but I have less to steal than he does, and given the differences between our lifestyles I suspect an element of paranoia. In his worldview there is no such thing as a middle class, and no such thing as a non-criminal under-class. The house that he flies home to every weeknight is a fortified compound, buffered by terraced ponds and beds of hostile, spiky shrubs. His self-watering lawns are patrolled by two pure-bred fighting mastiffs, which roll over on demand for Zé and his family, but would take the leg off an uninvited guest. His palm trees contain motion–sensitive cameras connected to the hub of technology in the guardhouse: if you disturbed so much as a blade of his grass, Zé would know about it. And that's just the beginning. Before you even get to the house you have to enter the compound itself, which is defended by bundles of oiled razor wire and a tooled-up crew that resembles a private army rather than a team of security guards. It would take a thief with Special Forces training to get past the outer walls, let alone breach Zé's last line of defence, and even if you did, you wouldn't find him – he'd be sealed in his tungsten panic room long before you got in, along with every other member of his family, and every object of value. Zé Fischer Carnicelli trusts nobody but himself, however many people he employs to protect him.

For the very rich, like him, a pall of fear almost as heavy as the pollution hangs over this unmappable metropolis – but if, like me, you have less to protect, you can get high on the energy of the place, and allow it to fascinate and excite you. Town planning never happened: there wasn't time. The city ambushed its inhabitants, exploding in consecutive booms of coffee, sugar and rubber, so quickly that nobody could draw breath to say what should go where. It has been expanding ever since, sustained by all that ferocious energy. And here, just as in the universe, anything could happen.

Derelict skyscrapers are not uncommon in the city centre, because when they get old it's easier and cheaper to build afresh somewhere new than to knock down and start again. These bricked-up towers rot into squats and vertical shanty towns, awaiting the eraser of redevelopment. In some neighbourhoods, there is so little green and so much concrete that during afternoon storms the streets simply flood. The roads themselves become gutters, as if the buildings were the beings for whom the city was intended, and humans their waste.

But turn a corner and you might find lush foliage, pristine pavements, smoked-glass security gatehouses, and deep, glinting swimming pools. For every wrecked no-go area there is an optimistic new condominium; for every rotting ruin a daring new spire. The city is being reclaimed all the time, either by the forces of development or those of deterioration:

the only constant is its power to change. Mobility is celebrated to the point that whole highways are named in honour of Workers and Immigrants. That is why for every desperate hopeful arriving today from the northeast, and every Japanese, Italian, or Lebanese who pitched up in previous years, the city is a stronghold to be stormed; a glaring citadel of opportunity, with swarms coming from all sides to hurl themselves at its ramparts, prepared to end up dead on the walls if they fail. But they must not fail.

# A Handful of Beans

*I am less than a year old. The hunger has been at full pelt from the beginning. Wails rip out of my wide-open mouth on behalf of a panicked, churning stomach. Quietly, my mother sings, trying to calm me down. Somebody came by earlier and asked if she would consent to be photographed with her baby. She doesn't understand why this rich white woman, the wife of the supermarket man, wants to visit her, but it would be impolite not to offer her something when she comes. She puts on her best blouse and prepares some beans and rice.*

As I am rarely allowed to forget, I was born in Heliópolis. Exactly how I came into being has never been satisfactorily explained, but I have heard enough versions to last a lifetime of the key moment, when Dona Rebecca, Zé's English wife and Melissa's mother, came to the slum on a mission of mercy and found my proud, beautiful mother nursing her newborn child.

Today, things have improved: the district is called Vila Heliópolis, and has the official status of a neighbourhood rather than a favela. The fact that it has a name at all gives you an idea of its size: names confer legitimacy, and slums don't make it on to maps or the destination boards of buses unless they are unavoidably sprawling. Many of the larger ones, cities in themselves with apartment blocks and tens of thousands of inhabitants, now have full sanitation, electricity, internet access, banks and shops. But there are always starter slums, which appear overnight under bridges, in corners, in wrecks and ruins. And when I was born, every one was a shit-hole.

I know what it was like: I've seen pictures. From a distance, you can't imagine anyone living in such a place: the area has the chaotic texture of a landfill site, a rubbish dump. Zoom in a little, and the teeming detail begins to emerge: tangled outbreaks of television aerials; dense thickets of unofficial power lines; walls and roofs of remaindered breeze-block and stolen brick and found iron sheeting and repurposed doors; structures that should never work but somehow do because they must. Inside, a mattress; a gas ring; electric current tapped from somewhere but seldom paid for; cold food when the gas runs out; no food when there is no cold food. And from each dwelling, the constant, slow trickle of *água preta*: the seeping shit and piss and waste water of people, with nowhere for it to go.

At that time, the Uproot Foundation did not exist, so Rebecca did not have an entire charity to act on her behalf. She was just the wife of a supermarketeer with political aspirations who did not like what she saw. She requested a favela visit to check out the conditions first hand, and Zé sensed an opportunity for publicity. He arranged the trip right away, and sent along a photographer and a journalist to make sure it was properly reported. The first photograph of me ever taken shows Rebecca and my mother exchanging awkward flashlit smiles over bowls of beans and rice.

Ever risk-averse, for all his willingness to exploit his wife's good nature for political ends, Zé made several decrees to Rebecca before her visit, all of which she ignored. Chief among them were that she should drench herself with insect repellent to ward off dengue fever, that she should on no account consider eating or drinking, and even that she should stop her nose with cottonwool on account of the smell.

But Zé had reckoned without his wife's compassion, and my mother's determination. A lightning flash connected them as they locked eyes over my bawling form – a shared longing to get this boy out of there. When my mother's gaze met Rebecca's over the outstretched bowl of food, Rebecca accepted it without hesitation, said her prayers, and sat down to eat. And this is where the miracle occurred. For although she didn't know where her next meal was coming from, or maybe because of that fact, this defiant young woman had somehow cooked the most delicious bowl of *feijão* that Rebecca had ever tasted. How, Rebecca asked, had she infused the beans with so much flavour when she could afford so little to flavour them with? The answer, my mother replied, was in plenty of cooking time, a few scraps of onion or tomato, some bacon fat if you were lucky, and a good measure of raw determination to make sure your son didn't go hungry.

When Rebecca got up to leave she wished us luck and planted a kiss on me as I lay in my mother's arms. But even as she closed the door, Rebecca was assailed by visions of the hardship my mother would endure to provide for me. Recently a mother herself, she probably had the infant Melissa in mind. The sight of us had plunged a knife into her heart, and every step she took away from us gave its hilt another twist. She turned back, stepped neatly over the trickle of effluent that snaked over the concrete outside our hut, and offered to take us away to her farm in the countryside.

My life was transformed by that moment, and Rebecca's decision to knock on our door a second time probably saved me from an unpleasant, predictable fate. The *favelado* who becomes a foot soldier for a drug gang may be a cliché, but that's because it happens every day. It is therefore no exaggeration to say that Rebecca saved my life.

Look what can happen in a generation: my mother lived in a flimsy shack, and I have my own place and my own car, and I can speak and read and write better than most of the playboys you'll meet, because I paid attention in school. But this is no normal case study. What happened to me does not happen. And unless you're extremely good with a football, it definitely doesn't happen if you're male.

I sometimes wonder whether Rebecca would have turned around again if my mother's cooking hadn't been so good. What if she had not been able to conjure something delicious from a handful of beans? I ask myself that question, allow myself to contemplate an alternative outcome for a moment, and then I go back to my business, grateful that this lucky path is the one I was asked to tread, and secure in my belief that a life dedicated to the preparation of good food is a life well spent.

Favelas are subversive by definition. A community stops being classed as one when its streets make it on to official maps, which is never allowed to happen so long as the land is occupied without being owned. The result is whole cities of squatters, with strong fingers, and dirt under their nails from clinging on – the fingers of second-thoughts suicides who try to claw their way back up the cliff. But these people never made the decision to jump: they woke up on the edge of the precipice, with nowhere to go but down. Consequently, the way we left Heliópolis stamped out the possibility that my mother might ever again relax. Because she had cooked our way out of the slums, and because cooking was what had caused the miracle of our new existence, she feared that to stop preparing food might send us back, and that it was therefore safer never to stop.

And stop she did not: she became a production line of cakes, stews, roasts and soups, mastering the signature dishes of Italian, French, and latterly even Japanese cuisine. Food had saved her, and food became her mode of expression. Her hatred and determination, her relief and joy, were beaten into soufflés, stirred into risottos and baked into pies. I could gauge her mood through what she was making: something simple but soothing, like *pão de queijo*, cheese bread fresh from the oven, meant contentment, equanimity; richer treats, such as *brigadeiros*, tiny chocolate bombs with payloads of condensed milk, signified something closer to happiness. If she was frustrated or angry, the conflict would emerge in bold clashes of spice and sugar: clove and orange, chilli and ginger, coconut and saffron. When these exotic pasties and sweetmeats came my way, I kept quiet, loving the sparks they generated on my tastebuds even as I knew they meant I should keep a low profile.

She spoke about what she wanted to speak about, or she did not speak at all. Whatever my father, or life in general, had inflicted upon her, she had reacted to it not with bitterness but by retreating into this world of industry, of calloused hands, of blood and flour, of sweat and cinnamon. It was as if she feared that to speak unguardedly about herself would release something she could never take back; that any admission of suffering would weaken her permanently.

When I think of her now, tending her hives in the sunshine, threading chicken hearts on to skewers in the steam of the kitchen, or picking figs against a backdrop of green foliage, what I see most clearly are her dark, brown eyes – eyes that seemed always to be looking down, as though she lived in a permanent state of deference simply for being alive. But, at least when I was a boy, it meant that her eyes always found me.

We lived together in the kitchen, so I was always within earshot. I became used to speaking without looking up, knowing that the reply would come as surely as if her voice were in my head. If she was working hard, the replies were short and blunt, particularly on Thursdays and Fridays, when the weekend was imminent. But occasionally, when she was relaxed, she spoke for hours, in a soft voice that seemed to come from a different person.

I couldn't cross the kitchen within range of her without receiving a light touch on the arm, or a tousling of the hair, as if I were a battery that charged her in quick, opportunistic fixes. More often than not these caresses were accompanied by the silent dispensation of something delicious: a spoonful from the *feijão* pot, a hot *empada*, an outstretched fingertip coated with thick, sweet *doce de leite*. In this way, whether she felt like talking or not, her love arrived constantly in spiced biscuits and sticky cakes, in slowly simmered stews and flash-fried garlicky greens, in piquant sauces and hot, salty chips. I had the services of a gourmet chef at my disposal seven days a week, whereas the family, for whom she was there and by whom she was paid, only got to enjoy her work at weekends. I ate like a prince but ran free as only the child of a servant can. And I had no father to tell me otherwise.

Rather than offer one definitive version of him, and create one specific repository for my resentment or my longing, my mother offered shadowy, multiple fathers, who floated over the table, conjured by her words. Sometimes he was a Portuguese nobleman she had met in Oporto, with whom she had lived when learning how to cook. This father she painted as a distinguished gentleman, playing the clarinet in his dressing gown, a glass of sticky green liqueur by his music stand, while my mother danced slowly in front of a popping fire to the high, mournful sound. I imagined them together in musty, shuttered rooms; a lumpy bed with an iron bedstead; a choked garden outside with a broken fountain. But he wasn't always European; at other times he was variously a Berber tribesman or a Sephardic Jew with whom she had led a nomadic desert existence, learning her trade in plush silk tents that flapped in the breeze. I knew that she had no more been to Oporto or the Sahara than I had, but it didn't matter. In this way, we travelled the world together, with our missing husband and missing father by our side.

It was a fine game to play as I sat in the doorway of the kitchen listening to the twitter of songbirds in cages, but no more than that. Only once, at the age of five, did I ask the question, although I don't remember it as being the moment when some urgent desire for the truth finally burst through. I recall it rather as an idle enquiry, something that occurred to me with the same naïve level of interest as if I were asking who had planted the trees in the forest outside. She was kneading dough, and had scattered the kitchen tabletop with flour that puffed out in tiny clouds in time to her strong, insistent movements.

'You're a lucky boy,' she said, smiling grimly. 'You have no father to boss you around – you just slipped down a rainbow.'

At the time, it seemed as credible an explanation as any of the others.

Once she let slip a genuine fact. It was my birthday, and she revealed that it was my father's birthday too. I knew it had to be true because of all the fantastic claims she had made, this was the only one she ever tried to retract.

'That was just a joke,' she said. 'Forget I said it.'

I did not forget. If she didn't take back palpably false stories about fathers who were pilots and nomads and thieves, then why take back this one? And I have clung to the fact that my father's birthday was the same as mine ever since, certain that it is the only thing I know about him, without knowing why my mother so regretted telling me.

It was a mixed farm: palm hearts, bananas and a small Brahma beef herd. Zé bought it partly as a way of establishing some agricultural credentials in preparation for his bid for office, but mainly as a place to spend weekends. Silvio, the farm manager, had been apprenticed as a young man to the previous owner, and he knew the land better than anyone. His job was to run the place, without ever letting Zé feel that he wasn't in charge – a diplomatic posting on top of all the back-breaking work of the everyday.

Weekend guests might never have known that it was a working farm at all. All the equipment was kept out of sight by Silvio's house, so it wouldn't interfere with the serious business of the weekend's fun. The only time any machinery came out was when it was required for the administration of leisure apparatus: when a goalpost had fallen over, or to clear a mudslide from the side of a plunge pool after heavy rain.

And whatever else he might be doing, if the power went down at weekends Silvio knew where his priorities lay. Whether he achieved it by climbing poles to get at the power lines, cursing waist-deep in storm drains or kick-starting the back-up generator in the forest, keeping the electricity going was all that mattered – lest Silvio face Ze's outrage at finding the light over his pool table extinguished, his caipirinha ice melted.

Although he sometimes muttered dark things about the guests who came to mess the place up, Silvio held an antique, feudalistic respect for the system that infuriated me. I wanted him and my mother to lock all the doors and take control of the land – they who made it work. One day, when I was twelve and had heard of Che Guevara, I suggested it.

'Why don't we seal the place off and start a revolution?'

'Seal it off how?'

'Fences. Blockades.'

'How's that going to stop a helicopter?' he said, tipping brandy into his coffee.

# Warm Rolls

Melissa dresses quickly and sprints up to the roof, while I cower in her bed, ready to throw myself into the wardrobe should Zé knock on the door. He doesn't come down. Time is everything for him, and it's wasteful to shut down and restart your engines just because your daughter hasn't conditioned her hair. Panic over. I could go back to sleep if I wanted, but I don't like being in the apartment alone and there is always the possibility of Ernesto.

Ignoring the doorman's suspicious stare, I let myself out of the building and go to a nearby Italian café that serves good coffee and freshly baked rolls. I think of Melissa as I pick up a warm roll and tear it open. Two of my favourite smells together – fresh bread and Melissa – one in my hands, and the other still on them. Distracted by this, I linger over breakfast longer than intended, but my boss is at a meeting all morning, so I'll not hurry.

My car is a dented beige Gol, spotted with outbreaks of dark rust. The wave of air that engulfs me when I open the door is so hot that I wait for five minutes before forcing myself inside. When I take to the freeway, boiling petrol fumes stream through the front corner window, up my left arm and into my face. I shift my thighs on hot black plastic, and wish I had a better car.

Thanks to his relentlessly pessimistic view of the city, Zé advises that I vary my habits and try new routes to work, to avoid falling into a routine that might be exploited by kidnappers. I have taken this advice to heart: not only does it justify erratic arrival times, but lately it has also enabled me to explore the forlorn area surrounding our new office building. This morning, I turn off the freeway at random to explore an unfamiliar square. Down the narrow corridor between two bright orange tower blocks I glimpse some blasted shop fronts and an old stone fountain – enough to make me want to take the next exit and have a look around.

I pull in at the entrance to a dilapidated high-rise car park, where a man in oily blue overalls and a red baseball cap steps forward to assist me. I step out of the vehicle's torrid atmosphere into the cool gloom.

'I'll only be half an hour,' I say. 'Don't park it far away.'

He nods, peels off a pink duplicate ticket from a damp pad and hands it to me. Then he drives my car at speed up a ramp, into the rattling, clanking iron cage of the lift.

'I said only half an hour!' I shout, too late. The lift has already started. I watch its rusty exhaust pipe quivering as, with a high-pitched hydraulic whine, the car ascends to be buried on some high floor. It will take the attendant time to retrieve it, which will mean he can charge me more.

Shaking my head and clutching my pink ticket, I step outside into high, mid-morning light. Dazed and blinking, I realise that my sunglasses are being winched up in the lift along with the car, wonder what I am doing here, and have second thoughts. But it will take time now for the guy to come back down, then more time for him to re-ascend and collect the car. Looking back up at the flyover, I see grid-locked cars edging painfully forward against a backdrop of giant roadside advertisements: cereal mascots; confectionery creatures; a backlit Marlboro Man waving his lasso. Wasting half an hour here can't do any harm. This might be my only chance: these days, whole neighbourhoods are reordered overnight, and today's discovery might not be around next week. I cross the street, under the merciful shade of the flyover, and enter the blinding square.

The light is maddening, so bright that I stare down at the cracked mosaic pavement to escape it, and the burnt sugar fallout from the raging overpass is irritating my eyes and nose. All of which combines to make this dusty, monochrome space feel like somewhere I should not stay for long.

Since the city took off in the nineteenth century, wave after wave of developers have ripped through it, obliterating what lies in their path. But occasionally, the past remains in isolated fragments that seem as if they have escaped the halo of a nuclear explosion. This square is one such tatter – and only half of it, at that. Once, there would have been symmetry: a fountain surrounded by four handsome stone benches. Now, one bench has been stamped on by a raised concrete plaza that fronts the first of the orange tower blocks, while in place of the other is an angular capsule of black, reflective panels, which I recognise as one of the new ultrasecure ATM machines – a cold, dark shard, disturbing the cosy grime around it. It is as if the city has taken a bite of the square and will return again when it is hungry.

A single-storey colonial-style building, lately a slum, survives on the older side. Its walls have been posted over so many times and in so many colours that they have faded to one texture and to a colour that is all colours. The carved stone over its entrance reads MDCCCLXXX, topped off by an angel flanked by two bugle-playing cherubs. It would have been grand here once. I picture carriages; ladies with parasols; men in dark suits with pearls in their neckties.

I sit on a bench, imagining that if I strain hard enough I might hear one last gasp of this past, but I can't get comfortable. My eyes won't adjust to the light. My throat is dry, still catching on flyover fumes. The alcohol that led me into Melissa's bed last night is thudding in my head. I am on the point of retrieving my car and heading to work when I notice what is happening on the opposite side of the square.

At the foot of the tower nearest to me, two women – both short and buxom, with electric-yellow hair – have left their office for their first cigarette of the day. They're chatting happily, not gasping down the smoke in haste, but inhaling with panache. They lean across the doorway, relishing the light and the heat, gossiping and touching each another on the arm as they speak. They do not see the boy approaching them.

I saw him entering the square, from the shadows to one side. He stands out because of his tattered clothes and a pronounced limp, which he did not have when he first appeared. The ladies in the doorway will not know this.

I can't hear what is said between them. I just see his frantic hands, his imploring arms. The women hear him out, then shake their tinted hairdos and ostentatiously turn to resume their conversation. The boy keeps performing even as he leaves them, dragging his foot along the pavement in such a contorted way that his bare, street-blackened heel does not sit on the sole of his paper-thin flip-flop.

There follows the tiniest chess gambit, played out in the black and white of the square – a strategic flicker that flares as briefly as sunlight off an opening window. The boy catches sight of me on my bench, and wonders how much I saw. When did I notice him? Is his cover blown, or can he try again? The look is fleeting and sly, but he drops out of character for it, and I register this because I saw him before the limp, before the overture of anguished sobs with which he approached the women.

I watch him come over, testing his act with my full

attention. He can't be much older than fifteen, but he is a good performer. I should be walking away before this encounter starts, but I'm curious. The boy wants something from me, which means, in theory at least, that these are circumstances I can control.

'Good m-m-morning, S-S-Senhor.' The voice is husky, not yet broken, but given an unnatural shove in that direction by too much cigarette smoke. His ripped yellow T-shirt has been washed a thousand times, but not lately. The smell – body odour, *cachaça*, a whiff of urine – barges into my senses. A thick vein throbs in his neck. His leg jigs up and down, a bare heel tapping in the dust, still only half-sitting on the flip-flop sole. His face is so dirty that he might be black, or white, or both, and while he doesn't look thin he is probably malnourished. Everything about him says he's running on very little to lose.

'Mmm . . . mmm . . . aaa . . .' Panic, or a convincing imitation of it, shudders through his body, making his head quiver. His breathing shoots out in fast, irregular bursts, like the panting of a trapped animal. The tortured, lip-chewing contortions of his mouth imply a grave problem: something so bad that it is paralysing his speech. The skyward glances hint at prayer, as if he were imploring the heavens to intercede and somehow resolve this unthinkable situation.

'Calm down,' I say. 'Tell me what is wrong.'

His mother is dying. She is in hospital and he needs the taxi fare to get there to say goodbye. He'll pay me back. He offers me a fake watch that dangles off his wrist as surety. Light glints off its face, dazzling me, making me blink.

More colourful stories occur to me immediately. *My brother has been bitten by a snake, and I must rush him to the Instituto Butantan for an antidote. I was mugged by rogue gold-dealers. My girlfriend is choking on candyfloss in the park.*

'I will drive you,' I offer, getting to my feet. 'My car's parked right here. Which hospital?'

He's thrown, but has the composure to remember his stutter. He is angry: why won't I just give him the money? Don't I trust him?

'No,' I say. 'You're trying to con me.'

The stutter goes. The foot straightens on its sole. 'You think you look so innocent, brother?' he says, looking at the skin of my arm. 'With a change of clothes, a bad night's sleep and some mud on your face, you'd look just like me.'

He's right – certainly in this bleaching light, which makes cars and tree trunks white hot, and their shadows black as ink.

'And that means I should give you money?'

'Yeah.'

'Why do you perform like that? Isn't it easier just to mug people like everybody else?'

'I'm not a thief.'

The sunlight is giving me a headache. I want to retrieve my car, get to work, and sit in my air-conditioned office with a bottle of ice-cold water and some painkillers.

'I have to go to work now,' I say, turning towards the car park. 'Good luck.'

I walk away slowly. I don't want to give him the impression I am escaping; I just want to end the encounter.

'What gives you the right to walk away?' he shouts, his voice cracking. 'You can't leave me. Give me money. Whatever money you have.'

Suddenly, the light, my itching eyes, the heat, the dehydration, Melissa – all of it combusts. I turn, and stride up to him, and push him hard in the chest. Melissa's face flashes before me. The deep blue water of her eyes.

'The right? What gives you the right to demand money from me? If you want money, you have to earn it.'

'How do you earn your money, brother?'

'That's none of your business.'

'I bet you were born with it like all the rest. You have no idea what it's like for people like me.'

'Shut up! That routine of yours: does it ever work?'

'Of course it works.'

'Make it work for me now. If you do, I'll go right up to that ATM and withdraw double the amount you make.'

'Fuck off, man.'

'I mean it. In fact, forget the routine. Get the money however you like. I don't believe people would take you seriously in any situation. You're just a kid, with a fuzzy moustache and a whiny voice. Come back here with some money, and I'll double it.'

My rage is genuine. I want to put him in harm's way. I want him to take risks.

'You shouldn't tempt me, my friend. Something bad could happen.'

'What do you mean?'

'I mean I've got something here you can take seriously.'

He's showing me the handle of a mean-looking kitchen knife, which juts from a pair of too-big trousers held up with rope.

'Please don't get that out,' I say, trying to hold his eye. 'It's a bad idea.'

'Don't worry, rich man. I'm not threatening you. Ha! How pathetic. I'm just showing this to you so you know I mean business. And so you know that if you try to run away instead of doubling my money then this is what will come after you.'

'I'll be right here.'

He stares at me with bloodshot eyes, fighting the impulse to get out the knife and use it on me. Somehow my anger enables me to hold his gaze in spite of the fear.

'I have no cash,' I say. 'And you won't get me into that ATM without a fight. It's your choice.'

He pauses before leaving, pushing his face close to mine. I can smell weed on his breath behind the sugary reek of the *cachaça*.

'You obviously never wondered where your next meal was coming from,' he mutters. 'Or there's no way you could do this.'

I've still got a roll in my pocket from the café. I contemplate offering it to him, but that might only antagonise him further.

I shrug. 'Do you want the money or not?'

He turns and stomps off across the square. As soon as he's gone I regret what I have done. My irritation, which had nothing to do with him and everything to do with Melissa, made me goad him. And maybe something in the physical similarity between us, and the way he drew attention to it, made me realise that my own temper could be used to ignite his. I could see the buttons I needed to push. Now, gazing across the desolate, dusty square, I have an impulse to follow him, give him cash, and take back the challenge.

But I do not. Instead I watch him hanging around, looking for his next mark, talking angrily to himself, replaying the situation and getting incensed in retrospect. He approaches passers-by, but they ignore him and walk on. He paces around under a palm tree, agitation building. Even at this distance I can see his pride kicking in.

I look away, wondering what the time is and thinking that I should be getting to work. Then I look back, and suddenly I want to move as quickly as I can, to release him from this situation. Because now I see that he has given up waiting for members of the public, has gone up to the security window in the base of the orange tower block, and is already engaged in animated conversation with the guard. A tall, dark man in his twenties, he looks down at the boy sceptically with his hands on his hips. He wears a brown uniform and a cap, and the polished wooden handle of a pistol juts from a holster on his belt. This is exceptionally unwise. Private guards are untrained, underpaid and bored – just waiting for an opportunity to draw their guns.

Briskly, I cross the square. I can see the impassioned gestures; the boy's desperation to make the world go his way; the building unwillingness to let this end on anything but his own terms. He will be embarrassed when I step in. He'll hate me even more. But I'll pay him off, anything to prevent him doing something stupid. I hear their raised voices over the laughter of the two oblivious girls in their doorway, and I speed up.

I don't see how it starts. I just know that something bad is happening the way you always know. Feral danger signals go off in me. Sweat runs down my collar; the skin on my neck cringes. The event accelerates into my consciousness as it gains weight in the world, and suddenly what's going on over there is all that matters.

The boy has gone for broke. He's waving his knife in the guard's face. The guard – probably stupid, definitely scared – shouts, telling the boy to put it away, and reaching for his gun.

I hurdle one side of the fountain to cover the distance as quickly as possible, to try and undo what I have begun. I want to scream, to tell the boy not to run. Running is like an invitation to those people to pull the trigger. But it is as if my throat has seized up.

The boy is beginning to recognise the scale of the mistake he's made. As he turns away he sees me approaching, and thinks I'm after him too. His eyes flash wide at me, beaming panic, and he breaks into a run.

I yell at the security guard not to shoot, but there is no way he will let this opportunity pass. The boy threatened him with a knife. Whatever happens now, he is in the clear.

The boy runs badly. He hurls the knife to one side, embedding it in the trunk of the palm tree. But his blundering, flailing gesture comes too late: smoke puffs out behind him in the light.

The sound of the gun is flat, almost soft: *TAT*. And it's over. The handle of the knife keeps wobbling after he falls, like a diving board after the jump, even after the damage has been done, and the boy's shoulder is perforated, and the little mosaic tiles around him seem to be floating in glossy, black blood.

The guard stands motionless for a second, his mouth a perfect O, taking it in. He will say that he didn't intend to shoot the boy – just to scare him – but he will be commended for his actions nonetheless. It is what he is paid for. These days, you can't take chances.

The women scream. The victim screams. The cars on the flyover continue to lurch and blare. Just one more frenzied city drama in a thousand, to be forgotten and absorbed into the oozing traffic, and perhaps mentioned in passing over lunch.

The boy lies face down, his legs splayed and twisted, dark blood-soak spreading across his T-shirt. He raises his head a fraction, and in the heartbeat between one howl and the next, his stare finds mine. Then the guard places his boot on the boy's head and pushes his face back to the ground.

When the guard gets out his phone to call the police, I look at the pink car-park ticket in my hand and realise there's nothing more I can do but get to work. I'm late enough as it is.

# Jacaranda Honey

The farm buildings spilled extravagantly over the lip of a wooded valley at one side, and lapped against the base of a steep hill on the other, as if they had been constructed on the top step of a giant staircase. You got vertigo whichever way you looked, whether up at the lone buzzard surfing thermals at the top of the hill, or down through the trees towards the silvery glint of the river. The main house, a grand plantation-style residence, was adjoined by seemingly endless guest bungalows and staff quarters, giving the impression more of a village than of one residence. There was room to spare – over a thousand hectares of it.

Our world, however, was the kitchen. My mother used to say that the range hadn't gone cold in a century, and she may have been right: no matter how hot the day, the fire blazed. The kitchen, with its huge stone floor slabs, hollows worn into them from years of industry, was the heart of the house, and my mother its constant attendant. Nobody set foot in there without her permission, not even Zé or Rebecca. It was imbued as heavily with her personality as her wooden spoons, her saucepans and her table, on which everything was chopped and prepared, and which Silvio planed down every few weeks so that its surface remained pristine, renewing the top when the old one was exhausted. She was up at six every morning to stoke up the fire and throw open the doors on to the veranda that overlooked the valley outside, from the eaves of which her collection of songbirds hung in cages, making beautiful, pointless noise.

Guinea fowl pranced in the yard, their bulging feathered ankles like boots. Honey, flavoured by jacaranda pollen, was produced in hives round the side of the kitchen, and was often the object of raids by gangs of howler monkeys daring enough to believe they could get past my mother. A giant tortoise disappeared every winter, and re-emerged in the spring, ponderously ravenous. Nobody knew where she slept, or how long she had been alive.

Below the house and its outbuildings were a clay football pitch, a tennis court and a swimming pool fed by water that ran off the hill and down the valley. It was as well to look around before diving in: shoals of fish gulped lazily at the algae, frogs spawned in the water, and Silvio claimed he'd even caught a young caiman that had made its way up from the river, waiting patiently in the shallow end, 'hoping for a bite of the good stuff'.

This set-up might have propagated disease had the water been stagnant, but Silvio was cleverer than that. He'd created a miniature ecosystem of pools and channels, linked to the natural watercourse, so there was constant circulation. Water flowed naturally down the hill, but it was diverted on the way for the purpose of irrigated entertainment. And, in creating this little miracle, Silvio also incorporated what was the farm's showpiece, the feature designed to show Zé's fun-loving side to his guests for maximum effect: a long water chute, dug into the side of the hill, which Silvio had smoothly concreted over and painted in stark municipal blue. A powerful pump drew water from the muddy pool at the bottom of the slide so that the cataract that emerged at the top was powerful enough to flush even the plumpest of

Zé's drunken weekend guests to the bottom, where they plunged into the frothing brown pool at great speed. Silvio would scrub the chute every Friday before the family arrived, checking it over to ensure no leaf litter had accumulated.

'Better make it flow fast, hadn't we Ludo?' he'd say. 'Don't want any of those rich old turds getting clogged in the pipes.' His wheezing laughter would roll down the valley. Then, at the flick of a switch, the surface of the pool, unbroken all week, would bubble and pound into action. And the weekend would be about to start.

Whatever I was doing on Friday afternoon had to stop in time for me to join the line-up that greeted the helicopter. I had reason to be excited; this was not for me, as for others, the prelude to onerous duties, but a starting-pistol shot that launched two days of pleasure.

The drone would come first: distant, separating itself slowly from the rest of the background noise – somebody in the next valley mowing grass, perhaps – but then the sound would build until the machine shot in over the trees. Our line would straighten. The sky would darken with the grey blur of the blades. My mother would fuss with my hair. And then it would be over us, and our hair would be whipped up anyway by the down-blast of whirling rotors. Clay from the football pitch would be pulverised and thrown into the air. The goalpost netting would shudder. Wheels would extend, and touch hesitantly down in the centre circle of the pitch. A door would unfold and a set of metal steps would unfurl to the ground, the bottom one biting into the clay like a spade. And there they would be: the first family of the ranch. You almost expected them to wave, or for a lapdog to bound out to complete the picture.

Rebecca was always first to emerge, her arms outstretched to receive me, her face broadcasting joy and kindness. The expression was a constant; you never surprised her looking sour or bitter, or forced her hastily to put up a façade of concern. She'd met Zé as a young woman on a postgraduate assignment with the Red Cross, and in spite of the wealth she had married into, she had never forgotten what brought her to our country to begin with. In addition to her work with the Uproot Foundation, she was on the boards of three orphanages, and if she was ever tetchy or distant you could guarantee it was because of some worry connected with another person. She wore pale, unrumpled linens, and expensive cosmetics whose oily scent made me feel queasy in her embrace (I preferred the soap-scrubbed non-smell of my mother, but kept this to myself). Whenever she was in the room it was as if an angel had descended, to look willowy and concerned, and empathise, professionally.

Next, Melissa would burst down the steps, aching either to pick up where we had left off the week before, or to introduce some new discovery she'd made over the past five days. She loved being a child, she loved the farm, and she loved her playmate. Through all that has happened, she has always made me feel wanted, included. She would never ignore me, whoever else might be in the room, which is not necessarily true of the rest of her family. From as far back as I can remember she has been well meaning and affectionate, to the point of being clumsy in her enthusiasm. She would break things with love – as when, at the age of six, she accidentally sat on a newly hatched chick that she was trying to hide in her pocket and smuggle home to the city. Her lack of cynicism means that the world can sometimes let her down. During those carnivorous weekends on the farm, it wasn't unusual for a whole pig or even a young steer to be barbecued slowly over a huge charcoal fire. I would watch transfixed as the flesh went dark and the smell rose, ask to ladle hot fat over the meat, and be offered first refusal on the more exotic cuts (hearts, livers, brains). Melissa, by contrast, had reached the age of seven before she connected those fragrant carcasses to the calves that stumbled around in the fields, and it was months before she again ate meat.

Last to descend: José Ícaro Fischer Carnicelli, or as he was known to one and all, Zé Generoso. The nickname derives from his legendary hospitality and the large donations the MaxiMarket chain makes to the poor. But on occasion I have detected a whiff of sarcasm in the way it was muttered by Silvio, or by my mother – as if for every act of magnanimity or largesse, Zé was chalking up your score, that there was always some future reckoning in his mind at which your position was constantly under review. He was a professional though: athletic, good-looking and amiable – even if he did have a tendency to ask the same question of each member of staff every week, as if every person was only linked in his mind to one area of concern. (Because my mother occasionally had trouble with a bad leg, that was her question; because Silvio's sister had at one time been ill, the question Zé asked of him was, 'And how is your sister?') He would wait for his family to disembark, then move fast, as if embarrassed by the attention. Melissa later explained this to me: if everyone around you moves slowly and you move quickly, you communicate that your time is at a premium, and that you can afford to pay others to waste their time on your behalf. They did it at Melissa's wedding, too – made the godparents walk down the aisle painstakingly slowly at the start of the ceremony, before pounding down at the last minute with presidential haste themselves.

It wasn't as if we were lined up like the domestics of some French château to greet the master, but there was an

unspoken understanding that Zé didn't like it if the comple-
ment was incomplete.

'Good afternoon everyone,' he would say, briskly trotting
down the steps, unpretentiously carrying the family's
weekend bags. Then he might pause, look around and say,
'But where is Silvio?'

'He wanted to be here,' someone would chip in (usually
my mother). 'But there are cows in calf.'

'Tell him to come and see me, will you? I was hoping to
talk to him about fences this weekend.'

The pretext would almost certainly be improvised – just
an excuse to see the errant individual – but in this way Zé
was able to give everyone a discreet seigniorial once-over,
like a trainer checking the teeth of his dogs.

The arrival was always picturesque, theatrical: Rebecca's
silk scarf flitting about her face like a monster butterfly;
Melissa a shot of colour from the gloomy interior; Zé grinning broadly behind his mirrored sunglasses at the door,
which he would sometimes open early as they flew in over
his land. When he emerged and established that all were
present and correct, he would gesture vaguely back at the
helicopter and turn to whoever was around, saying, 'Let's
get this thing out of the way so we can play some football,'
as if he were a salesman stowing his briefcase. Then he would
grind his handmade Italian shoes into the red clay, and mutter:
'Down to earth. Down to earth, at last.'

I loved it all: the anticipation of that first hint of rotor-
noise; the drama of the arrival; the Friday night smells of
aftershave, cut limes and barbecues. When the helicopter
was towed away by tractor into its shed beside the football
pitch, and the doors closed on it, the weekend could start
for real.

Zé could never wait to get on the football field. He would
ditch his suit for a T-shirt and a pair of indecently flared blue

satin shorts, frayed at the edges – some relic from his university days – and begin organising teams from a line-up of guests and employees. He saw no reason to blunt his competitive edge just because there were children on the field, and was quite happy to send us skittling across the clay – often Melissa, who being tough took it well, or me, who as an employee had no choice but to take it well. The least dangerous situation was when he was refereeing, but it was a position he hated because of the requirement for impartiality.

His enthusiasm was so blind and so masculine that it verged on the dictatorial: if he wanted a cold beer, everyone had to have one; when he was in the mood for steak (which was much of the time) then he couldn't fathom the idea that you might not be. My mother had accustomed herself to his capricious approach to the weekend's catering, and had worked out subtle but firm ways of dealing with it without making too many last-minute changes. For example, when she had been preparing a seafood platter, Zé might declare after one or two drinks that he'd gone off the idea of lobster, and wanted red meat instead.

'Must we have all this seafood? *Fish don't pull wagons*, as my father used to say. Bring me beef!'

'Senhor, I have spent the afternoon, and a lot of your money, on this dish. Will it go to waste?'

'Very well. Serve both, my angel. And make sure you keep back plenty for the boys. How is Silvio to round up my cattle if he has no strength? Keep him three lobsters, you hear? Force them on him!'

Guests would arrive in armoured 4x4s or mud-spattered jeeps: tanned men with bellies and moustaches, who chatted by the pool all weekend gripping beers and caipirinhas; stunning wives on sunloungers with tinted hair and manicured nails and cosmetically enhanced bodies, rotating in the heat like rotisserie chickens. Sometimes a second or a third helicopter would land. On big weekends there'd be a whole tournament of football, and Zé would have people to impress and points to score. Once there was even a visit from the president.

Melissa and I would dip in and out of the weekend's activities. We spent hours floating in pools talking nonsense. We lost ourselves in the woods. Often, we took to the tree house, a creation of Silvio's high in the branches of a giant fig tree, which gave us an unfettered view of the proceedings below, and allowed us to lie in sleeping bags spying on the guests, our giggles muffled by the din of roosting starlings. During Saturday night parties that went on late into the night, Melissa and I would watch things get more boisterous – more than once we saw Zé trying his luck with other women, but it didn't seem to upset her – then fall asleep together as, no matter how much we wanted to stay awake, our exhaustion kicked in.

But time was always running out, and however much fun was had over the weekend, the family would soon be packing up and heading back to the city. On Sunday afternoons, as they turned their attention to the week ahead, the mood would change. Melissa would become grumpy and distant, and our games would seem suddenly irrelevant.

I had no memory of the city. I knew I had been born there, but nothing more. The place had developed a life of its own in my head. I would ask Melissa questions. Were the buildings as high as mountains? Was the pollution really so bad you had to keep the light on all day? Were there animals? To the family, though, the city represented reality, from which this weekend amusement park was nothing but a welcome distraction. When the Predator was wheeled out from its shed, the transformation from football pitch back to helipad was the surest sign that my world was again about to deflate. As the light faded, Melissa and her parents would disappear into the house to pack and freshen up for the journey. And then it would be over. Staff were not required to line up to say goodbye – Sunday evenings were businesslike – but I would stand there anyway, watching in silence as the helicopter lifted off, spun its nose round and, with the core-jangling scream of a Formula One car, shuttled wastefully back to the city.

However much I dreaded its departure, the sight of the machine never failed to excite me – seeing it surge upwards and spin carelessly around with lights flashing in its underbelly made adrenalin burst in my stomach. Every week, I stood there until the lights and the sound had disappeared, and the family in its smug flying capsule was enfolded by the night-blue horizon.

I would speculate on what was happening up there, imagining the conversations they might be having as they sharked away across the trees. Did they talk about me, about the weekend just gone? Or was I already forgotten? I would feel momentarily lonely, and then head for home, where I knew that my mother would be preparing something comforting from the weekend's leftovers.

Whatever impression was given on the surface, we were there to provide a service: a weekend fix of excitement and authenticity; of being 'down to earth'. Back in the city, it was as if we didn't exist. But my week was another world too. While Melissa slept soundly in their fortified compound – I pictured flags fluttering on a turreted castle – I would lie awake, listening to the disputes and confrontations of the natural world outside, projecting stories on to the sounds I heard. Loneliness should be hard to come by in the forest, but the white noise of animals getting on with their business was never a consolation. It only reminded me how sure most living things were of their place in the world, while I was not.

# Peanuts

Back at the high-rise car park I hand over the pink ticket, now almost illegible from the sweat of my palm. The attendant is gone for ten minutes, and does not look me in the eye when he finally drives my car out of the lift and presents me with the bill. I am too dazed to remonstrate with him.

The Marginal highway: eight lanes of stewing anger and alcohol vapour beside an evil trickle of green water in a ditch that was once a river. Amid the rubbish, where the water is deep enough, floats a one-man favela: a platform on old lashed-together tyres bearing a body, huddled in sleep, free from everything except the foul liquid that surrounds him. In my rear-view mirror, a gallery of demons flashes past – the faces, contorted with emotion, of those trying to beat the traffic by suicidally cutting through it on mopeds. Frantic to clock in, they contribute their energy to the city in the hope that it will offer them something in return. Meanwhile, kings and princes roar overhead, skimming towards the horizon, perusing the morning newspapers.

Sweating on to my plastic seat, I am dreaming up an excuse for being so late to work when the freeway provides one: a crash, four vehicles ahead. I hear the bang of hot, colliding metal and see a rising black wisp of tyre smoke. The cars in front brake hard, slowing and swerving into a vehicle concertina.

We are experts at traffic jams. We've taken them to new levels. Even when there aren't accidents, traffic lights on sagging metal arms blink and change while car soup simmers beneath them. But the energy doesn't disappear just because the flow is blocked; as in a human artery, it is re-routed. A grid of trapped vehicles activates every vendor, huckster, implorer and charity case within a kilometre-radius, and the resulting teeming sideshow makes you forget you had anywhere to go. The incident up ahead is barely two minutes old when five young boys materialise to wipe windscreens, sell peanuts, peddle flowers. One, barefooted, juggles fire on the shoulders of another, both grimacing with concentration. Everything is an opportunity.

Guilt begins to wring out my guts like a wet cloth. I thrust cash at the boy with the peanuts, averting my eyes from his face. Instead, I look upwards, at two black vultures congregated on the high X-bars of a streetlamp, hoping for carrion. Everything is an opportunity.

I have had enough of this. I pull out between the traffic and put my foot to the floor. The car lurches forward, and the wing mirror loudly slaps the car in front. The driver honks his horn and swears through his open window. I keep driving, tearing open the package of nuts with my teeth and tipping them wildly into my mouth. Somehow I make it through without hitting anyone else and I drive past the accident, where blame is being tossed about in loud voices over broken glass. The two drivers look over in astonishment, as if I have broken some unspoken rule of the road by presuming to drive through their argument.

I have a recurring nightmare in which Melissa probes around in my belly button with one of the sharp metal skewers my mother used for weekend barbecues. She stares intently into my navel, manipulating the skewer, and I feel its cold metal point enter my stomach. Eventually, she achieves her object-ive, and unknots my umbilical cord. My intestines gush to the floor like a string of raw sausages.

Not a complex dream – just a recurring one.

Last night's stopover was a rare treat. I don't get the call so much now they are married. I am not permitted even to have the idea that Melissa and I should see each other; it has to come from her. I had finished work for the day and was contemplating a solitary evening on my balcony when she rang.

'My husband has abandoned me,' she said. 'Want to come over and order a pizza?'

'I'll cook,' I said.

I haven't been to the penthouse much lately, but I lived there for years, and I still have my key, so it seemed ridiculous that I was regarded with such suspicion when I arrived. Like any stronghold of the wealthy, Melissa's building is defended by bored young guards reading comics behind bulletproof glass, craving melodrama and an excuse to let off their weapons. Even though Melissa had told them to expect me, they insisted on looking through my groceries from the Municipal Market before they let me through.

I knew something was wrong when she met me at the front door and kissed me on the lips. She only does that when Ernesto has pissed her off.

'It's been so long,' she said, when we separated.

I took in the dazzling, infinite city behind her, and put the food on the counter. 'This view,' I said. 'You forget. Especially at night.'

'What's in your bags?' said Melissa, pouring me a glass of wine.

'Santa Catarina oysters, and pork chops.'

She made an appreciative noise, and handed me the drink.

'What have you been doing?' I said. 'You look almost as if you're . . . shimmering.'

Melissa has a lot of her mother in her, and is very white. But unlike Rebecca, she is never pale. At the beach she sets herself out to bake all day, though her genes protest. When she returns, her freckled skin glares with outraged heat for twenty-four hours before it swallows the damage and moves on. But last night, she seemed to be positively emitting light.

'I've been working,' she said. 'There's a new spa treatment at the shopping mall: gold, frankincense and myrrh. I'm doing a piece on it.'

'It sounds gruelling.'

'It isn't as pleasant as it sounds. The gold exfoliation process is very abrasive.'

Melissa calls herself a lifestyle journalist, but she seems only to write about the kind of lifestyle that very few – herself among them – can afford. Zé was keen for her to become a political journalist after college, but in her own words, she 'got sidetracked'. She tends to say that this is OK, because 'Ernesto does the socially responsible stuff for both of us'. It's a consolation I sometimes offer myself when I contemplate the vacuity of my own work, so I can hardly blame her for it. Ernesto's shoulders are so broad that everybody feels entitled to perch on them.

'Abrasive or not, you look . . . nice,' I said, trying not to let on how exciting it was to see her again. 'If a little thin.'

Her blue-green eyes flash when she's angry – mermaid-infested waters. 'Don't start on that.'

When we lived together she would eat nothing for days, then command stacks of burgers and toasted sandwiches. She also can't sleep alone with the light off and showers about five times a day, which means her hair is more often wet than dry.

The wet hair is just one of the things that get me. There are others: her perfect teeth; her short, clear-polished nails; her white jeans; the sprinkling of freckles on her nose; the striped shirts she wears at home. Traditionally these were Zé's cast-offs, but, lately, they're Ernesto's, which I like less, although his are too big for her to use as anything other than nightwear. I also love her continued devotion to the plastic watch she has worn since we were kids – a constant, tiny reminder of our shared childhood.

'I don't want to talk about me,' she said. 'Tell me about your day.'

'Why are you acting as if I'm your husband? I haven't even seen you for months. Where's Ernesto?'

'He's away in the interior. Something for work. I don't know.'

Her lingering pause invited the question. 'Is everything OK between you?'

And that's how it started. She was always going to get me in the end.

Ernesto is an anthropologist. For years, he has been studying for his doctorate, the thesis of which looks into the motivations of the hordes of desperate migrants who come to the city each year looking for work, and their (usually dismal) experiences on arrival. He spends long periods of time in rural villages, amassing an ever-expanding quantity of interview material, and shows no sign of stopping. It's as if he intends to keep going until he has heard the personal story of every single person who has either moved to the city or is contemplating doing so. When at home he divides his time between interviewing favela inhabitants, fulfilling the demands of his teaching post at the university and organising various community projects. His wife pines at home in her tower, and he stays away for days before returning stinking of sweat and the slums. But his commitment to the welfare of others is the bedrock of Melissa's love for him, and she has fought many battles with her father on his account.

He has never accepted a job working for Zé – not even indirectly, for the Uproot Foundation, which would suit him. At some point during his transformation from Spoilt Rich Kid to Academic with Troubled Conscience he came to the conclusion that he needed to make his own way in life, which infuriates Zé, because it means he has a son-in-law he can't control. Ernesto's self-righteousness works to my advantage, so I'm not complaining, but normally Melissa wouldn't hear a word against it – which is what made last night so unusual.

Normally, it goes like this:

'You never see him,' I point out.

'His work is important,' she says. 'I wouldn't want to be the one to stop him doing it.'

'What about his marriage? What about you?'

'I don't need saving. I have everything I could want. Thanks to you.'

And then she kisses me, and I forget what I was saying.

I know perfectly well that she is a hypocrite. All that talk of how much she values Ernesto and the work he does doesn't stop her from frequenting shopping centres so exclusive that you need an appointment, and being almost as wary of the pavement as her father. I never point this out to her, of course. I might miss out on the kiss.

It may sound cold, but I don't want the responsibility of working out how to deal with the kid I might have been – the one who lived in a wooden crate and spent his formative years playing in the sewage pipe, or jumping rubbish on his bike. Big ideas scare me. The thought of doing something that actually matters is enough to bring me out in a rash. Instead, I pay my taxes and I give to charity, in the hope that someone worthy like Rebecca or Ernesto will tackle the big issues on my behalf. Meanwhile, I spend my days gently informing women which cleaning products are most deserving of their hard-earned wages, and showing kids who want to be the next football hero how one choice of boot might be wiser than another.

The posture of cool that supposedly defines life in my office is belied by a corporate culture every bit as backbiting as you'd find outside a 'creative' industry. Our building may be a reclaimed squat, our reception desk may be the wing of a Vietnam-era American bomber, and my boss may sometimes wear designer trainers, but we might just as well be toiling away in some bureau of nightmares with acres of anonymous desk space and the façade of a Soviet ministry. At least that would be honest. Although a veneer of funky self-assurance coats every employee in the building, you don't have to scratch hard before it chips off in your hand. Under the surface, everyone lives in fear. Fear of being found out, of not being found out. Fear of the possibility that the white goods, mobile telephones and confectionery they are paid to promote might be all there is to life.

But what a life! I marvel at what we achieve. Our communication for a certain vitamin-enriched, hormone-injected dairy brand is so successful that rural farmers are selling off their own milk and eggs in order to go down to their local MaxiMarket and buy the enhanced versions. Enraptured by what we tell them, people have been known to have perfectly good teeth knocked out of their mouths so they can benefit from the glamour of a false set. We are magicians!

Take cereal: our client bulk-buys the crop, which it gets

at a knockdown price, converts it into air-dried flakes, adds flavouring (it's more cost-effective to use artificial sweeteners than home-grown sugar cane), then sells it on, informing consumers exactly how and when the cereal should be eaten. In return for the addition of this lifestyle data, our client receives roughly fifteen times the worth of the original raw materials – and that's where my fee comes from. Alchemy exists; we call it branding, that's all.

Zé got me the job after my unexpectedly early return from the United States. Through his friendship with my boss, and a veiled threat that he might one day look elsewhere to advertise the MaxiMarket chain, which is by far the most profitable account the agency handles, he saw to it that I got to work on the most interesting brands in the building: a chocolate company owned by an American multinational, the nation's leading detergent, and two children's breakfast cereals. It can be a ruthless place, so this status as the *filho de papai* is invaluable, even if the Papai in question is only an adoptive one.

I have known my boss, Oscar Cascavel, all my life. He plays tennis with Zé every other week, and he was a regular weekend guest on the farm. But he still makes me nervous. He's an amoral little monster who dry-humps you in the corridor when his serotonin is up, and trashes your day for fun when it isn't. A guy who used to work here told me that Oscar actually fired him by telephone from a urinal. He said he heard the automatic flush kick in as the call ended. When you think you're alone in the lift and his arm shoots in just as the doors are about to meet, it gives you a shock every time. But for the sour tang of sweat and coffee breath that precedes him, the first warning of an encounter is the sight of this fist, followed by his fist-sized Rolex, and before you know it the conversation has started.

'Good afternoon, Ludo. Heavy night? Floor nine, please.'

Shit. I was sure he wouldn't be around to see me arrive. The shooting in the square has made me very late.

I push his button, forgetting to hit floor two, which means I have to pass my own floor and ride with him all the way up.

'Don't joke, Oscar. At four a.m. this morning I wouldn't have been able to recognise you.'

'What I wouldn't give for your stamina. How's business?'

One of the few things I learned before my MBA was abruptly curtailed is that if somebody worth impressing asks, 'How's business?' you should never reply, 'Good.' Your career prospects shrivel the instant the word is out of your mouth. Offer instead a cautiously optimistic statement, quantified by the fluctuations of some unexpected market force. The interrogator cannot fail to be impressed by your appreciation of the subtler factors affecting your business, and he or she will walk away thinking: *Hmmm. I'm lucky to have dos Santos on my team. He's no fool.*

'Chocolate's firing on all cylinders since the peanut limited editions, but my spies tell me we can expect retaliation before the end of this quarter. As for cereal, you know as well as I do that it's a dirty fight, but the new guidelines on salt intake for the pre-teens should work in our favour.'

Just as it was for the boy in the square, confidence is the key. Oscar decides I'm in control of the situation and switches off before I've even finished the chocolate assessment. It's one less thing for him to worry about, so he can zone out of the conversation.

'Good,' he says. 'Well done, Ludo. And I believe I'm seeing you for a briefing in ten minutes. I'm sure you haven't forgotten.'

With that, he breezes out of the lift before my prepared speech has run half its course. I know how quickly consumers make their purchasing decisions, and buying into people is the same: it happens in seconds. And today, Oscar was a buyer – though things would have been different if he'd been in a bad mood.

The Rolexed arm shoots back in. The doors jerk open apologetically.

'One more thing, Ludo – I have a job for you. There's a guy in town called Dennis Pinto. Smart cookie. Been running detergent all over the Pacific Rim. He's half-Australian – left here with his mother as a teenager – but he's thinking of moving back, and he's over here for a few weeks to check us out. From the sound of him I think he'd be an asset.' The lift doors try closing again but Oscar's arm punches out once more. 'His father's an old friend of mine, and I'm supposed to meet him for drinks at his hotel tonight to make him feel at home. But perhaps it would be better if you two hotshots hung out together. I'm sure he would rather meet up with someone closer to his own age than an old blowfish like me. You should have plenty of energy after your lie-in, so make sure you show him a good time. I'll cover your expenses. OK? He's staying at the Windsor. See you in nine minutes.'

The lift doors snip off my reply like scissors. It doesn't matter. He'll be metres of carpet away by now, ruining somebody else's morning.

He knows exactly what he's doing, the bastard. He doesn't like this cocky business chat following straight on from my boasts about how hungover I am. Most of all, he doesn't like the fact that when he first met me, I was nothing but the son of the cook at Zé's weekend *fazenda* – and now I'm snapping at his heels. And because, inexplicably, his old friend Zé has actually adopted me, he can't even fire me. *All right*, he's saying. *Stick your head over the parapet if you dare, but I will shoot it off.* He can't fire me, but that doesn't mean he has to respect me. To him I will always be that farm boy in the kitchen. Nothing more.

\*

In its relentless effort to teeter as close to the cutting edge as possible, the agency recently relocated to one of the city's grimmest frontiers, a district of hastily constructed high-rises, shabby tenements, and, on all the available patches of wasteland, favelas. Big or small, under every bridge, behind every rusty fence, you'll find them: improvised burrows of wood, cardboard and brick. Washing on the line. A plant pot here and there. Mongrels rolling in the dust. The shanty towns in this city are sedimentary – not brashly spilling down hillsides, as they do elsewhere – and many of them are far out of town, out of sight. They can be vast, but they can just as easily grow in crevices and forgotten corners – wherever there is a gap, like silt.

Everyone calls our office the Beehive, though it is no longer a squat. The term is usually applied to high-rise slums, or other fallen buildings colonised by the needy, where multiple families share one toilet and sleep four or five to a room. The building is therefore on its third and most confusing life yet. (It used to be said that the economy was like a bumblebee, because somehow it worked though logically it shouldn't have been able to get off the ground. The inhabitants of beehives and favelas are similarly paradoxical: they shouldn't, in theory, be able to survive, but they do.)

Until we took it over, our office was abandoned and condemned, and inhabited by ghosts who made it their own. Usually, the fate of a building like this is to be razed to make way for new, sanctioned accommodation. But the agency stepped in. To the bafflement of the authorities, when all the 'marginals' had been moved on, the company bought the doomed building as well as the site. They strengthened the floors and fumigated it for pests. Then they sprayed clear epoxy resin over every surface to fix it before bringing in the chrome chairs, the bleeping terminals, that eye-catching piece of war memorabilia. And now we hammer out flimsy approximations of the global strategies handed down to us by our brand over-lords surrounded by frozen graffiti: impulsive obscenities, disposable ideas, cartoon art, and the ominous tags of a local gang known as the Shadow Command.

The result is a workplace close enough to some of the city's black holes to benefit from a perception of frontier danger, but not so unsafe that you'll get knifed popping out for lunch. We gaze down from our sealed windows over the chaotic contours of a mid-sized favela, and never give it a second thought. We could be somewhere leafy and upmarket, surrounded by glittering designer brands, but we choose this instead: it has more cachet. This kind of self-conscious cool is a relatively recent development – and as with other foreign imports, we sometimes go too far in our eagerness. Sensing a pose of ironic detachment to be important, we rushed to acquire one at the expense of all sensitivity. Even as they raise their eyebrows at how far we have taken things, our international clients find the place thrilling – and they love having their meetings on cantilevered Italian chairs while perusing the desperate scrawl of the unfortunates who used to live here.

Events sometimes burst the bubble. When the block was restored, a beautiful old avocado tree nearby was preserved and nourished, and now spreads out over the fortified guard-house and beyond the office compound, covering the street with its canopy. Not long after we moved in to the building, a cyclone blew a huge branch into the street. So many people came out of the favela to harvest the bounty that there was almost a riot, and one of our security guards was forced to draw his gun.

But fixes of real life like that are rare. For the most part, we sit at our terminals like drones, waiting for strategies to blip in from London or New York: slick multimedia presen-tations of nonsense words devised to sum up the brand, to which we are invited to devote ourselves: *Eatertainment*; *Funteraction*. If they are meaningless even in English then how are they supposed to make sense in our language? But I'm not paid to ask questions. I exist to reassure my distant masters that their ideas work in this market: to provide local evidence in support of their conceited impositions, regardless of the truth.

My response to the realisation that my job is pointless has thus far been to worry as little as possible, to spend my office days how I like, and to do just enough to slip under the radar. I pass the time sleeping and reading in toilet cubicles converted from the last-resort hovels of those with more tenacity than I can imagine, and try to avoid the comparison between their lives and mine even as it stares me in the face. The occasional client pops in to the office to make sure we're implementing his or her strategy, and they might have to be taken for lunch, but otherwise my days are spent staring at the terminal at my desk or organising meetings whose sole purpose is to fill the diaries of their attendees with reassuring appointments.

I remember the Windsor Hotel. In spite of the name it is, like several hotels in the downtown area, run by Italians. It looks old-fashioned now, but was once a beautiful place: thick carpets, dark marble, and a proper bar with a multi-coloured array of backlit bottles. And it was the setting for a precious childhood experience.

For a week or two after I had left the farm but had yet to be enrolled at school in the city, nobody knew what to do with me. So Zé used to take me with him to work. I suspect he liked having the boy he had saved around as a PR asset. One day, he had a meeting in the Windsor Hotel, in one of its private rooms, and he took me down from the helipad to the ground floor and asked me to wait for him in a small, mirrored chamber off the main lobby.

'I think you might find what I'm doing up there very boring, Ludo. Why don't you stay down here and have some lunch while you wait – ever eaten a club sandwich?'

I shook my head. Hotel food wasn't my mother's style.

'They're good here. Sit down. I think you'll like it.'

It was a typically smart move to leave me in that little alcove with such an exquisite and time-consuming new distraction. I was still reeling from the size of the city to which I'd been transplanted, but even in the grip of all the new sensation I remember the shock of realising that I had been denied something so pleasurable until now. This heavenly confection of lettuce, mayonnaise, grilled bacon, chicken breast and sweet tomato, that lasted so long due to the ingenious decision to use three slices of bread instead of two, and to toast them (but not too much) – what else had I been missing? Clever Zé. You have to hand it to him. He knew me well enough, even at fourteen, to know that no matter what the big, bad city had to offer – I could have wandered out on to the streets at any time – setting a triple-decker sandwich and a cold Coke down in front of me was all that was required to keep me occupied. When he came back, his business concluded, I had not moved. I was sitting back, listening to the music of the lobby and staring at myself in the mirrors, a plate with four neatly lined up cocktail sticks on it before me.

The doors ping open on a nervous pack of blinking clients. Somehow that memory has taken me all the way back to the ground floor. I don't want to look as if I can't operate the lifts, so I emerge and make as if to leave the building. Then I go round the back of the wing of the American bomber, greet the receptionist, and open the doors to the back stairs. Hot air blasts my face as I leave the air-conditioned zone. The stairs stink of stale smoke, sweat and eucalyptus-scented cleaning fluid.

I start taking two steps at a time to get to the second floor, then realise that nobody is watching and I might as well waste some more of the day. The cleaner is tramping down the stairs dragging a green refuse sack, a tinny-sounding little radio hanging from her belt. I pick up my pace as I pass her, issuing a cheery 'Good morning'. She ignores me. She's found me asleep on bathroom floors too often to take me seriously.

But I have something on her, too. I know that she feasts on the uneaten food she clears from the meeting rooms. I caught her in the act. She looked stuck to the door, immobile, as I passed her in the Technicolor concrete corridor. Then I realised it was because she was trying to eat something off the side of the tray she was meant to be clearing. Halfway through the door, her urge for a leftover *empada* on the side of the plate had overwhelmed her, and she had bitten into it with the tray still in her arms.

'Can I hold that for you?' I said. 'That way you could use your hands.'

I wasn't trying to be sarcastic – I meant it – but she didn't see it that way. She looked at me through frightened eyes, her mouth full, a guilty smear of sauce emerging from one side, then stomped off without a word. Her contemptuous looks when we pass each other in the corridor have been shot through with suspicion ever since. I suppose she fears I might report her to someone.

I only have to deal with two more corridor encounters before I reach the safety of my office: one brief exchange about football and an unsuccessful attempt at flirtation. Finally, I close the frosted glass door behind me and check the time. Twelve-fifteen: just in time for Oscar's meeting. My associates will either assume that I'm arriving now because I've been out at a chocolate meeting, or else I will tell them my hangover story and in their desire to collude in my irreverence they will overlook the fact that I have missed a morning's work. And so the days fly by. Practise your confidence tricks on the street and you risk getting shot by trigger-happy security guards; do it in the office and you get put on the board.

I am thinking how everyone in the building is a confidence trickster, that it's *what we do*, when I look down at the phone on my desk to see a blinking red message light. Sweat springs in my palms and all that confidence is briskly annihilated.

Someone is leaving abusive messages on my work phone. It happens often enough to be unnerving, but not so often that I have bothered to do anything about it. It must be someone I know, because whoever it is insults me by name, and his tone projects real, targeted hatred. The words, when they come, are delivered in a rasping, guttural whisper, often separated by long periods of silence during which all I can make out are strange background noises: rushing water, machinery and, occasionally, what sounds like birdsong.

Sometimes there are no words at all. Other times I can't understand them because the whisper is too quiet, the phrases too mumbled. But usually if I wait long enough, I'll make something out, and get a taste of the venom. Insults. Warnings. Threats.

> *You're in serious trouble, Ludo. I've found you out. I've*
> *   seen you.*
> *What squalid hole are you hiding in tonight?*
> *Change your life. Before I change it for you.*
> *You better do something about this soon. You better.*
> *Or else.*

I have met the odd self-righteous madman with a cross to bear about the industry. They get almost evangelical about it, which is ridiculous – we aren't Nazis, for God's sake. So the first time it happened, I thought I had a lunatic. I congratulated myself on being big enough to have my own personal hater, and deleted the message without a second thought. But it keeps on happening. And now I'm almost used to it. Almost.

*Who could hate me that much?* I thought at first. Then, after the arrival of the third message, it came to me.

If he knew more than I thought.

If he had known all along, and was playing some sort of bluffing game with me and Melissa.

Ernesto might hate me that much.

# Feijoada

We have an epidemic of helicopters now. There are over 200 helipads in the city, and on Friday nights the skies darken as the wealth takes wing to retreat to its weekend homes. It wasn't always like this, but Zé was one of the earliest of the very rich to take to the air. And for all the family's non-chalance, you could tell that the ability to fly never got dull. Sometimes, on Sunday evenings when they left me waving particularly morosely, Zé would get the pilot to recede a little, then come in low and buzz me at high speed. I would feign exhilaration, dust myself off and go inside feeling as if something had been unnecessarily flaunted in my face. I know it was only a helicopter. But I wonder how much it contributed to the state of things between me and Melissa. Seeing her float away like that week after week, emphatic-ally, according to all the evidence at my disposal, a superior being – how could I fail to raise her on a pedestal?

There were practical reasons why it was necessary. First, Zé's job made time a precious commodity; second, the family didn't have the time to drive out to the farm every weekend. But there was a third reason why Zé wanted to keep his family safely up in the air. In addition to accounting for that raising of barometric pressure when they left on Sunday evenings, it also explains why they retreated so religiously to the farm every weekend, and why they were so ecstatic on arrival.

It happened in the city, on a school day. Only infrequently did the family enter our lives during the week, so when the kitchen phone rang, and my mother heard Zé on the line, she knew that something was wrong. Rebecca sometimes called her to discuss menus and arrangements for the weekend, but never Zé.

*I am nine, and sitting in the kitchen licking cake mixture from a spoon: dark chocolate thickened with condensed milk. The phone goes, and my mother crosses the room wiping a hand on her apron. She answers normally, tired, bored. Expecting Silvio. But when she hears the voice on the other end, respect stiffens her voice. Then comes the blood-chilling sound of my mother praying. So this is what the end of the world sounds like.*

There exist hybrid faiths where she came from, and she tended to keep the specifics of her beliefs out of my sight. All I know is that on the day Melissa was taken, my mother made sounds that I had never heard before. Horrified, I asked what was happening, and she told me, using her voice to say that I should not worry, while every other part of her screamed that worrying was exactly the right response.

I had a slingshot, a proper one, with a brace that extended to the forearm. It came equipped with lethal ball-bearings, which I had soon exhausted missing mice and frogs around the farm buildings. But I had learnt how to use it to convert inert objects into deadly projectiles: stones, dried seedpods, stray bits of wood. That afternoon, after the phone call, I took the slingshot into the woods, and spent an hour firing at trees and fruit and birds, imagining every quarry to be the invisible foe I hated so much, and feeling more powerless and angry with each shot I missed.

Melissa was ten. The MaxiMarket chain was hitting the headlines for the speed of its expansion, and this financial success, combined with the public relations dream of Rebecca's foundation, had made the family newsworthy. A full colour spread appeared in a widely read gossip magazine. It included one photo of the three of them posing on the farm with a horse, and another of Melissa chasing around with a butterfly net, her blonde tresses perfectly backlit by the sunshine. It got bad people thinking.

Class had finished for the day, and Zé's driver had not yet appeared, so being Melissa she bounded off out of the jurisdiction of the guards, in the direction she knew her ride would be coming from, and waited at the lights. That's where they grabbed her. A car door opened, and everything went dark. I can picture her calmly looking around as the bag came down over her head. She wouldn't have been scared so much as interested in this new development – whenever she drew blood on the farm she was always more fascinated than afraid.

She did not scream or shout to begin with – not until she decided to get away, and threw her terrifying seizure. She never said a word against her captors, and refused even to attempt a description of them to the police. All we know is that they were taking her somewhere, presumably to formulate their demands, she faked the fit, and they threw her out of the car. I remember seeing her re-enact what she did to escape: contorted body, guttural sounds, a steady stream of froth emerging from the mouth. It terrified me even though I knew it was an act. When the kidnappers lifted the bag from her face and saw what was happening inside, they panicked. Luckily their car was not travelling at high speed. She got away with a sprained ankle, a black eye and a deep cut to her left eyebrow. The man who found her and called the police was a young mechanic named José Luís Oliveira, who lived nearby in a one-room house built by his father. In his gratitude, Zé bought the man a new apartment, and posed for photographers with him and his wife on handing over the keys.

Sometimes, before the kidnapping, Melissa didn't come, opting instead to spend her weekends at the beach houses of her city friends, many of whom thought Zé and Rebecca eccentric to retreat at every opportunity to a bug-infested ranch (Ernesto, I later discovered, being the principal offender). When this happened I would watch in vain for the dart of colour and energy that I so wanted to emerge from the helicopter, and Zé would place a hand on my shoulder as he beat down the steps, and say, 'Not today, Ludo, I'm sorry. Call of the surf this weekend.' After the kidnapping, the farm came into its own – as a 1,000 hectare comfort blanket for the entire family – and Melissa's absence became a rarity. For all their gorgeous Friday evening appearances on the helicopter steps, the predominant emotion inside each of them was one of relief.

Not that this was evident in Rebecca's behaviour. On the first weekend back, when Melissa limped down the helicopter steps with a dressing over her injured eye, my mother embraced her so tightly that I wondered whether she would ever let her go, while Rebecca remained typically disconnected. All weekend, it was my mother who fussed over Melissa and prepared her favourite dishes, while Rebecca behaved as if she had decided not to treat her differently, or even to refer to the abduction at all. It was as if Rebecca was almost annoyed with her daughter for getting herself into trouble – that this one child had created an inconvenient distraction from the needs of all the others out there.

Zé merely demonstrated his relief by saying much less than usual. I think he so badly wanted the incident not to have happened that he couldn't bear to mention it. Money was spent trying to track down the perpetrators, but there was nothing to go on; Melissa couldn't even tell the police sketch artist whether they were white or black. And I know that this powerlessness would have infuriated Zé. To have control wrested from him so definitively in any situation was unheard of, and would remain unspoken of too.

In the weeks that followed, Melissa did not wet the bed, become wary of strangers or exhibit any other sign of trauma, so everyone believed what they wanted to believe, and the event was buried. My mother found this shocking enough, but when Rebecca took her aside and told her that her continued preferential treatment of Melissa should stop as it might lead her into bad habits, it caused my mother to do something unprecedented: to criticise her saviour.

'Dona Rebecca should be talking to the child more. She should be holding her tight, and not letting her go,' she said quietly, into the sink, as if even to give voice to such disloyal thoughts was tantamount to blasphemy. And then, so faintly that I wondered whether she had said it at all, she added, 'Only an Englishwoman.'

Later, accompanying Rebecca on her orphanage visits, I noticed that when dealing with the kids she tended to disdain affection in favour of problem solving: dressing wounds, taming hair, treating warts. When the children wanted a hug and nothing more practical, she would stand up, smooth down her linens and find a pretext to leave, the impression being that if her kindness were to be widely distributed, it could not be frittered away on single physical encounters. Her husband, by contrast, would reserve all his charm and tactility for the person he was talking to, even as he conducted his life with total ruthlessness.

But an event like that doesn't just go away. However un-affected Melissa might have seemed, an arrow had been fired high in the air by what happened, and it had to come down eventually. That I was the only person to realise this is directly attributable to the fact that it was *feijoada* day.

If cooking *feijão* is an exercise in loading the beans with whatever flavour you can summon, then *feijoada* is about overkill: freighting them with everything and seeing what comes out. Every mouthful is different, and the dark, glossy sauce is enriched by every dried, salted, fresh or smoked cut you throw in. On *feijoada* day, Zé could spend the afternoon poring over the shuddering, bubbling clay pots my mother brought out, from the 'new' cuts which he liked well enough – smoked pork sausages, loin chops and belly, jerked and salted beef, salt pork – to the 'old' cuts to which he was devoted, and which for him were the main event – ears, tails, noses, trotters, tripe. Then there were the accompaniments: heaps of finely shredded green kale fried in garlic and oil, toasted cassava flour, pork rinds, plantains, rice, glistening slices of orange. And endless ice-cold jugs of passionfruit, *cajú* or lime *batida* to help it all on its way. On *feijoada* day my mother could not rest – she was on duty the whole time, keeping everybody topped up with fat and protein and alcohol.

An invariable after-effect of this ritual was that it put everyone to sleep for hours, which is the only possible way we could have managed to go missing for a whole afternoon so soon after Melissa's ordeal. If they'd lunched lightly they would have been scouring the farm for guerrilla kidnappers when we didn't turn up. Instead, guests reclined on loungers under the eaves of the pool house, some drinking coffee and brandy and watching the rain outside, others groaning or snoring, while Zé browsed the table for any remaining worthwhile morsels. And we disappeared.

The storm had been building all morning. Clouds heavy with rain massed over the valley; hummingbirds flickered from plant to plant, getting their business out of the way before the onslaught. Rebecca was not enjoying her weekend. Two of her lunch guests were significant donors to the Uproot Foundation whom she wanted to impress, and one of them was a high-ranking Church official. Fearing that her husband and his friends, who invariably got drunk on *feijoada* day, might let her down, Rebecca compensated by concentrating as much as possible on those elements of the lunch that she could control. She asked my mother to clean down every surface several times in advance of the visit, and to make sure that the *feijoada* be more spectacular than ever.

Just before her special guests were due to arrive, Rebecca was on the veranda aligning magazines and setting down dishes of peanuts and *pão de queijo* when Melissa, who had been quiet since the kidnap but was now starting to recover her energy, came sprinting out of the house and wrapped herself around her mother's leg, hotly pursued by me and the ice cube I was intent on putting down her back.

'Leave me alone!' shouted Rebecca. 'What's got into you?'

Melissa squealed. 'Ludo has an ice cube!'

'Snap out of it, will you? I'm meeting some very important people today – people who are going to help save a lot of children who are much less lucky than the two of you. Kids who have the kind of lives you can't imagine.'

Melissa was struggling not to cry.

'Come on,' said her mother. 'I know you had a horrible time, but you're OK now, aren't you?'

Melissa nodded, still fighting tears.

'And you have to remember that what happened to you is nothing compared to what some of my kids at the orphanage go through, or the ones that live on the street.'

'I know that, Mamãe.'

'You're incredibly lucky. Don't ever forget that.'

'I won't.'

Rebecca heard a car arriving, checked her hair in the patio doors and walked into the house.

I had been watching the exchange silently from the doorway, and now, wordlessly, I approached Melissa, whose eyes blazed with powerful, childish indignation.

'Sorry,' I said, dropping the ice cube and wiping my hand on my shirt.

'It wasn't your fault.'

'What shall we do now?'

'I don't want to be here,' she said. 'Let's take off.'

'What about the *feijoada*?'

I had been enjoying the build-up, watching my mother soak the beans and the salt cuts, helping to stoke the fire all afternoon, getting high in the kitchen on the smells of flesh marinating in lime juice and garlic and on the sight of Silvio arriving with bags of bright pink noses and strings of freshly stuffed sausages.

'They'll be sitting there for hours. And my mother is in a terrible mood. We should escape. Bring your slingshot.'

The meal was served under the eaves of the pool house so everyone could watch the storm as it came up the valley, and the main course was just arriving as we escaped. Roars of approval went up as each new delicacy emerged. Melissa and I were forgotten. Leaving the laughter of the lunch table behind us, we crept into the forest, fine rain soaking our faces. The darkening skies and dense greenery sapped the light. The rush of the river was only a distant backdrop, and all the noise that mattered seemed to be right beside us: the calm beat of raindrops hitting foliage, the shuffle and scamper of forest creatures. Enraptured by the hot, wet atmosphere, we walked in silence, failing to notice how steadily the rain was intensifying.

We came upon a recently fallen tree not far from the outhouse that contained the back-up electricity generator.

Its roots had left a deep red hollow in the earth, already slick with mud.

'Let's live wild for the day,' said Melissa.

'What's "living wild"?'

'Living off the land. Killing our food,' she said.

This was out of character. It wasn't all that long since the sight of a dead animal had been enough to upset her for days. But something in the intimacy of the steady, warm rain and the dark green canopy overhead was conducive to strange behaviour. We could do anything here, and the world would never know.

Soon, the rain was coming down so hard that water gushed down the hill, making a cataract out of the path.

'We can't get back up,' said Melissa. 'So we'll have to stay.'

We took off our clothes and hid them behind a rock. Then we covered ourselves in mud and leaves, and daubed on to our bodies what we decided were the markings of Tupi Indians, comparing how they looked on the different shades of our skin.

Apart from my mother's, which I had never scrutinised closely, Melissa's was the only naked female body I'd seen. There was nothing more or less than I had imagined; a crucial component was missing, which I had expected, and an abrupt vertical fold was there in its place, which I had not. But for a glance at me Melissa didn't seem interested in the differences between us, so I followed her lead and concentrated on the game instead. We staked our claim on the land. We found berries that Melissa claimed were edible and which I well knew were not, so we only pretended to eat them. We laid branches over the hollow in the ground, and called it our 'base'.

'Let's be the first Indians. We're Adam and Eve, and this is our new world,' said Melissa, her eyes glaring starkly from her blackened face.

'OK,' I said.

She gestured at the slingshot hanging from my arm. The river roared somewhere behind her. 'Now you have to kill something for us to eat.'

'What shall I kill?'

'Anything. That bird.' She pointed at a green parakeet twittering in a tree.

I took aim, and let fly. The bird's calls stopped abruptly. I saw a flurry and a flash of leaves, and thought it had flown away, but then came a thud as it hit the ground.

'Good,' said Melissa. She leapt over to pick up the body. 'It isn't quite dead, so it can be our prisoner. Put it in the hole.'

I jumped into the rising orange water to lay down our victim. Slimy, pungent mud slid between my bare toes. I breathed in the smells of rain and steaming earth, enjoying inhabiting this version of myself – a boy who killed things in the jungle, and defended his friend from harm.

'Now you get in the hole too,' said Melissa.

'Why me?'

'Because you're my prisoner as well.'

It didn't occur to me to do anything other than go along with the game, so I crept into the hollow in the ground, and let her cover it with leafy branches. Crouching in the puddle inside, I started to get cold, and shouted to Melissa, asking how long I was supposed to stay down there. Abruptly, she burst through the roof of leaves over my head, and landed beside me.

She stared at me in the dripping gloom. 'Now you have to lie on me.'

I did as requested. Her skin felt warm against mine. She lay rigid, her arms at her sides.

'You have to move back and forward.'

'This is stupid,' I said. 'I know you don't do it like this.'

'How do you know?'

'I've seen how animals do it.'

And suddenly she was screaming, and I felt it too. Fire ants were sweeping over our bodies in a red wave of pain. They had been living in the base of the fallen tree, and without the protection of the trunk the rain was drowning them in their nest.

'We should get in the river,' I said, my skin alive with them. I got to my feet and ripped away the covering branches.

'No,' she said. 'This is natural. We have to leave them. Sit down.'

The jags of pain in my limbs, my fingers, on my genitals, merged into an all-over heat. I remember crying, but thinking that there was no way I could jump into the river if Melissa did not. I remember finding the red of the bites shocking against her pig-pink complexion, and thinking that the colour was somehow more at home on my skin, because it was darker.

As the afternoon progressed and the killing began in earnest, I felt that we were taking our revenge with the sling-shot for what the ants had done to us. Somehow, the pain made me shoot better, and with every bird I brought down, the bites seemed to glow brighter on my body. I began to appreciate the link between the wounds that nature had inflicted on me, and the revenge I was exacting on it in return. Everything we saw was condemned by Melissa and fired at by me: two thrushes, a kingfisher and a rat. We even took aim at an infant monkey unlucky enough to come into view. Melissa had a sweet little potbelly at this time. I can see her now, coated in mud, stomach out, jumping around in the undergrowth, pointing her finger at the unfortunate crea-ture I was to kill next.

Silvio, the only person not occupied by the *feijoada*, had set out when the rain started to come down hard. By the time he tracked us down, our naked bodies were shivering and mud-streaked, and broken up by bright sores from the ant bites. Our 'base' had become a mortuary of feathered bodies, their plumage limp, their colours muddy. Melissa and I stared at him from the hole. He stared back, smoking, rain dripping from the brim of his hat, as if we did this every afternoon. But his smile was absent, and he spoke calmly, as though he'd found us preparing to leap from a high ledge.

'Why don't you both have a swim in the river, then get dressed before I take you back up to the house,' he said, glancing briefly at the dead animals, at the slingshot hanging from my hand.

By the time we had returned from the river – damp, cold, meekly dressed – he had disposed of the birds and filled in the hole. At the house he gave us calamine lotion for our bites, and told Zé and Rebecca, who still lolled round the lunch table watching the rain, that we'd gone for a swim and lost track of time. He never told anyone what he'd seen.

Against all logic, it was Zé's belief that you had to follow *feijoada* with a very big dinner. 'Sometimes,' he would say, 'I think I only enjoy eating it so much because of the room it makes in my stomach for the next meal.' That evening, we ate like monsters, everything the grill could offer, and every one of my mother's sumptuous side dishes. Smiling sweetly at each other, coasting on the exhilaration generated by the rain, the ant bites, the killing, we snapped at chops, sucked on bones, devoured steaks. I remember competitions: how quickly we could each eat a burger, how many chicken hearts we could fit in our mouths at a time. Our faces glowed in the lamplight of the veranda, grease on our chins. I lay awake all night, unable to sleep, partly because I was still immersed in the rapture of the afternoon, but mostly because my belly was taut as a barrel, and I was bent double with indigestion, and the still-glowing pain of the ant bites.

★

There were no barriers between me and Melissa. Nor was there any sense that the pleasures we enjoyed on the farm belonged to her more than they did to me. You might think, though, that some sense of propriety would have made our friendship embarrassing for Zé and Rebecca, or for my mother. It didn't. I think the Minister and his wife liked the fact that their daughter had a companion waiting there in the queue to entertain her for the weekend. In letting them continue unimpeded with their entertaining, it was a service as valuable as Silvio's gardening, or my mother's skill in the kitchen. I did sometimes feel guilty about abandoning my mother, especially when things were busy – during the visit of a special guest, perhaps, or, in the days when he was in government, when some initiative of Zé's had met with public or official approval. At these busy times, I might see my mother hard at work, and leave Melissa to help her carry heaving dishes of food to the table for lunch.

'You aren't paid to do it like I am,' she would say. 'Go and play with Melissa. You can help me during the week, when she's not here.'

It was during one such weekend that I burst into the kitchen with a loaded water pistol in pursuit of Melissa and found my mother resting uncomfortably against the draining board, with a male guest standing strangely close. He was a regular visitor; Melissa and I laughed often about the stink he gave off when returning from one of his sessions with Zé on the tennis court. He hadn't filled out to the extent that he has now, but his belly was already as round as a bowling ball, and he wore a chunky Rolex that was too big for his wrist. As I clattered inside and the door hit the wall, he stepped swiftly away from my mother and turned to me with his hands up.

'Don't shoot!' he said, wide-eyed, putting his hands in the air to reveal sweat patches the size of fried eggs under his arms. His blue shirt lifted in the process, revealing an oblong section of hairy brown belly that protruded between his belt and the shirt as if being forced through a letter box.

'Sorry,' I said, used to apologising whenever I burst in on my mother during work hours. She had tapped me round the head with ladles and spoons for less – and once, when I skipped school, with a copper saucepan that was the first thing to hand. I expected some sort of stinging blow now, but this time she did not even look at me. She kept her eyes on the man, who was beginning to look nervous.

'That's OK. Go on, get out of here,' she said.

I left the room, quietly puzzled. I knew all too well that tight-lipped look of fury, but her words had shown me that, for once, it wasn't directed at me. As I ambled into the yard outside, Melissa directed at me the full force of her pump-action water cannon, so the incident went to the back of my mind. But I remembered it later that day when I saw Oscar Cascavel sitting in a corner, rubbing a nasty saucepan mark on the side of his face.

# Crab Linguine

'Before we start this briefing I want a two-minute update from one of you on where we are with chocolate cereal.'

Oscar is stressed. Someone higher up the corporate ladder has been bullying him and we'll pay the price. He will want to stay here, rebooting the confidence that crashed during the ear chewing he's just received, and he'll believe that the positive outcome of the session will hinge on the hours we devote to it, which means we could be here some time.

'Who wants to fill me in?' he says, dancing around nervously, like a boxer.

'Well,' I say. 'They didn't give us much room for manoeuvre. It's a kids' product, as you know. In order to fit in with the Global Brand Template we have to incorporate the concepts of "play" and "fun". We also have to mention chocolate.'

'OK. Where did you come out?'

'Our starting point was *Playful, Chocolatey Fun*. Then we looked into *Fun, Playful Chocolate*. Neither of those seemed to take us into new territory. I think we're all pleased with where we are now.'

'Which is?'

'*The Playful Way To Make Your World More Chocolatey.*'

Oscar pauses dramatically on his way round the room,

screwing his eyes up and repeating the expression silently to himself. Behind him, the teeth of a vicious graffitoed cat are closing around a cowering mouse. Beside it, in small letters, is scrawled *I don't want any more cheese. I just want to get out of the trap.*

'That's bold, cutting out "fun" altogether,' says Cascavel. 'Think they'll allow it?'

'We're giving it a try.'

'Good work. Now,' he says, 'to the business of the day. We have a new *pro bono* brief.'

He pushes a button on the keypad in front of him, and automatic shutters descend to black out the windows. The screen on the wall flashes into life, to reveal a high-resolution photograph of a favela, shacks and cells intermingling as they tumble shockingly down a steep incline of red earth.

'It's not often that a brief arrives on my desk that makes me think *This is revolutionary*,' Oscar goes on, pacing in the gloom and making shapes with his hands that are meant to communicate inspiration. 'We're only marketeers, after all. But this one is different. What's more, in spite of the fact that it will be work for which the agency will not charge a fee, it has the potential to open up more untapped markets than any piece of communication in our history. It's not just going to benefit the client in question – it's going to benefit every one of our existing clients.'

He pauses behind my chair. Not being able to see him makes me uneasy. His hands clap down hard on my shoulders.

'Tell them, Ludo.'

I squirm out from under his sweaty palms. 'Sorry Oscar – I have no idea what this is.'

'You're serious?'

'Absolutely.'

'I'm amazed. The client from whom we received this brief

is a consortium composed mostly of members of your family.'

People round the table laugh.

'Never heard of it,' I say. 'I haven't seen much of the family lately. Apart from my sister.'

'The brief is not from Melissa, lovely as she is,' says Oscar. 'It's from someone else. With characteristic generosity, your father has come up with a striking new initiative. He plans to open a chain of subsidised supermarkets in the hearts of each of our largest favelas.'

He clicks another button, and the screen is filled with a logo similar to the MaxiMarket one, though in more garish colours, and larger. More childlike. It reads *MaxiBudget*.

'I am sure that I'm not the only one who detects the influence of your mother here,' he says, continuing to address me.

'Rebecca is my adoptive mother.'

'Of course. It was – ' He breaks off, and stares at the wall. 'It was a great shame about your mother. She gave pleasure to many people.'

'Thank you, Oscar.'

The moment of humanity disappears as quickly as it came. Feeling awkward, he scrabbles to recover his position by turning to flippancy. 'For one thing, she would have been useful to us on this brief. We could have pulled together a little focus group.'

I can cope with the remark, but I wish he wouldn't give me all this special attention. There are six other people round the table, and the way he speaks to me – in spite of what he's saying – is only going to reinforce the general perception that I did nothing to earn my job here.

'Ludo's *adoptive* mother, Rebecca Fischer Carnicelli,' he goes on, 'has always acted as her husband's conscience, and the MaxiBudget initiative is to be launched in partnership with her charity, the Uproot Foundation, of which Ludo was an early beneficiary. Am I right?'

'More or less,' I mutter.

'But on to the brief,' says Oscar. He clicks the pad on his desk again, and we cut to a grubby child pawing at the window of a brightly lit produce counter heaving with bounty. The pineapples look stunning. The papayas emit tropical sunshine. The bananas make you want to burst out laughing.

'See this child?' asks Oscar, in a faintly aggressive way. He waits until someone says 'yes', in a small voice.

He pauses, gazing at what would be a view of the infinite, yellow city were it not for the blinds. He takes a deep breath, before spinning round to face the room.

'We are going to feed this child,' he says, high on how sensational his words are. 'I don't need to tell any of you what a big idea this is. This girl – look at her again – represents a section of society that is marginalised, and consequently it's a group we have never been able to reach. Through MaxiBudget, we will not only acknowledge them and offer them affordable food, we will open a dialogue. These people are a giant untapped market. They are just waiting for their chance to rise up and consume. And the MaxiBudget stores will be . . . *training grounds*, if you like, for these consumers of the future. Training grounds. That's great. Somebody write that down.'

The next slide he clicks to details the new corporate identity for the MaxiBudget chain. I am as familiar with the MaxiMarket equivalent as I am with my mother's face, with the layout of the paving slabs round the pool on the farm. All through my childhood, this image held sway – it was on every notepad on which my mother made a shopping list, and every pen she wrote with. An impressionistic stick cartoon of an open-armed figure embracing the shining

MaxiMarket logo, drenched in its sunbeams. It was on the stationery I took to school, on the clothes I wore – I suppose it was what rescued me. Without that Godlike presence, there would have been no farm, no helicopter to get there, and no need of a full-time cook.

And here it is entering my life again, albeit in strange, altered form. The same sunbeams emanate from a similar logo, except that it's not just one figure embracing the glow but a faux-naïf image of an entire family, huddled together for safety. What's more, where the stick-man in the original MaxiMarket logo looked sleek and cool, this family has somehow been drawn in such a way that they look emaciated. (Is it my imagination, or is there something of the Holocaust about them?) And they are, of course, not so realistic that you should ever question whether they're black or white. That's a minefield of which MaxiMarket likes to steer clear.

Oscar has lit an acrid cigarette, and is basking in the light of the screen. 'As you should know, some supermarket chains already operate in the larger favelas, but never before has a commercial brand gone into partnership with a charity in such a committed fashion, and never before has a household brand sought so openly to associate itself with those who do not, in theory at least, own their homes. The middle classes have this wariness of favelas, imagining them to be little more than hotbeds of drug crime and disease. And in some ways, they're right. But not everyone born in a favela is a criminal. Most are trying to live normal lives, but their neighbourhood prohibits it. Take Ludo here. He's a charming young man, a go-getting businessperson. There's nothing scary about him! He's so beautiful sometimes, I just want to fuck him.'

There's a murmur of obsequious laughter underpinned by a note of disgust that Oscar could never discern. If it weren't for outbursts like this, I think people would resent the special attention I get from him. As it is, I get sympathy for being the object of his peculiar fascination. People know, because I've told them, that much of it is to do with my mother – and Oscar's continued bafflement at how I have somehow managed to rise out of the station into which I was born.

He's still talking. 'And that's my point. Attitudes are changing. People like Ludo are on the up. The favelas are the beating heart of the samba, of the *capoeira*, of God knows what else. These days, it sometimes feels as if they are the heart of everything. And this is what I want you all to think about when developing this campaign. Try to find something that captures the spontaneity of these people. Their *joie de vivre*. Has anyone taken the time to look out of their window during a traffic jam lately? It's like Carnival out there.'

'That's not spontaneity, it's desperation,' I say.

'Whichever term you prefer, Ludo, you're the wordsmith. My point is that this should be a colourful, joyous campaign. Something that will resonate. First thoughts by tomorrow please. And I don't need to tell you, Ludo, that I am expecting particularly great things from you, with your insight into this world.'

'As you know, Oscar, I grew up on a farm,' I say.

'I know, but . . . before that. You know what I mean.'

'Do I?'

'What I mean is that you, of all people, should throw yourself into this one. See if you can spend some time in one of these places. Meet the people. Go on one of those tours, perhaps. Get reacquainted.'

Someone pipes up. 'So all of this is *pro bono* work? It's unusual for us to be doing this much for free.'

'Here's the clever part,' says Oscar. 'In return for providing all the communication for the MaxiBudget chain for nothing, our agency will receive exclusive rights to promote our brands in every one of the new stores. Which means that only our clients will have access to this new market. And that's work we *can* charge the full rate for. The thing pays for itself!'

Now a genuine laugh splashes round the room. A knowing, indulgent one.

He holds up a hand, acknowledging the laugh, and halting it. 'Seriously, guys. At the moment these people buy their produce from the man with a dirty wheelbarrow who runs along at the end of their road. Their meat, when they can afford it, is often carved up in the street and rarely refrigerated. Sometimes, they even work on a bartering basis: meat in exchange for favours. It's immensely un-sophisticated. When MaxiBudget launches they will have the opportunity to buy from a clean retail unit right there in their community. Just like the rest of us.'

'Where does that leave the guy with the dirty wheel-barrow?' I say.

'If you're going to be clever, Ludo, then I'll fire you right now and you can go back to the gutter with your relatives.'

There's a shocked silence. Oscar licks his lips, where tiny white marks of dried saliva have accumulated. He clears his throat.

'Sorry. But you were way off the point. Right,' he says, turning on the room and plunging the end of his cigarette into the plate of pastries on the table. 'Class dismissed. I want something interesting on this by tomorrow afternoon. We have the client coming in to discuss it, and I want you all buzzing with fresh ideas.'

'Who is the client?' I ask, nervously.

'Don't worry, it's not Mamãe or Papai – *adoptive* – they've hired a new guy, just for this. Now, get lost, all of you. I don't want to see any of your faces until we have something special on this. Ludo, please stay.'

The others file out. One of them gives me a sympathetic look at the door.

'You know, your problem isn't that you don't do the work,' he says when the door has closed. He's standing with his back to me as if he were surveying the view, even though the blinds are still down. 'It's that you don't *look* as if you're doing the work. If you don't start behaving more profession- ally, then people who walk the walk better than you will start to surpass you. At that point, it won't matter who your father is. Do you understand?'

'I understand.'

'Sort yourself out, will you? Make me proud. And here.' He gets an envelope out of his pocket and slides it across the table towards me. 'Expenses for your evening with the Australian. Show him a good time, OK?'

I return to my office to find the red light on my phone blinking, and press the button expecting another instalment of whispered voice-hate-mail. But it's only something work- related. Perhaps my enemy is getting bored.

I should try to get home before going to the hotel. This shirt has been on my back for two days, and can't take another evening's onslaught from my toxic body. But Ernesto returns tonight, and I need to see Melissa again before he does. I have to keep her topped up – to remind her of me one last time before he reclaims her attention. If I leave her alone in his company for long enough, her life might seem simple again, and she will forget there was ever anyone other than her constant, gigantic husband.

Thankfully, the office is fitted out with a bathroom and a fresh supply of shirts – we are a service industry, and are equipped for unforeseen entertaining – so I shower and slip on the least offensive item in the cupboard. The shirt has been cheaply laundered: when I slide it out of its wrapper it smells of a sickly, chemical agent, and the material makes my skin crawl when I put it on. I swear if I had the money I would send my clothes to be laundered in Paris, like the old Amazon rubber barons.

I open Oscar's envelope to find a bundle of currency, and a small zip-lock plastic bag of white powder. I tap some of it on to my tongue, which immediately numbs to the root. Oscar will never explicitly allude to this arrangement, but I know what I have to do.

I dial Melissa's number.

'What do you want?' she says.

'I need to see you,' I say.

'You can't. Ernesto's back. Anyway, you saw me this morning.'

'He's there now?'

'He went to the university.'

'At this time?'

'He has something big on tomorrow. Ludo, I have to go.'

'I'll be there in twenty minutes,' I say, putting the phone down before she can protest.

I leave my car at the office and take a cab to Melissa's. During the journey the new shirt begins to irritate my skin so much that I can't sit still. By the time I have arrived at her chrome tower, I am ready to tear it off. Tonight the guards wave me on up.

'You shouldn't still have a key to this place,' says Melissa, as I open the front door.

I lean in to kiss her cheek, puckishly reaching for her breast at the same time, but she spins away so that both advances glance off.

'I preferred yesterday's welcome,' I say.

Ernesto's bags sit unpacked near the front door. I picture

him dumping them as he arrives home, scooping her up and taking her to bed. I picture the surface of my half-drunk glass of water on the bedside table, rippling unnoticed as they fuck away his absence.

'Don't worry, I can't stay long. I have to take an Australian out for dinner.'

'What are you doing here?'

'I need to borrow a shirt.'

'Of Ernesto's? It will dwarf you.'

'At least it won't make my skin come out in a rash.'

'Ludo –'

'Just let me borrow a shirt and then I'll leave. If he does come back that will be the reason I'm here – an office emergency. He'll be pleased to see me.'

'I don't want you here.'

The phone rings, rescuing me. She leaves the room, and I hope it's him, telling her he'll be some time yet. Forgetting for a moment that I no longer live here, I tidy the place up, washing two glasses and retrieving a cushion impacted into the furniture by Ernesto. God, but he's enormous. It might have been shot into the sofa by a cannon. This is not news to me, of course; I've slept on his side of the bed enough times to know the indentation he leaves. When the mattress hasn't been turned for a while there's a hollow on his side you could skateboard in.

I head for the bedroom. As usual, the concentrated fug of Melissa in all the clothes and bed linen, the mother-lode of pheromones, makes me sway momentarily in the doorway. I note with approval that she hasn't had time to change the sheets. There's still some of me in here yet, then. But she's tidied, and lit candles, and a pair of Ernesto's trousers lies on the floor. I kick them under a chair, and throw open his wardrobe.

Swathed in the least tent-like of Ernesto's soft cotton shirts

I emerge to find her at the granite kitchen island studying a recipe book. Two huge crabs steam in a saucepan on the stove.

'The "Welcome Home" dinner,' I say. 'How lovely. What are you doing with these?'

'Go away, Ludo. This is hard enough as it is.'

'Let me help you,' I say, rolling up the sleeves of Ernesto's shirt. 'You know I can do this better than you. You can still take the credit.'

She takes a gulp from a glass of white wine, but can't hide her relief at the offer. She never was much of a cook.

'What were you going to do?'

'A crab salad,' she says. 'He's been in the interior for three days, so I thought he'd be sick of red meat.'

'We can do better than that,' I say. 'Pour me a glass of wine. You can't give the man a salad for his homecoming. He needs something more nourishing.'

She admits defeat, and gets out a wine glass.

'I promise,' I say, getting to work on cracking the crabs and extracting their steaming, fragrant flesh, 'that I'll be gone in half an hour. You can sit and talk to me while I work, and then I'll be gone.'

She sits down, shaking her head, but relieved to have the job taken out of her hands.

'What did you do today?' I ask.

'Not much. Shopping.'

'Guess what happened at work? I was briefed on Zé's new supermarket chain for the poor.'

'I haven't heard anything about that.'

'No?' I take a rolling pin to what remains of the claws and torsos, pounding them open. 'Seems to be a big deal. Oscar says it is, anyway. Thinks it will give us a whole new generation of consumers to brainwash.'

'Good on Papai. And Mamãe, too – I bet this was her

idea. Then again, I suppose it isn't such a new idea: that surgeon in Rio has been doing free cosmetic work for *favelados* for years. The samba schools built a whole float in his honour when he retired.'

And there's your reason. So-called Zé Generoso never does anything out of pure generosity. His gifts come with conditions. Your running total is totted up at the check-out, just as if you were in one of his stores, and if he's subsidising you for now, it's only to help you graduate to the next level, where he can charge you the full whack. Meanwhile Melissa's out blowing the proceeds on luxury brands while her father burns it up overhead on helicopter fuel.

I open the convex sliding door leading to the balcony. 'I bet you haven't been watering my herbs.'

When Melissa and I lived here together, before the penthouse became her marital home and our relationship strayed beyond the fraternal, I grew herbs in terracotta troughs on the balcony, hoping to summon the ghost of nature from the smog of the megacity. There was coriander, parsley, thyme – all struggling on with nothing to sustain them but my ministrations and the evil city air. Now that I have been banished, the shrubs are a sorry sight: rows of dead, dry clumps, their leaves crumbling to dust at the touch.

'Thought so,' I say. 'But wait! There's life in this parsley.'

It's a miracle. Just what I need. God knows how much flavour it will have, but I won't be eating it. I twist off the living shoots that remain, and step back inside.

'Sorry about your plants,' says Melissa.

'Don't worry. I hadn't exactly pictured you or Ernesto out there at first light with the watering can.'

I shred the parsley, and prepare mounds of chopped garlic and red chilli. Then I take down the frying pan from a hook above the black granite work surface. My hand remembers this pan: the knot in its wooden handle, its patina. Its familiarity is heart-wrenching. It was one of my mother's on the farm, bequeathed by me to Melissa. It was the pan that instigated our first kiss.

Suddenly I want to get out of here. Initially, I wanted Ernesto to come home and find me cooking his dinner, a scorpion in his nest, but now I don't want to see them together. So I make the sauce quickly, softening the garlic and adding the chilli and the crabmeat before turning the heat right up and flinging my glass of white wine over the mixture.

'I'm late for my Australian,' I say. 'Add the parsley in a minute. Then cook some pasta – linguine if you have it – and toss that sauce in it for a minute or two before serving. It will be delicious.'

I leave before she has the chance to forget to thank me.

The Windsor Hotel has gone downhill. The plush leather banquettes on which I devoured my first club sandwich look old and lumpy, and are ripped in several places. The sophisticated off-white walls I remember are closer to washed-out lime green, and the mirrors look stained and tacky.

Entering the bathroom to wash the smell of crabmeat off my hands, I find a very old, very black man sitting on a chair by the basins, a small plate of tips by his side. When I enter he leaps up to brush my shoulders, squeeze soap on to my hands, anoint me with aftershave – whatever I request. It embarrasses me. I tell him to stay seated and, realising I'm carrying it in my hand, I offer him the shirt from the office.

'It's clean,' I say. 'And brand new. I have no need of it.'

He shrugs, feels the material with the tips of his fingers, and thanks me. I'm sure it's a better gratuity than he's used to, but as soon as I've left I worry that I have patronised him. The hotel uniform he is made to wear seems, at his age, to be an assault on his dignity as it is, and maybe I have made things worse by offering him my cast-offs.

The white coats. The gloves. The slicked-back hair. The jump-to, cheery enthusiasm. We may as well just come out and say it: the toilet attendants in places like this are encouraged to look and act like slaves.

'Plantation chic,' I murmur, climbing the stairs, thinking I should write that down. It might come in useful for a campaign.

Then I worry that I am patronising the man even more by thinking like this. Maybe he's perfectly happy. Maybe he takes pride in his job. Maybe he finds sitting down there on his chair a relaxing way to make a little money in his old age. I spend plenty of hours myself hanging out in toilets trying to make the day go faster.

In the bar, I order myself an unsweetened caipirinha, and settle into a seat discreetly located behind a battered marble column, revisiting my club sandwich memory in order to forget about the toilet attendant. A pianist somewhere echoing and distant knocks out a slow, swinging version of 'One Note Samba'.

The waiter delivers my drink along with a dish of warm smoked almonds. He clears his throat nervously.

'Would it be too much trouble, Senhor, for you to pay for your drink in advance? We've had problems lately with people running off without settling their tabs.'

Yet more evidence that things aren't what they used to be. But I don't mind. There's something inherently nostalgic about this dilapidated place, even without the memory, and it's good nostalgia, the kind that's like a warm bath, not the kind that makes every vital organ in your body ache. I curse the Australian in advance for being about to spoil my mood, and resolve to come back to the hotel again when I'm not meeting anybody. I could stay here for hours, staring at my reflection in the ceiling, anaesthetising myself with *cachaça* and thinking of Melissa.

But I still can't get my mind off the toilet attendant. It takes me at least half of my sharp, numbing drink before I realise why. It's because he reminds me of Silvio.

# Homemade Stew

*I am eight. A weekend party is in progress. Snatches of music and laughter rise from the pool house. My mother scuttles from pocket to pocket of the party, meeting expectations, tidying as she goes. Melissa is not here. Escaping the crowds, I close the door behind me to take refuge in the large, white salon. The silence refreshes me. Cigarette smoke and the fumes of an overturned whisky glass blanket the smell of the furnishings. On the back of a glossy magazine, I see a small pile of icing sugar. As is the norm during large parties, I have been expelled from the kitchen, and I feel hungry and hard done by. I swipe a finger through the sugar and put it to my mouth. The taste, not sweet at all, makes me wince. I am experimenting with moving my mouth in different ways, contorting it, unable to feel anything, when my mother enters the room minutes later.*

*'The sugar tastes funny,' I say.*

*'That sugar isn't for you,' she says, hoisting me away from the low table with one strong arm and depositing me at a safe distance before wiping away what's left with a wet cloth. 'Come back to the kitchen and I'll give you some of the good stuff.'*

*When I go to the kitchen I am unusually unhungry, and I can't sit still long enough to read a sentence or watch even a minute of my favourite programme. I run to the woods and howl at the moon.*

*

There was no school nearby, and no time to travel to one, but Zé Generoso and his wife wouldn't have dreamed of denying their workers an education. So I learned to read and write alongside my mother and the rest of the staff in the farm's own schoolroom.

It's not difficult to come top of the class when your only competition is workmen anxious to get back to herding cattle or boring waterholes, but I knew I wasn't stupid. And Rebecca, who gave regular English lessons to the staff ('Like I'm ever going to use it,' laughed Silvio), had noticed that I picked things up more quickly than most. It was a running joke that I was the farm's 'little genius', that I was 'wasted here'.

Zé and Rebecca were not great readers, but they couldn't invite illustrious guests to stay for the weekend without having a few walls of improving literature. In addition to a political library, there to communicate that Zé knew his place in history – though I never saw him reading a book – the walls of the sitting room were stocked with literary classics, in English and Portuguese. There was plenty of chaff, and much duplication (at least three copies of *Great Expectations*, for example), but I was never short of something new with which to while away the time. When school was over for the morning, and often as a way of avoiding being roped into kitchen or farm work, I would sit in the cool room, perched carefully on one sofa cushion so that I wouldn't have to tidy up too much to cover my tracks, and read; not always understanding everything, but turning the pages fast, and covering a lot of ground.

Not everyone appreciated how smart my mouth was getting. One high-spirited Saturday afternoon, just after my fourteenth birthday, I answered back to a younger, though no less creepy, Oscar Cascavel. He'd drunk one too many caipirinhas over lunch, and when he sensed I was laughing at him, he decided to teach me a lesson. After a high-speed chase around the farm, he finally cornered me in an outhouse, his lungs rattling like one of Silvio's ancient diesel generators. He was so furious that he actually pinned me to the ground with his knees, like a schoolboy. The weight of him bruised my arms, and the swarthy, hairy mess of his stomach loomed over me, but I didn't make a sound.

And then, panicking a little, I remembered some stupid routine I'd learned years ago from Silvio, where my eyes would roll to the back of my head, and my teeth chattered. Melissa and I had used it on each other during play fights as kids. It was meant to make you look mad, to scare people into letting you get away, but I hadn't done it for years.

It did not work on Oscar. 'What's the matter? Are you subnormal? Stop that.'

I stopped, shook my head, and opened my eyes properly.

There was venom in his whisper, and his shortness of breath made his voice quaver. 'You won't get out of it that easily. Think you're so clever, my little *favelado*? Let's see.'

The Rolex rattled near my face as he scrabbled at his belt buckle. He pulled the belt from its loops in a swift, swishing movement, and folded it once, gripping the ends in his right fist. He held it over me, shaking it as he spoke. I stared up at him, resolved not to respond, not even to flinch, when the strike came.

'What's six times nine?'

'Fifty-four.'

'What's the capital of Canada?'

I blinked, brain racing. 'Toronto?'

'Who wrote *The Masters and the Slaves*?'

I stared at him, desperate not to show my fear. He shook the folded belt again, glaring back, his face bright red. 'I'm warning you. Who wrote *The Masters and the Slaves*?'

This was lucky. I knew the answer only because I had seen the spine of the book on the shelves. 'Gilberto Freyre.'

'And what makes you think I'm not going to hit you anyway?'

I spoke fast, getting the words out quickly before I lost my nerve. 'If you do, Senhor, I don't know how I will explain it to Zé Generoso and his wife. I may also have to tell them about the way you try to touch my mother in the kitchen when you come here. I may only be a little *favelado*, but I am loved in this house. And so is she.'

Kneeling hard on my arms, he spat something unintelligible and got up to retreat, leaving me on my back in the outhouse, chest rising and falling like a manic piston. He visited the farm again many more times, but those were the last words we exchanged before my first day at the agency ten years later.

Idiot. I bet he still doesn't know what the capital of Canada is.

I'm sure the decision wasn't taken lightly. Rebecca probably agonised over it for months, particularly over the question of whether what she had in mind was respectful or not – a line she was terrified of crossing. And then, one afternoon, not long after my unpleasant run-in with Oscar, when my mother had finished cleaning up after lunch and was relaxing with her *cafézinho*, Rebecca came to the kitchen and offered to take her son away to the city.

My mother came to me bright-eyed that evening, and said, 'Something wonderful has happened.'

'What?'

'Sit down, and I'll tell you about it.'

That evening I ate slowly, staring at the wall, wondering what it all meant. My mother wouldn't have dreamt of showing me how she really felt, but her sadness was as evident in the chicken stew she ladled on to my plate as if the meat had been simmered in her tears.

The exact terms of the 'adoption' were never explained to me. I have never seen the paperwork, if any exists. I expect Zé steamrollered through the red tape as always, with bribery and string-pulling. Whatever the specifics, I did wonder why the family had to adopt me to help me. If it was simply a question of education, why not just borrow me from my mother during the week, rather than steal me away from her completely? It was most likely a stipulation of Zé's. He never liked being a minor shareholder. And although he wouldn't have said so, I think he felt the lack of a son everywhere, from the football field to the boardroom. Given Rebecca's ever more consuming preoccupation with the children of the city, I might be his only chance to have one. Perhaps he also saw how unlikely it was that Melissa would want to take over his business, and wanted to offset that disappointment by hedging his bets.

In this way, Zé's and Rebecca's colonisation of me, that had started when I was less than a year old in Heliópolis, was made complete.

My mother never came out to see off the helicopter on any normal Sunday, and the day I climbed the metal steps myself for the first time was no different. We said our farewells in the kitchen, my clothes and exercise books packed in a bag on the worn stone slabs. The birdcages under the eaves were ominously silent during our final embrace. But I felt no sadness. I was suddenly, keenly aware of how little there was on the farm to keep me, and I knew I would be back soon enough. Most importantly, I couldn't believe I was really about to go up in the helicopter.

Instinctively I stood to attention beside it as the others filed in, but Zé slapped my back and pushed me towards the doorway.

'In you get! Tonight Ludinho comes with us!' he shouted

over the noise of the rotor, as if this revolution in my life were a Sunday evening entertainment he had contrived for himself.

The whirling blades put me in mind of decapitation, and I kept my head down as I climbed inside. Once seated, I stared from the window at the bright orange clay of the football pitch, and the marks in it made by that weekend's sliding tackles. Melissa and her parents took their seats, and belted up. The family helicopter at that time was so basic as to be almost military, and its stark interior and flashing lights all fed my fourteen-year-old imagination with the impression of a drop behind enemy lines.

First the football pitch, then the entire farm shrank away. The ponds in which I had floated away the hours became tiny; the water chute that had seemed a kilometre long was reduced to a thin blue scratch in the land. I tried to find the individual light I knew was my mother's kitchen, and wondered what dish she was cooking in which to hide her pain.

As we spun around in the direction of the city, Melissa tapped me on the knee and pointed out a rippling herd of white cattle, the dust cloud it was kicking up in the dusk. The pilot knew it was my first time, and he banked low over the animals to speed them up. Zé noted my expression of wonder with proprietorial happiness, as if he'd just bought some new gadget and it hadn't failed to deliver.

I remember the high whine of the engines, the smell of the fabric seats, Melissa's teeth gleaming at me in the gloom. I also remember the studied, calm manner in which everyone else behaved. Even though bringing me with them must have been a novelty, it wasn't long at all before all three wore detached expressions. Zé read a document he had taken from his briefcase. Melissa played an electronic game. Rebecca stared blankly out of the window, as if she were already turning her thoughts to the millions of children in the city who needed her attention, now that the problem I represented had been safely resolved. I tried to disguise the outrage I felt that all could affect such nonchalance while fields sped by beneath us, and the city drew ever closer. I tried to suppress the electric, nervous energy that lit up my body and made it impossible to sit still. I tried also not to look too overawed and excited, to remain unobtrusive, lest they should realise how much change I would bring to their carefully orchestrated lives and ask the pilot to spin round and take me back to the farm.

The city starts innocuously enough from the air – but it starts so early. It starts when you are nowhere near the city. For a long time, rolling green pasture and red earth and forests are all there is to see, broken up by herds of white cattle, clumps of cacti, termite mounds bigger than men. Then you begin to spot homes, and the spores of favelas, in creases in the land. And suddenly there are whole shanty cities.

Many times on that first journey there were false dawns, when we sped over settlements on the outskirts that merely contained tens of thousands of inhabitants, not tens of millions. And then we hit the real thing. No matter how often you see it, nothing prepares you for the scale. It's like having a blindfold whipped from your eyes every time – as impossible to comprehend as an entire country. That first night, as we reached the edge of that galaxy of fuming green lights, a speck in the sky, I nurtured a secret, shameful feeling that I had somehow graduated to the position of a god.

'Down there,' shouted Zé, at one point, looking up from the document in his hand, and gesticulating. 'Roughly, at least: The City of the Sun!'

I looked at him blankly.

'Heliópolis,' he explained, over-emphasising the syllables

so I could hear him over the roar of the engine. 'Not as bad as it was, but still tough. We're working on it though!' He flashed me a political smile. 'The inhabitants are to be awarded the land they live on, so technically, it is no longer even a favela.'

I wasn't sure exactly where he was pointing, but imagined I saw an area with dimmer and fewer lights than the rest. I nodded. And it was gone.

This city may not be the most beautiful, or the most poetic, or the most formally perfect, but it is the biggest, the loudest, the dirtiest, the most brazen. Twenty million souls and rising, and there is nothing to stop it seeping across its plateau, and nothing to get in the way of its commerce. It is an ever-expanding lung, whose oxygen is money – which is not to say that the air is evenly distributed. On the contrary; the money accumulates in specially created pockets. Like Angel Park.

The word 'community' doesn't do Angel Park justice. It is a self-contained city of 30,000 people, with shopping malls, schools and a private police force that never goes off duty. Guards in black uniforms sit with potted plants and loaded guns behind reinforced glass in the 'reception areas' that dot the perimeter fence. If you're a resident, they act like your best friends; to anyone without an appointment, or to some delivery boy to whom they feel superior – even to the police – they are less than welcoming. And God help you if you are a genuine intruder: they are bored and armed, and they live in a consequence-free environment.

If you wanted to, you could live most of your life in Angel Park without having to leave. Private highways mean that inhabitants can safely traverse areas not contained within the community to get to school or work. And when life's amenities are for some reason not contained within its walls, like the grand city church at which Zé and his family worship, then out comes the helicopter again. When Zé wants to pray, he flies.

The marketing literature that seduced people out of the safety of their tower blocks when the first gated communities were developed made much of the fact that everything a successful middle or upper class family might possibly want could be found inside: you could live, work and relax there; breed, exercise and die there. Even more comforting – though not, of course, explicitly stated – was the understanding that this was a safe environment in which your kids could make their mistakes. They could lose their virginity, sample a drug or two, even joyride Papai's car if they wanted, and all in relative safety, because the real police – the police with consequences – never got past the front door, and the only function of the park security was to keep real life at bay. Plus, you knew that whatever your kids were doing, they were doing it with the right sort of friend.

The grounds around the communal driveways that linked homes with the ancillary services were prettified with landscaped ponds and waterfalls. Unreal rocks and imported earth had been used to make them look natural, but they ended up looking every bit as fraudulent as the environments devised to fool animals in zoos. There were two shopping malls, an ice rink and a grand cinema complex that showed all the latest releases, approved for screening by committee and advertised in the compound news-sheet.

Life in Angel Park is life with the sting removed. The more you accept what passes for reality behind its walls, the less likely it is that you'll know the real thing until it breaks down your door. Impulses and feelings are all very well – but every one of them has been anticipated and rendered safe, and its potential consequences catered for. When your overindulged son wraps your Porsche round a lamp post, all he has to contend with is a security force whose paymaster is you, his parents, so he can never really get into trouble. And you can live your life without coming into contact with the favelas, or any other unsavoury aspect of the megacity outside. Behind the gates, it even smells better. The chemical fumes of the city recede, replaced by the aromas of cut grass and cinnamon candy, and the warm smell of freshly bathed Caucasian babies. That, in any case, is the theory.

A car met us at the heliport. I looked around anxiously for my bags, but they had been silently spirited away. The car that met us smelt of polished leather, and shot off down a pristine, empty road. I turned to Melissa, who was sitting beside me, watching my reactions.

'Are we sharing a room?' I asked, afraid of treading too hard on her turf.

She smiled. 'Wait and see.'

We passed through a set of smooth, automatic gates, and the absurdity of my question was revealed, because there was the house: steep and huge, and familiar to me, though at first I couldn't understand why. Then I realised that it had the same façade as that of the giant doll's house that Melissa and I had played with on the farm. With its three storeys and its four reception rooms, I had always thought it unreal, a fantasy place. Nothing like it could exist in real life, unless it was a hotel or a palace. As we drew up beside the sumptuous spray of fountains outside the front door, I realised that all along the doll's house had been an exact replica of this place; a lavish true-to-life gift and not, as I had imagined, the whim of a fanciful toymaker. The question of whether I would have a bedroom of my own was embarrassingly redundant. I couldn't believe that I had thought this was the real world, and that what they had wanted from the farm was something manufactured, when in fact, they lived in a doll's house set in the grounds of a guarded amusement park. No wonder Zé said 'down to earth' every time they landed at the farm – they lived on another planet!

By the time I was shown to my room, my bag had been magicked up there already, and was being unpacked. The settling-in period I had prepared myself for was not, it seemed, necessary. Here were my clothes, pitifully arranged in a massive darkwood closet that smelled of eucalyptus, beside piles of far more expensive ones that had been purchased for me; here was my toothbrush, leaning jauntily from a mug by the basin alongside Melissa's, for all the world as if we'd brushed together that morning. When I introduced myself to the maid in my room, she, like the chauffeur who'd brought us from the helipad, called me 'Senhor'. It made me squirm. Already I felt homesick for the wood-smoke smell of the farm kitchen, for Silvio bursting in with a lewd remark, and most of all for the prickly yet willing object of those remarks, my mother. The room was silent and plush. Everything smelt new. Those few things I'd brought with me were swamped. I paced around the room for a moment after the maid had gone, wondering whether I should stay put or go downstairs. As soon as we arrived, the other three had marched off purposefully in different directions, and my desire to blend in was so strong that I wanted to fall in with their behaviour in spite of having no business to attend to – even less than I thought, now that my bag had been unpacked for me. Because the maid was there, I didn't even have the opportunity to be ravished by the size of the room, to test the sponginess of the mattress with a nervous giggle. Everything was so casually supervised that I couldn't even give vent to my wide-eyed, farm-boy amazement.

Zé poked his head round the door. 'You should be comfortable in here. Did they get you some clothes?'

'Yes, thank you. For all of this…' I began.

But he'd already left the room and was pounding down the first-floor corridor (red carpets, chandeliers, black and white 1960s photos), assuming I was following him. I ran to catch up.

'I think we should do a quick tour of the property. You need to familiarise yourself with the security measures, in case you should ever be here when the house is empty.'

It seemed unlikely – I'd already met two members of staff and I had only entered three rooms of the house – but I followed him downstairs.

'You'll need to know the locations of all the trip lasers – I set them off by accident myself sometimes, and I swear that *Intruder Beware* voice scares me to death every time – and we'll need to drill you through all the relevant alarm codes and passwords in case the park security guards ever turn up. They wouldn't hesitate to shoot you if they didn't know who you were. Then there are the searchlights – they have the power of a million candles each, and you should know how to operate them. And you must learn the attack calls for the dogs.'

I'd seen two mottled, stocky hounds pacing around the garden as we pulled up. They hadn't looked all that threatening.

'Don't be fooled by the sight of them,' Zé went on. 'They're Fila Brasileiro fighting mastiffs, and they're lethal. They're bred to control livestock – so a man is nothing more than a snack as far as they're concerned.'

'Control?' I said.

He sniffed. 'Aggressively control. Then of course there's the panic room – I'll show you how that works later on.' He handed me a shiny, thin aerosol can. 'And this is your Silver Bullet. Keep it on you at all times. I get them custom made, and we all carry one. They spray a substance forty times more powerful than Mace into the eyes of your assailant, and coat him with a sticky ultraviolet paint for the purposes of identification after the event. *Don't leave home without it!*' he added in English, with a cheery American accent.

I must have looked uneasy, because he paused in the middle of a large sitting room decked out with white carpets and gold mirrors, and said, 'Ludo, you look terrified. Don't worry. This is just how things are in the city.'

I nodded. 'Carry on. I'm listening.'

'That's almost it. All we need to do now is teach you how to handle a gun.'

'I can shoot,' I said quickly.

'Not a rifle, like on the farm. Here, you'll need to know your way around a handgun. Just in case. What I always tell Melissa to do if anyone gets inside is to take up a defensive position in one of the bedrooms and bring the intruders down one by one as they come in. But don't worry: I've asked Ernesto to take you out tomorrow morning for a shooting lesson.'

*Ernesto?* I thought. *Who the hell is Ernesto?*

'But for now,' Zé went on, 'it's time for dinner.'

And then something reached my nose that made my body quiver. A warm smell of meat and onions slowly simmered in wine, herbs and cream, and distinctively spiked with nutmeg. It was a Sunday evening favourite for me. It was the smell, comforting as one of her hugs, of my mother's chicken stew.

I saw Zé stride forth into the kitchen, arms outstretched, and disappear from view. Then I heard him say, 'Dinner! What delicious food do you have for us this evening, oh cook of my dreams?'

They'd brought her too! Without even telling me! God knew how they'd got her here so fast – maybe the helicopter had gone back to fetch her – but it didn't matter. What mattered was that she was here. I flew across the polished marble of the hallway and into the kitchen, ready to give her the embrace of her life. My mother stood at a large, spotlit stove with her back to me, wearing the same blue smock she had worked in ever since I could remember.

Zé wheeled round as I entered. 'And this, Claudia, is Ludo – our new member of the family.'

The woman who was not my mother turned around and held out her hand for me to shake. She wiped it first on her smock, which I now realised was standard issue uniform for all Zé's kitchen employees and not something unique to my mother. And, much more horrifying, neither was her recipe for chicken stew.

# Club Sandwich

A candle burns on my table. As I wait, and hope that the Australian has forgotten our meeting, I dip the fingertips of my right hand one by one into the molten pool around the wick, relishing the hot, sharp pain followed by the feeling of delicious intimacy as each fingertip is coated in solidifying wax. I peel the caps off in turn, and let them fall to the table, where they land like petrified flower petals. I scoop them up and drop them into the breast pocket of Ernesto's big, baggy shirt, not wanting to appear too bored by my guest's late arrival.

I make a bet with myself that I can identify him when he walks in. It's a little unfair. I would know when he's here with my eyes closed, so much does he jar with the faded elegance of the place. There's something almost obscene about how healthy he looks: his tanned, blemish-free skin; the dog-dick, coral pink of his tongue against the bright white of his teeth. His T-shirt clings like sandwich wrap to a pair of repellent, inflated pectorals. His trousers have huge saddlebag pockets in their sides, as if he were on safari and needed kit to hand for every possible scenario. Was he expecting an untamed wilderness, or does he just dress for the outback all the time?

'How you going?' he says, in English. He's been drinking

already. He walks with a swagger, and when he sits down, his feet swing out loosely from his ankles like cars on a fair-ground spinner.

'Well,' I reply. '*Cachaça* makes excellent fuel. We even power the cars with it here, as you may remember.'

He laughs, and sits down.

'When were you last here?' I say. 'Should I be speaking to you in English?'

He laughs, and switches languages. 'No – my Portuguese is intact. Although it's been a few years.'

'Your English – you've picked up quite an accent,' I say, playfully.

'I have. But speaking this language again – it's wonderful. I can hear the Carnival drums already! Let me tell you straight away, I'm excited about working back here – and I would love to make the move permanent if I can.' The waiter arrives. 'Could I get a beer thanks.'

'Bring him a caipirinha as well,' I say. 'He's home now!' The only way to make this experience bearable is to get him drunker. He's physically fit, so it shouldn't be hard.

My task for the evening is not simply to entertain him. He is on the verge of accepting a secondment to the agency, so in theory I'm vetting him as much as schmoozing him. That's what I tell myself, anyway. The truth is that to deny him the position if he wants it would be out of the question. His father is another old buddy of Oscar's, so that is pretty much that; showing him a good time is my only option. It won't be easy – my real feelings are snapping about in my throat like snakes, ready to strike – but the fact that he has to feel charmed doesn't mean I can't have some fun at his expense.

Within the hour, he is well oiled, and talking. After my second caipirinha I order a bottle of Californian Pinot Noir, but the Australian decides to stay on beer and spirits. While

I'm ordering the drinks he also leans over to request 'the largest cigar in the hotel' from our waiter, and slobbers on the end of it like a dog with a twig when it arrives.

'I love it here,' he says. 'I've been reading up on how the market works. Tiny ideas for tiny minds: it's like being a god. Back home, consumers expect to be entertained before they'll even consider hearing your brand name. Over here, it's like the good old days – you tell them to do something and they do it.'

I smile. 'We like to think it's more complicated than that. Now, what would you like to eat this evening?'

'What's on the menu?'

'Everything!' I say. 'Nowadays. In that area, I expect the city has changed beyond recognition since you were last here.'

The regulations prohibiting imported goods have long since gone. And now that chefs can obtain saffron for their pilafs, *bouquets garnis* for their *bourguignons* and *porcini* for their *risotti*, the plates of the city's diners are home to the real thing and not poor local approximations. It's just a question of which restaurant is most likely to blow his mind.

'It's your first night in the gastronomic capital of the continent,' I say. 'And I have a generous expense account. So the question is, what would you like? We could hit one of the *churrasco* places, but this city also has some of the best Italian and Japanese restaurants on the planet – not to mention Lebanese, Portuguese, Indian, Korean, Spanish, French. Or if you're looking for something a little simpler, they say that more pizza is eaten here some evenings than in the whole of Italy. Just say the word. I can get us a reservation anywhere.'

He takes a pull on his cigar, and blows a thick, bottom-heavy smoke ring, the larger half of which dips down towards the table and lands like a toxic bomb in my glass of wine.

'To be honest, I'll have plenty of time to explore the city. For tonight I'd be happy just holing up here and ordering a club sandwich. What do you say?'

My eyes glaze over and I take a big gulp of wine. 'Of course.'

I can't bear to order one for myself, but I request the sandwich for him, hoping for his sake that he enjoys it.

I try not to look at it when it arrives. I want to avoid the comparison. I don't want to know whether this sandwich is better or worse than the one I remember, or the same. I just don't want them connected. But simply by ordering it the Australian has barged in on the memory, and lashed himself to it.

He gets drunker and more boisterous, and doesn't touch the sandwich. To avoid thinking about it, I retreat further from him into the comfortably padded room of good red wine. As he talks on, my mind wanders, to the boy in the square this morning, to the man working the bathrooms downstairs, to Ernesto. To Melissa.

'The problem with first-world markets is that clients are constantly trying to find new ways of discovering whether or not advertising actually works. Here, you know it works – I've seen what happens when a good campaign rolls out. The sales skyrocket. They treat us with the reverence of Romans before the Oracle. I love that.'

As he talks, he picks up one quarter of the sandwich, gives it a critical glance, and takes a large bite, spilling much of what is left behind. Then, right in front of me, he dismantles the other three quarters, browsing their insides for wads of chicken breast, which he absentmindedly tosses into his mouth between puffs of his cigar, and leaving the rest.

'What are you saying? That consumers over here are un-evolved? Halfwits?' I ask.

He pauses mid-swallow, fearing he's upset me.

'Because I might have to agree with you.'

He roars with laughter.

'But you've hardly touched your sandwich.'

He grimaces. 'Tell you the truth, I eat a lot of club sand-wiches, and this one isn't that great.'

It does look tired: limp lettuce, grey bacon, old bread. I feel exhausted just looking at it.

'I feel we have let you down,' I say. 'There's still time for us to get a table somewhere.'

'I have a better idea.' Stage whisper. Foul cigar breath. 'How about a pick-me-up to help me get over the jetlag? That will soon take our minds off food, eh?'

If he's leaping right in like this it means that Oscar prob-ably tipped him off. I feel like an errand boy, and am tempted to toss the bag on the table and leave him to get on with it, but I manage to keep my cool and lean back in my chair. It's the first time in forty minutes that his conversational requirements can't be met by a serious nod of the head or a conspiratorial chuckle of acknowledgement, so I make use of the opportunity to keep him quiet. I'd have expected this from a New Yorker, a Londoner. But an Australian? I thought they were meant to be clean-living – all yoghurt and fruit shakes and jogging.

'You want cocaine?'

Fearing he has misjudged the situation, he backtracks. 'I don't know. I mean, Oscar said –'

'Of course.' His smile returns. 'You can find most things in a hotel like this.'

He raises his glass. 'Excellent.'

'Just one thing,' I say. 'If you have a taste for drugs, you must be careful. It doesn't do to get mixed up with the police in this city. They shoot first, and do not get as far as the questions.' I drain my glass of wine, and stand up. 'I will ask around.'

What he wants is right here in my pocket, but I need some time away from him, and I can't stop thinking about the sandwich. Things are bad enough for the hotel as it is without that kind of ingratitude. I feel I should offer the chef an explanation, which is convenient as the kitchen is probably just where he thinks I would go to get drugs. He's probably read a magazine article trumpeting the virtues of the new fusion restaurants in the city, and is picturing fashionable young chefs boosting their culinary creativity with powders less wholesome than cassava flour. Never mind that the idea of barging into a crowded hotel kitchen and demanding drugs from a bunch of semi-geriatric second-generation Italians is laughable – I want to give him the impression that's what I am doing. I leave the bar, cross the hotel lobby and enter the restaurant.

It's a barren, dessert-trolley sort of a place, fringed with foreign couples, and with one rowdy business dinner at the centre. I'm trying to work out where the kitchen is when our waiter comes in from the bar bearing the remains of the club sandwich, and I follow him through a set of swing doors.

We enter a cramped, steamy kitchen, where a crackling radio plays bossa nova. Several large aluminium pans bubble away on the stove. One young chef is twisting and cutting small red sausages and dropping them into a pan. Another grates cheese. A third, older man is seasoning a huge sea bass, which must be for the businessmen outside. They're in the middle of a joke and are laughing as the waiter enters, with me, unseen, on his tail.

'Excuse me,' I say to the waiter. 'Can you tell me who made that sandwich?'

The waiter spins round, then looks down at the tray in his hands, and back at me. 'I beg your pardon, Senhor?'

'That sandwich. I want to speak to the person who made it.'

'Was there something wrong with it?'

'Nothing at all. It was good. I just want to tell whoever made it that it is not being sent back half-eaten because it is unsatisfactory. The person who ordered it was not in a position to appreciate it, that's all.'

The waiter looks around him to see if anyone else is on hand to deal with this situation, before turning back to me. 'Sir, you really shouldn't be here. Guests are prohibited from entering the kitchen.'

I shout over his shoulder at the chefs. 'Whoever made that sandwich – it was delicious, OK? It was very, very good.' They look up from their work in bewilderment.

'Thank you, Senhor,' says the waiter. 'We appreciate the compliment. Now I must ask you to leave us.'

'It was great! Hear me? It was a *life-changing* sandwich!'

Red-faced, I burst back through the swing doors and into the restaurant. I should go down to the bathroom to cool off for a second before going back to the bar, but I can't bear the thought of running into that attendant again.

I stride into the bar, trying to contain my indignation. The Australian's excitement is palpable from the doorway. His saddle-bagged thighs are trilling up and down like the fingers of a cocktail pianist. He's probably high already on the excitement, and thanks to my warning about the police, the perceived danger of what is about to happen.

I slap Oscar's bag of powder into his hand, and say something cheap like, 'Amazing what the well-equipped kitchen has in stock these days.' And he's off to the bathroom with a spring in his step. I picture him snorting and spluttering away down there, and pity the poor attendant in advance for his next client. Then I order a large whisky and try to get as much of it down as I can before he returns.

He springs back into the bar after a while, beaming. There's a white crust around one nostril. I motion for him to wipe it, and hand him a napkin.

'Thanks,' he says. 'Not partaking yourself?'

'Thank you, no.'

'So, your boss, good old Oscar,' he says. 'Remarkable man. Very persuasive. Knows how to get a man motivated.'

'He certainly does. He is skilled in the art of terrorism.'

'Know what he told me about this city once?'

'What?'

'He said, "For seventy dollars, you can fuck someone who's more beautiful than anyone you've ever fucked. But for 200 dollars you can fuck someone who's more beautiful than anyone you've ever *seen*." That idea didn't terrify me, I can tell you.'

'Yes, that does sound like him.'

He gives me an arch look. 'Is it true?'

I could feign incomprehension, but I can't bear to open the door to more of his leering, unsuitable conversation. 'So I am told,' I say. 'You're interested?'

'Is it an inappropriate request?'

'Probably. Are you asking it anyway?'

'Maybe.' He almost looks bashful, then laughs.

'You may have to give me a little time,' I say, finishing my drink.

'I'm going nowhere,' he says.

The belt of heat that strikes me outside the hotel is welcome, though I know I will soon be ready to retreat back into air-con. I head for a square at the foot of one of the city's tallest buildings. During the day this area is respectable – the tower is open to the public, and tourists pay to go up it and attempt to take in the vast yellow forest of scraper-chaos that surrounds them – but at night, the plaza near its base is anarchic and alive. Everyone here is hustling in one way or another: the gold dealer standing with his *Buy or Sell* sign, his mouth and ears full of dodgy product; the apothecaries plying their witchy potions and rainforest remedies from mobile stalls; the street performer who claims to have a cobra in a bag; the transsexual prostitutes loitering on the corners looking disarmingly stunning. Not one is what he seems. Not one can be trusted.

I cross the plaza, fending off advances from two fortune tellers and a hooker, and head for the green light of an all-night pharmacy. The kid behind the counter is bored and sleepy, and after I have named a couple of brands they don't have, he swivels his ancient black and white computer terminal in my direction so I can browse the stock myself. It doesn't take me long to find what I'm looking for.

On my way back across the plaza, I approach one of the transsexuals. S/he's wearing long blue tights, gold shoes and a pink fur coat, from which juts a shelf of tanned, pumped-up cleavage.

'Looking for something special?' s/he says in a husky voice.

'Not tonight,' I say. 'But I'll buy your bra for fifty.'

'Souvenir-hunter, huh? That sounds like easy money to me.' The bra is whipped off in a swift movement and I proffer one of Oscar's banknotes.

'You don't want to *know* what I would have let you do to me for that.'

'You're right, I don't. Good night.' I stuff the bra in my pocket and re-enter the hotel.

'Sorry about the delay,' I say.

'I hardly noticed you'd gone. I've been getting stuck into that stuff since you left.' He's squirming around, taut-mouthed and goggle-eyed. 'I think people might be wondering what

I'm up to. They keep staring at me when I go to the bathroom. Any luck?'

'It took time to find someone nice. But she will join you in your hotel room later.'

'Lovely,' he says, thrashing about in his chair as if he were tied to it.

Several hours later, I'm picking around the Australian's bathroom while he lies face down on the bed in the next room, snoring. At my suggestion, we brought a bottle of Johnnie Walker up to the room, and while he was getting excited about his visit from the call girl I slipped enough crushed-up Temazepam into his drink to counteract the cocaine. It wasn't as easy as it looks in the movies – a conspicuous white residue clung to the inside of the glass – but he was so drunk he didn't notice, and even requested a refill that washed down the dregs. He will be out cold for hours, but now that I don't have to talk to him, I'm in less of a hurry to get home.

It's a well-appointed suite: the bathroom shelves heave with lotions, oils and creams. There is even a special dish next to the bidet with a bottle of something unbranded on it, called 'Intimate Cleanser'. I unscrew the lid, sniff it briefly and replace the bottle. His wash bag bulges with a great stockpile of Australian contraceptives (clearly he has grand plans), bright vitamin supplements that look like they are designed for kids, protein powders and mists and lens solutions. I go back into the room, unhook the phone, and dial Melissa's number.

'Do you know what time it is?' she hisses.

'I wondered how the crab linguine went down.'

'I can't talk now.'

'I bet you overcooked the pasta, didn't you?'

'Ludo, I have to go.'

'You shouldn't give linguine longer than five minutes, especially if you're keeping the heat on when stirring in the sauce.'

'I'm putting the phone down now.'

'Did he eat it all? I bet he did –'

'Goodbye.'

'Wait. I didn't tell you. I saw someone get shot after I left you this morning.'

The phone is dead.

I stand at the window. The city lights spin off kaleidoscopically in every direction. My head reels.

Looking down to see powder chopped out on the TV I decide to have some for the journey home, and one quick jolt becomes two or three. I bounce round the room, relishing the sparkle in my synapses, the sudden commotion in the front of my brain. I turn on the TV to see if it wakes the Australian up. Nothing – my work is finished.

*I am twenty, talking to Zé. We're having a nightcap together, on the farm, and he's come over all patriarchal, imparting wisdom.*

*'Cocaine is a good business,' he says, circulating his brandy balloon. 'Know why? Because it has a very high value-to-bulk ratio. It's like gold. Or fur.'*

*'And how would you know about that?' I ask.*

*'I don't, of course,' he says immediately. 'But I can see why these people take the risk. The pay-off makes it worthwhile. Good night.'*

'And good night to you, *mate*,' I mutter to the comatose Australian, heading for the door. As I touch the handle I feel a warm trickle down my upper lip. Oscar, it seems, needs a better supplier.

I go back into the bathroom, and linger by the mirror, fascinated by the sight of the blood. Instead of applying tissue to my nose, I pick up the Australian's glass, which I have carefully washed, from its paper coaster by the sink, and let the blood accumulate in it drip by drip. I don't know what I had planned to do with the transsexual's bra – leave it in the bed, perhaps, to confuse him – but the nosebleed has given me a nastier idea.

I begin to feel guilty as soon as I leave the hotel. He's not all bad, the poor guy. It must have been hard for him to be bundled away from here as a teenager and taken to a strange new country just because his parents didn't get on. I know also that when you work internationally like he does, your job is simply to oil the hamster wheel, to keep your subordinates working hard and reassure your bosses that things are going well without doing anything yourself. Who can blame him for wanting to let off steam? I shouldn't care how fucked-up an evening he wants to have.

But that prostitute he wanted could have been my mother. And the mistake he might have made, if his trusty foreign Australian prophylactics had failed him – and from which he would have walked away just as casually as he discarded the remains of his club sandwich – that mistake could be another me.

The taxi I hail stinks of fried food, and its seats bear the patched-up wounds of many years' service. For security, the window can't be wound down more than a couple of inches, so I sit with my face pressed to the aperture, enjoying the blast of hot wind in my face like a dog smelling its way home, the blood drying to grit in my nose. Without consciously deciding to, and even though it is nowhere near my apartment, I direct the driver to the square with the fountain in it.

'I was here this morning,' I say when we arrive. 'A boy got shot.'

The taxi driver shrugs. 'It happens. If you're a *paulistano* you have to confront a little reality every once in a while.'

'It is my experience that we *paulistanos* try to avoid reality at all costs,' I say.

I ask him to park and wait. After some discussion and the promise of a good tip, he consents.

The cool blue of the evening and the deserted streets make it feel different to the blindingly hot spot where the boy and I danced around each other this morning. The fountain seems less substantial, and the square is defined more by the shadow of the tower blocks and the sharp angles of the invulnerable ATM kiosk than by its past life. It seems so different that initially I think I have made a mistake, that it is a different place. Then the two stone benches emerge from the shadows, and I find the wound in the palm tree, scabbed over already with smog-darkened resin. I recall the boy's eyes, gaping and pleading as the realisation struck of the danger he was in. There's no police tape round the spot where he fell; clearly the authorities have all the information they need. Where the dark pool of blood was this morning, the pavement has been scrubbed clean so that the mosaics gleam. Only this cleanliness shows that anything happened here at all – that, and the gash in the tree.

*You obviously never wondered where your next meal was coming from, or there's no way you could be doing this.*

I reach into Ernesto's shirt pocket, take out the wax flower petals I made at the hotel, and toss them at the base of the tree, where they break into fragments.

Apart from the jungle balcony and a bathroom, my apartment is contained in one room. I have a pull-down bed, a shelf of books, a computer on a desk, and not much else. The kitchen is the one area where I have made modifications to the studio set-up, and am properly equipped. I threw out the primitive gas ring that was here when I moved in and installed an oven of quality. I also brought in much of my mother's old equipment from the farm kitchen, including its antique, gas-powered refrigerator, which Zé had shipped here at my request. It dominates the room and makes constant noise, whirling and churning and gasping and sighing, but the sound comforts me, and the idea of throwing it away is heartbreaking.

I turn on my computer and make myself a coffee: tiny, strong, little more than a smear of dark flavour in the bottom of the cup. The cups are exquisite, a present for my mother brought by Zé and Rebecca from Italy. Their porcelain is so thin that the decorated dimples on the sides of each one are translucent. I knock back one coffee, then another. I take a bottle of vodka from the freezer, along with the slender crystal shot glass I keep chilled with it. When the computer is up and running, I sit bathed in its blue light, drinking shot after shot of the frozen vodka, relishing every mouthful of the numbing, syrupy liquid.

It used to be near impossible to find out anything about a shooting from which no death resulted. No longer. Until the authorities close it down, we have a site called *citybodycount.com* set up to monitor shootings in the face of police misinformation. The standard official report of most violent incidents is *resistance followed by death*, and this site exists to provide a little more background. It is here that I find a brief note on the event that I precipitated this morning:

*At 11.23 a.m. in the Praça Áustria, an armed robber was shot following an attack on a private security guard.*

The brevity of the report, and in particular the devastatingly non-specific use of the word 'armed', strengthens the urge I have been feeling all day to find the boy and somehow make amends. But given that he is almost certainly what they call a 'marginal', he will be impossible to find.

'Let it go,' I say aloud, licking the last of the vodka from the bottom of my glass and pouring another shot. 'It wasn't your fault.'

In fact, the person I blame is Melissa. It's only after unsatisfactory contact with her that I behave as odiously as I did this morning – or, for that matter, this evening.

I turn off the computer and open the sliding door to my terrace to enjoy my drink outside. I cultivate huge, leafy plants out here that almost block out the light, giving it a cavern-like feel, but they bring me as close to nature as is possible here in the city. Also, my hole in the wall of an apartment is right above the pool maintenance area, so that when the traffic noise dies down, you can hear water flowing through the filtering system, and, if you ignore the smell of chlorine, almost imagine yourself to be by a river. That, and the calls of my songbird, are what I cling to.

The bird is a refugee from the farm – a fat little monk parakeet who would not fly away when I tried to set him free. I have come to love his squawks and titters. He keeps me company on my balcony at night, when I sit in a wicker chair drinking *cachaça* and Coke and thinking of the farm until my head is too numb to recollect. The sad thing about songbirds is that the beauty of their cries is contingent upon longing – if mine ever found a mate then he might fall silent for good. Thankfully there's not much chance of that happening round here.

That said, exotic creatures are sometimes drawn to my jungle terrace. As I sit in the darkness with my vodka, something, a flying cockroach or a small bat, hits the shutters with a dull thud, picks itself up and flies away again. I hope whatever it is stays away from the swimming pool. The janitor is always picking sodden corpses out of the filter in the mornings, even though there is an electric snake that's supposed to patrol the depths scavenging for litter. It slithers smoothly across the floor all night, vacuuming the water and emitting a cold blue light. Not long ago I woke up to hear the snake gasping and sucking, and emitting a high mechanical whine of anguish, and went downstairs to find it grappling with a bat. I tried to free the creature, but it was half-drowned and struggling madly, and there was nothing I could do to stop it being devoured by the machine.

# Spray Pancakes and Spring Chickens

The only night sound in Angel Park was the faint hiss of conditioned air. At the end of my first day I lay in bed rigidly fixing on it, unable to sleep. It wasn't just the lack of animal noise that bothered me: for as long as I could remember I had slept in the next room from my mother, and overheard every murmur, every snore, every creaking bedspring.

I came down in the morning to an eerily empty house. Strewn about the granite hub at the centre of the kitchen lay the litter of three breakfasts: once-bitten pieces of fruit, half-drained glasses of juice, overturned yoghurt pots. Here was my first glimpse of the family in their city clothes. Whereas breakfast on the farm was a performance that could take all morning, with Zé installed behind the newspapers at the end of the table presiding over a steadily mounting pile of fruit peel, this meal had happened fast. The scene made me think of a sci-fi apocalypse – as if the family had dropped everything to rush off at the chilling sound of some early warning siren.

'Good morning, Senhor,' said the maid who was not my mother. 'Would you like some breakfast before your shooting lesson?'

'I can get it myself.'

'I insist, young man. How about a pancake?' She held up two aerosols: one of oil and the other of pancake mixture.

'I could manage one of those,' said a voice from the door.

Ernesto the man is very different from the boy who let himself into the house that morning and saved me from a batch of aerosol pancakes. Now, he sees his privilege as a platform from which he can change things for others. Then, he was awkward and uncomfortable, and made sporadic attempts at mimicking the brashness he observed in the delinquent kids he had grown up with. I didn't even know he existed until I moved to Angel Park. But here he was, as important a part of Melissa's life during the week as I was at weekends.

When I asked her later on why she hadn't mentioned him before, she said, 'Ernesto? He's the weekday you – didn't you know that?'

The expression was deliberately provocative. With his blond fringe and his big milk-fed frame, he couldn't have looked less like me. His plump cheeks had the effect of shrinking his other features, and although contact lenses have corrected it now, when I first met him he had a squint that afflicted him at random, causing his eyes to sink back into his face like currants into a loaf. But he was tenacious. If he sensed injustice anywhere, he would divert every pound of brawn into overturning it, from (in those days) a playground bully to (these days) the uncompromising might of favela drug gangs. At sixteen, he had the potential, but not the purpose, and this could come across as arrogance – the hauteur of a tournament bull misplaced inside the frame of a blinking calf. As he sat in the kitchen that morning eating the pancakes I hadn't wanted, I felt I had the measure of him already.

'Where's Melissa today?' he asked me.

'I think she went shopping with her mother,' I said, not

knowing at all, but hoping to imply that I had already become an integrated part of the family.

He sniffed. 'So . . . you live here now?'

'Yes.'

'You're sort of . . . Melissa's *brother* now, right?'

'I suppose so.'

This seemed to please him. Brother. Nothing more. 'OK, we'd better follow the Minister's orders and teach you how to handle a gun, so you can defend your new sister.'

He must have been aware of the zigzag trajectory of my past, but he didn't mention it. Meanwhile, I was concentrating less on his questions and more on how much accumulated cash was hanging off his shoulders – designer T-shirt, Italian jeans, new trainers that were at least a size too big to run in. It was when we got outside and I saw his car that I came closer to realising the kind of wealth we were dealing with.

'It's a Pontiac Firebird,' he said sheepishly. 'It's going to be mine, but I'm not legally allowed to drive it yet, so for the moment I can only use it here in the compound.'

'It's great.'

'It's OK,' Ernesto replied. 'It's nothing special.' His discomfort puzzled me. I was supposed to be the one who was new to the place, not him. Now, I understand that he was probably embarrassed; that he had heard where I came from and thought I was fresh off the streets. At the time I just thought he was weak – though I was grateful for the possibility of a male friend my own age.

We pulled out on to one of Angel Park's clean, white roads at a safe pace.

'Where are we going?' I asked.

He looked in the rear-view mirror through huge Aviators that made his face look even more fat and puppyish. 'Shooting range.'

Trying hard to let Angel Park surprise me as little as possible, I tried to picture our destination, anticipating a leafy gravel driveway, a brass plaque with *The Angel Park Gun Club* on it, prim folk wearing white suits in a panelled dining room. Instead, Ernesto drove us to a building site.

The outer reaches of the community, by which I mean the parts furthest from the city, were backwaters at the time – tracts of land owned by the developers whose potential had yet to be fully realised. They were thinking of the future – a future that has now arrived, along with thousands of vitamin-enriched, gym-toned residents – and they didn't want mere geography to inhibit their potential for success. There were therefore large areas of Angel Park that were little more than wasteland, the terrain where the mansions and luxury blocks of the future would be built. We were still within the jurisdiction of Angel Park Security, but as discreetly positioned as it was possible to be inside the perimeter fence. There were several half-finished houses here – their lamp posts yet to be wired in, their metal girders reaching imploringly to the skies for more concrete – and it was outside one of these that Ernesto now brought the car to a lurching, gear-grinding halt.

Lots of space here,' he said. 'We won't be disturbed. And I can't reverse park so it's good that we can drive straight out again.'

He turned off the engine and leaned over me to the glove box.

'Here she is,' he said, reaching inside and taking out a heavy object wrapped in an oily cloth. 'The Glock 17, chosen weapon of many a street hoodlum and gangster. And also of my father.' He pulled back one corner of the rag to reveal the gun. 'Let's go inside and heat this baby up. Bring that box of bullets.' He cast furtive glances in each direction over his sunglasses as we got out of the car.

We climbed a low fence and entered the half-built shell of what was destined to be a very big house, with a grand entrance hall and a sweeping spiral staircase. Our voices echoed round the empty rooms. Work had been interrupted on the building, but it still smelt of brick dust and plaster. Ernesto led me through the ground floor to a long, unpainted concrete corridor. Noticing empty shells on the floor, I realised this wasn't the first time he had come here for shooting practice.

He opened a bag he had brought from the car and produced a stack of gossip magazines. 'Now,' he said, 'who shall we shoot at today?'

Thus my first morning in the city was spent in the lobby of an unfinished mansion, being taught how to fire a handgun at the cut-out heads and bodies of politicians and celebrities. We shot at footballers, TV presenters, soap stars, Hollywood actors. Nobody was excused. We even found a picture of Zé, with half of Rebecca's face just peeping out behind the embrace taking place in the foreground between her husband and Pelé. After some discussion about whether or not it would be disrespectful, we pinned him up and gunned him down with the rest.

The gun scared me. It was cold and heavy when Ernesto slapped it into my hand, and I felt I barely had the strength to hold it straight.

Ernesto steadied my wavering hands. 'No, take aim more carefully. It's not like you've seen in films. They have a kick to them. Mel Gibson may be able to shoot three drug dealers without a second thought while rolling around on the floor, but nobody in real life has that kind of coordination, so you have to hold it with both hands and take proper aim.'

My first bullet ricocheted off the ceiling, and the noise made my heart lurch, but then I told myself that this was no different from using my slingshot on the farm, or from firing Silvio's rifle at birds. The city was intimidating me.

My next three shots took out one glossy cover photo apiece.

'Nice work!' Ernesto shouted. 'Sure you haven't done this before?'

'Melissa and I shoot stuff together all the time,' I said. 'I just haven't used one of these before.'

The mention of Melissa annoyed him. 'Perhaps you'll be safe enough after all. Here, give it to me. I'll show you how we do it in the city.'

As I passed him the gun, the door behind us was kicked open by an armed guard.

'Don't shoot,' I managed to shout.

'Gun down!' screamed the guard. He was no older than twenty-three, with a peach-fuzz moustache, and in spite of his forbidding black uniform, his pistol shook in his hand. He had probably heard our shots from outside, and been preparing himself for a brush with death.

Ernesto screamed at him. 'What are you doing coming in here with your gun drawn? You might have killed us.'

'Are you a resident?'

'Of course I'm a resident. So is my friend.'

'He doesn't look like a resident.'

'What the fuck do you mean by that?'

'Don't be cocky, kid. Who is he?'

'This is the adopted son of Zé Fisher Carnicelli, so you better show him some respect.'

'I don't care who you are. You can't shoot guns in here. You can't shoot guns anywhere. How old are you? How old is he?'

'I'm sixteen and he's fourteen, not that it's any concern of yours. Zé Generoso has asked me to teach this boy how to shoot so that he can defend himself when people like you let him down, and there are villains inside his house trying to kill him. You want to take issue with the Minister about it?'

'You shouldn't be firing guns,' said the guard, holstering his pistol. 'Give me your rounds and go home.'

Ernesto fumed as the guard drove off. 'Let's take a shot at his tyres.'

'He's taken your bullets.'

He kicked the wheel of his car. 'I hate people like him. Little dictators. Put a uniform on them and a gun in their hand and suddenly they're the king of the universe.'

He shut the boot of the Firebird on his collection of guns.

'It doesn't matter,' I said. 'At least I know now how to take out Madonna with a couple of shots to the head.'

'We'll talk to my father about it this evening. He's on all the residents' committees. We'll get that guy cautioned at the very least for speaking to us like that.'

'We?'

'Has nobody told you? My parents have invited you and Melissa over tonight for a welcome dinner.'

*I am fourteen, and not long in Angel Park. It's dark, and a serious thunderstorm is in progress. I've been over at Ernesto's, and when I return to the house the mastiffs are out. I have not yet learnt their attack calls. They come at me across the drowned lawn, gnashing, slobbering strobe dogs in stop frame animation, the shutter speed dictated by the lightning. Slipping in the red mud, I make it to the gatehouse, where a guard steps in front of me and shouts over the thunder the words that make them stand down.*

*Is everyone in the city like this – advancing on me in the dark, their true nature only revealed when the lightning flashes?*

'This place is weird,' I said to Melissa that morning, when Ernesto dropped me home after our shooting trip. We were sitting in the kitchen eating sandwiches, and the combination of eating and complaining was making me feel better. 'How could Ernesto speak to that guy like that? I thought he was going to blow our heads off.'

'He might have done, if you hadn't been residents,' laughed Melissa. 'It's happened before. People sneaking into unfinished houses, looking for somewhere to sleep. Things turn ugly . . .'

'But Ernesto spoke to him like he was a baby.'

'That's because Ernesto could get him fired. They aren't like the police. They work for us.'

'I would never speak to someone like that. Especially someone with a gun pointed at me.'

'You want weird? Wait until you see Ernesto's house.'

Although Melissa and her family were very rich, they were rich people I knew well, and for whom I had worked. Because I knew all their quirks and tics, I no longer defined them by their wealth. Plus, even if he was extravagant in some areas (helicopters, food), Zé prided himself on not being too pretentious. He was moderated by the influence of Rebecca – whose outsider's sense of outrage at the inequality around her made it impossible for her to surrender completely to their life of affluence. At my welcome dinner that night I saw properly complacent wealth, and its expression in the gleaming baroque horror of Ernesto's family home.

It was one of a sub-cluster of houses in Angel Park built to resemble miniaturised versions of European-style palaces: Germanic, English, Venetian and so on. Ernesto and his family lived in the one that was meant to look like a French château. As Melissa led me to their colossal hardwood front door that evening, I realised that the description of Angel Park as 'weird' did not by any means do it justice.

Melissa pulled on the enormous brass bell. 'Be prepared for the fact that they won't understand where you have come from at all. But remember: none of it is real.' Just before the door was opened, she kissed me on the cheek.

Five of us sat round the table: Ernesto's father Gaspar, his mother Olinda, Melissa, Ernesto and me. Although the evening was supposedly my welcome dinner, it took the form of a performance between Ernesto's parents. Gaspar sat at one end of the table asking me questions and telling me the answers, while Olinda reacted at the other end to her husband, alternately charmed and scandalised by his behaviour. I guessed the performance was for my benefit. In fact, as I learned later, they performed for each other on a nightly basis.

Whereas Rebecca was shaped by her coolness and her sympathy, and my mother by her steel and gristle, Ernesto's mother Olinda was a painted freak; an eyesore. Her cosmetically butchered face harboured nothing but fear and received ideas. That evening, while the rest of us were served fish in a thick, creamy sauce, I watched as three spring chickens only a few weeks old were delivered to her table. As she listened to the conversation, making faces when required, Olinda used her square-cut nails to excavate chunks of breast meat from the golden-roasted birds, which she tore into strips and fed to the cats swirling at her feet before rinsing her fingers in a pewter bowl of water scented with lime. Most of the time she didn't look down to see where she was dropping the meat, and more than once I heard wet thuds as it dropped on the carpet unnoticed by the animals.

I couldn't focus on the conversation. Not because of the room, or even the feeding of the cats, though both were distracting enough. I kept hearing a series of wet, staccato noises, like clusters of bubbles breaking the surface of water, just out of my line of sight, but close enough to make me wince and turn sharply every time. It took me half an hour to identify where the noise was coming from: it was the traffic of saliva as yet another false smile broke on Olinda's teeth. As for her, with every turn of my head she shot me an indulgent look, probably explaining away my erratic behaviour to herself as evidence of the strange foibles of the poor and muddled.

Still more distracting was the change that came over Melissa during the meal. It was as if she too were performing – adopting a dinner table persona for Ernesto's parents.

The violence of the city was alluded to regularly, but in an oblique, glancing way, with jokes, as if to address it with sincerity would be to plumb the depths of poor taste. Instead, their fear found expression in blasé jokes about hold-ups and kidnappings, in which even Melissa participated. I kept my head down and concentrated on my food.

'I hear you are originally from Heliópolis, Ludo. I was near there myself recently. The area has changed a great deal.'

'I wouldn't know,' I said. 'I have no memory of it.'

'Let me tell you, it would have been a squalid place when you were born. And violent, too. You are lucky to be out of there.'

'That reminds me,' said Ernesto. 'We got threatened today by one of those idiot guards.'

'What were you doing this time?' said his father.

'Firing your gun in one of the unfinished houses.'

Gaspar laughed. 'And the guard took exception? How unreasonable.'

Olinda shot him a delighted look as she tore up *poussin* flesh.

'It wasn't my idea,' said Ernesto. 'Zé asked me to do it.'

'He wanted you to teach Ludo how to fire a gun? Why?'

'So he could take care of himself in the city.'

Gaspar turned to me. 'I think our neighbour is being

paranoid. The security forces here in the community are well trained. As your run-in with them would prove.' His wife smiled. The noise made me jump. 'But of course, if you hadn't been rescued from Heliópolis, you wouldn't need Ernesto to give you lessons in how to fire guns. You'd have been the one teaching *him*.'

Olinda responded with a mock-appalled intake of breath, and dropped meat on the floor. Melissa laughed in a way I'd never heard before – an infuriating, indulgent chortle that was not hers.

Gaspar and Olinda were so closed off from everyday life that they had been forced to become infatuated with themselves. They had walled themselves up in Angel Park, but remained so afraid of the world outside that they didn't even dare look – however much they joked about it. Their food was similarly insular: grand but bland, rich but soulless. It was food that went far out of its way to avoid the national and the honest, and sought some bereft version of the international instead. It left me feeling sick and gasping for cold water. It frothed and churned in my groaning stomach all night long, just as the evening's small talk would gurgle away in my head for days afterwards.

I have often been shocked by Melissa's manners. My own were drilled into me during my time 'in servitude', as it might have been called in another century. My mother was strict on the subject, so I knew what was polite and what wasn't, and it never occurred to me that you could appear charming by being cocky or smart. I don't mean that Melissa was rude, just that her way of being polite differed radically from mine because it relied on the function of her charm.

That night I watched Ernesto with fascination. He ate his fish messily, then requested a second helping in spite of having left large sections of the first, whereas I had painstakingly collected every last speck of sauce from my plate so as not to appear ungrateful. And he lounged across the table, elbows out, gesticulating with his cutlery, and shovelled in his food with his fork upside down, which my mother had told me I must never do, because I was not some poor street kid who didn't know any better. Miraculously, I had been spared that life.

# Avocado Milkshake

Despite the late night, I wake up early. Things shuffle and stir on my balcony. A hornet peers through the shutters with one beady eye. A bright scarlet butterfly looms and is gone. Half-asleep, I imagine that the jungle has advanced on the city while I slept, and that on my way to work, instead of apocalyptic traffic and police brutality, I might encounter the crazy scale shifts of the rainforest: cats big as bears, butterflies broad as your head, fox-sized rodents, rodent-sized foxes. Tyres scream in the street, shattering the illusion. It isn't the first time nature has crept up on me like that. I still miss the farm every night.

Swinging one leg to the floor to get myself out of bed, I feel my foot brush against something. Blue-grey morning light confers beauty on a used tissue, which looks like a frothy white rose, rooted in the floor. Mercifully, there's no sign of blood, but a metallic taste is still evident towards the back of my mouth from the nosebleed. It's not altogether unpleasant: perhaps a rare steak for lunch.

I feel filthy, and I can't remember how the evening finished, which is a bad sign. I am conscious though of something in the air, some residue of unpleasantness, as of a drunken argument left unresolved. As of the cordite whiff that lingered in the air yesterday after the boy was shot. Also, I've slept in my clothes, and the body I discover when I peel off Ernesto's giant shirt is a *bollito misto* of steamed meats. Deciding that the shirt will need a professional clean before I can slip it back in Ernesto's wardrobe, I run my thumbs up my body, nail-side down. What arrives at my nostrils when I bring up my hands bears the too-human stench of an overcrowded bus or a staff canteen. I make for the shower to blast it away.

It's one of those mornings when the idea of work actually appeals. My bird trills away beautifully in his cage, my morning coffee tastes good and I'm even looking forward to the MaxiBudget meeting. Oscar will know I had a late night, so an early appearance will score points. I want him to register me, perky and alert, and compare that image favourably to whatever we see when the Australian creeps in.

To my surprise, and to his credit, he doesn't look too bad. He's ditched the saddlebag trousers for a suit, and looks only slightly haggard and withdrawn. If I didn't know that he woke up spattered in blood with an unidentified gold bra linking his wrist with the bedhead, I might think he looked well rested.

'Good night?' I enquire.

'Oh…amazing.' He laughs weakly. 'To be honest, I can't remember you leaving.'

'You don't remember?' I lean forward so only he can hear. 'How was she? She looked spectacular when she got out of the lift.'

He clears his throat and I notice sweat running down behind his ears.

'Good morning gentlemen.' Oscar has materialised. 'I hope Ludo showed you a good time last night?'

'Great,' says the Australian.

Oscar raises his palms in defence. 'I don't want to hear about it. I'm sure it would embarrass me.'

'I doubt that,' I say, picturing him pawing at my mother back on the farm. 'Let's just say we covered some of the city's key attractions.'

'Excellent. What I wouldn't give to be a single man about town again,' he says. 'Now, Ludo. Good news. Dennis is going to be working with us on the MaxiBudget project while he's here. We're going to put him right in the thick of it.'

'Who the hell is Dennis?'

'That's me,' says the Australian.

'Of course it is,' I say. 'Forgive me.'

'You degenerates!' says Oscar. 'Can't even remember each other's names. Pull yourselves together, and I'll see you at the meeting.' He turns and heads away down the corridor.

'Sorry about that,' I say. 'My brain is useless today.'

'So is mine,' says Dennis, smiling weakly. 'Thank you for . . . everything.'

'*No worries*,' I say, in English, doing a poor imitation of the accent. 'Welcome home!'

I will probably never know exactly what abstract nightmare he has conjured from the available clues – whatever his suspicions of me, he will not dare raise the subject again – but I doubt it's a relaxing one. This crucial victory obtained, my energy levels dip, and my brain registers the cold edge of a hangover. I must still have been drunk when I woke up.

The light on my phone is flashing, and I press the button to hear the message without thinking. The usual familiar background sounds float out of the speaker: the rushing water, the high machine whine. I can make out what sounds like someone settling into a chair, and lighting a cigarette. Then the whispered voice floats out, barely audible at all unless you're listening for it, which I am. I'm feeling tough enough to let this one run, to allow the bile to flow out, to hear what it has to say.

*I want you to really listen to me tonight. This is important. It's LIFE OR DEATH. Understand? It isn't even what you're doing to others that I care about — be a bastard to the whole world for all I care. Who am I to stop you? No. It's what you're doing to yourself that drives me nuts. How can you live with yourself? How can you do this, after the opportunities you've had?*

Is it such a crazy idea to think that it's Ernesto? There's nothing in his diary about it, but then I haven't dipped in there for a while. The sanctimony certainly fits. Suddenly, I'm convinced of it, and angry. How dare he talk about my 'opportunities'? I never asked to be taken off the streets and used as Zé's vanity project. I have the receiver in my hand, ready to dial Ernesto's number and ask him point blank whether it's him, whether he knows about me and his wife, when Oscar appears in the doorway.

'Well done, Ludo. You obviously really fucked up poor Dennis last night. But I hope you haven't forgotten about this MaxiBudget meeting. The clients will be here at midday, and I want something spectacular from you. Especially with your unique insight into this market.'

'As I keep telling you, I don't have a unique insight into this market.'

'It doesn't matter what you tell me. It only matters what I have been telling them. And what I have been telling them is that we have a success story right here in our office, who rose up from the slums to become a promising young executive. But one who hasn't forgotten where he came from. One who was born to work on MaxiBudget. Do you hear me?'

'I hear you,' I say. 'Don't worry. I'll have something.'

'Good,' says Oscar. 'I want to impress this guy. I want him to be bowled over by our insight before he's even explained what he wants us to do.'

\*

128

When he's gone, I blunder to a favourite bathroom cubicle towards the back of the building, overlooking the favela, enter, and with little ceremony curl up around the bowl and close my eyes. I've become accustomed to sleeping in here. I like the warmth, and the enclosure. Even the ambient noise has become associated with sleep for me, to the point that the blast of hand driers and any activity in the adjacent cubicles do not wake me up.

I don't know how long I'm asleep for – maybe ten minutes. Enough to get comfortable. Enough to leap with fright when the unlocked cubicle door swings open and a damp mop is thrust towards my face. I shout. The cleaner propelling the mop sees me and it swiftly retreats.

'Excuse me,' she says, backing out, trying to disguise her amusement. But the doors back there swing shut very slowly, and even though my eyes are gummed together I have time to see her shaking her head as she walks away, dragging her black bin liner with her.

*Time to do some work*, I think, springing up to give chase.

My face clings to the tile like chewing gum as I rip it off the floor, and leap, too quickly, to my feet. I almost black out as I follow her out of the stall and into the corridor. Hearing me approach, she stops and turns round.

'There are tile marks on your face. You should wait here a minute before you go back to work.'

'Could I ask you something?'

'Yes?'

'What's your name?'

'Flávia.'

Why have I never thought to find that out before?

Why have I thought to find it out now?

'Can I get you something to drink?' I say. 'A coffee?'

The offer is so weird that I suppose she can't think of a convincing way to say no. We walk through the office together. She hesitates before joining me in the lift. If people are surprised to see us leaving the building together they don't show it – or perhaps the sight is so alien that they just don't see it. I watch her from the side. She wears a huge black smock that hints at a big shapeless body beneath, and a powerful undercarriage at work. She walks slowly but deliberately, making more elaborate movements than are necessary, as if she were proceeding through water.

Presently, we're sitting on metal stools at a bustling corner *lanchonete* a few blocks from the office. Customers eat sitting or standing at a worn, semi-circular enamel bar. The seductive fug of grilling cheeseburgers is cut through by a zesty citrus tang thrown out by a juicing machine that takes up most of the back wall. An endless line of oranges rolls down a wire gully before each one is mechanically halved and eviscerated. The place serves great juice, and has a fast turnover. There's a sign boasting that when it gets to you, your juice is so fresh that it 'thinks it's still in the orange'. It's not the best way to sell orange juice, if you ask me. It makes me think of decapitated chickens running round farmyards, of eyes blinking in guillotined heads.

Flávia gives me a puzzled smile. I notice that two of her front teeth are broken. Her skin looks colourless and unhealthy. She is very tired.

'Why are we here?' she says.

'I wanted to get to know you a little. And get out of the office.'

'Haven't you got work to do?'

'Nothing important.'

I order a large orange juice for myself and, at her request, an avocado *vitamina* for Flávia. The avocado is peeled before us, its fat seed plucked out like an eyeball, and the flesh diced. In the liquidiser, the fresh green cubes vanish and blur in a whiz of sugar and condensed milk. The cold tumbler of glossy liquid is set before us.

'Do you have far to come? To work, I mean,' I ask.

She gives the name of a neighbourhood that is literally on the other side of the city, probably two hours away on the subway and more by bus.

'Really?' I say. 'You live all the way out there?'

She nods, sucking at a straw. The level of gloop in her glass smoothly drops.

'Is that really where you live, or just where your pay cheques go?' I ask, carefully.

My orange juice is good and pulpy. I swipe a finger through it and take a big mouthful of gunk, relishing the texture.

Softly, she spits out the end of the straw and fixes me with an iron expression. 'So that's why we're here. I knew it was too damn weird.'

'Wait –' The fingertip pops out of the side of my mouth.

She's off. 'Two can play at that game, Senhor. Tell your bosses I live in the favela and I'll tell them how you like to sleep off your hangovers on toilet floors. And yes, I know that won't do me much good, because you're the rich kid and I'm not, so they'll fire me and promote you, but I'll do it anyway, because what have I got to lose? My Lord, you people! Can't you even let a woman earn a living wiping your shit from the toilet bowl without demanding that she has a proper CEP code, and a fixed abode, and a tennis court?'

'Please relax,' I say. 'That's not why I'm here. I was just making conversation. My God.'

'Well, don't. I'm off. Coming here was a stupid idea.'

'Please don't go. Finish your drink.'

She had begun the lengthy process of removing herself from the bar stool, but now she stops. 'No bullshit?'

'None, I promise. I just wanted to get out of the office and talk to someone.'

We both pause while she calms down.

'So. What's it like?' I say. 'It's the one right here by the office, isn't it?'

'You really want to know?'

'Yes.'

'It's better than it has been, but it's still shit, if you'll excuse me. My son –'

The delicious char-grill smell finally gets the better of me. 'Would you like a cheeseburger?' I ask.

'You're not even interested in what I have to say.'

'Yes, I am, but I can't concentrate until I have one of those cheeseburgers in front of me. Do you want one?'

'It's only quarter to eleven.'

'Breakfast burger.'

She laughs, a little ruefully. 'If you're paying, sure.'

I order the burgers, then turn back to her. 'Sorry. You were talking about your son.'

Suddenly she is lost again, incredibly sad. 'It's nothing. It's just that he is never very far away from violence. That's all.'

'Is that true? I mean, one hears things, but –'

'Do you know what the life expectancy of a young man is where I live?'

'I admit that I do not.'

'Of course you don't. Why would you? It's better now I work at your office, but there've been times when I thought my boy and I might starve. You wouldn't know anything about that.'

'I know a little.'

'You know nothing! How could you know? I've lived in some Godforsaken places. I know people who live beside chemical factories and give birth to children without arms and legs. People whose water supply was poisoned by their own piss and shit. People who are afraid to fall asleep at night.'

'But things are changing, aren't they? *Favelados* are awarded their land these days.'

'What does that matter? Some areas of the favela I lived in before were recognised by the government. Others were not. All that happened was that the ones who owned their houses said they were no longer part of the favela, and tried to fence themselves off from the rest.'

'But you have amenities now, right?'

'I have water. Electricity, some of the time. I'm not complaining. I've lived in shittier conditions. But it's not exactly the Grand Hyatt, where I live. My son still has to read for school by candlelight sometimes.' She takes another hit from the *vitamina*, then says, 'You know your office was a squat?'

I nod.

'We lived there, before your company kicked us out. The toilets at the back of the sixth floor were a kitchen I shared with sixteen other people. You can see a scorch mark on the wall in the third cubicle along where my chip pan caught fire. And one of my son's drawings – of a hang-glider, I think – is still on the wall. By a soap dispenser. It's a crazy place, where you work.'

'How many children do you have?'

'Just one. Milton.' She smiles. 'You remind me of him, you know? If it wasn't for your stuck-up suit! But I don't want to talk about him.'

I weigh my words. 'He's . . . in trouble?'

'Of course he's in trouble! We're all in trouble. He's got nothing to eat, no money, nothing to do. It's fucked, the whole situation. And he sees these drug boys, the *traficantes*, strutting about. Is it any surprise he's attracted to them? Walking around, devil-may-care, waving their guns in the air! They've got all the clothes, all the dough, they do what they want! How do I keep him away from all that by saying "Go to school", "Stay here", "Eat this shitty bowl of beans"?'

Suddenly she is crying.

'I'm sorry. I –'

'You want to understand what it's like?' She closes her eyes, shedding twin tears that steal down her cheeks. 'I said I didn't want to talk about it. But you asked me. So you brought us here.'

'Brought us where?'

'My son got shot yesterday. Only a few blocks from the office. He was out in the street and he got shot by a mother-fucking security guard, just for asking for money. How can people be so ready to take us out over nothing?'

The *lanchonete* is suddenly small and vivid, and filled entirely by Flávia's wet, careworn face.

'My God.' The news seems to supercharge my hangover. I feel sick and giddy, and my head feels like it's filling up with heavy blood.

'Don't look so shocked, child. It's not your fault.' She sniffs loudly, and reaches for a napkin.

'Is he OK?'

She blows her nose. 'He'll be fine. This time. But of course, the people who helped with the medical attention were the *traficantes*. Every way you turn you need their help.

'I try to keep him on the right track. I threaten him. "If you fall in with those boys," I say, "then I'll kill you myself. Better that than the alternative – that you get shot by a policeman, or by some other kid who wants to take your place." But he doesn't listen to me. He has a horrible temper. He gets it from his father. I worry so much about what he might do if he fell in with the wrong people. And this is just the kind of thing that will push him over the edge. What am I supposed to do to stop it?'

'I cannot imagine.'

'No! You can't. A boy younger than mine was shot in the head, only four months ago. They found his body in the street, his brains drying on the wall. I knew his mother.' She is crying again.

'I'm sorry.'

She sniffs. 'Milton was lucky this time. But the point is that the scumbag who did it really didn't care if he was alive or dead. If it hadn't been for the two secretaries who saw it and called for medical help then I don't know what would have happened. I just don't know where it will end. The gangs. The guns. The drugs. Some things are getting better. But street names don't stop people getting killed. Sanitation doesn't stop people getting killed.' Her voice is now quavering with anger. 'And because we're mostly black – even though for some reason I can't understand everyone is proud of saying that the white can be just as poor – we mean nothing to the authorities. We might as well not have names.'

Still, I can think of nothing to say.

'We want to help ourselves. That's what the rich never understand. They assume we want them to do something, when all we want is to stop being invisible to them so we have the chance to get on.'

Still nothing.

'Forget it. Second thoughts, I don't want the burger. I feel sick talking about this stuff. I'm going back to work.'

'Wait –' my voice cracks.

'This isn't your problem. It's not right for me to talk like this to you. You live in a different world. Sleeping on floors coated with piss is a choice for you.' She makes herself laugh, bitterly. 'Sorry. I'm not in a good mood today. Thanks for the *vitamina*.'

'My best wishes to your son,' I call.

She turns slowly, like a supertanker adjusting her course, and meets my eye. 'He's not your problem. Don't worry about him. You can't make the world better all on your own.'

At the door, she calls over her shoulder, broadcasting it to the street, 'And stop drinking so much.'

All I can think as I watch her walk away is: *How could you come into work today?*

I sit at the bar for a while after she has gone, contemplating the network of cracks that break up the surface of its cream-coloured enamel, and sliding my empty juice glass around in a small puddle of condensed water. Seeing that Flávia didn't completely finish her *vitamina*, I suck briefly on the straw, tasting the sweet avocado mixed with something more bitter that must be her saliva. Then the cheeseburgers arrive, steaming and savoury, and though I have lost some of my appetite, I can't ignore them altogether.

I eat, feeling the fats and sugars detonate within me with each greasy, meaty swallow, combating the hangover head on. I finish the first burger, pluck a napkin from the chrome box on the counter, and dab my mouth a little before embarking on the second.

'Where have you been, you little shit?' Oscar is standing in the doorway of my office. 'I warned you about this meeting, and you haven't done a stroke of work, have you? The MaxiBudget people are here, and your computer isn't even warm.'

'You told me to prepare for the meeting, so that's what I've been doing,' I say. 'I've been meeting with someone from the favela.'

'Prove it.' We're pacing down the corridor, past a beautifully painted graffiti mural of a mermaid, undermined by a later occupant with the spray-on title, *Suck My Fish*.

'Her name is Flávia. She cleans in this building, and I've just taken her for a drink. She's perfect for this project: has a son, is struggling to make ends meet, goes hungry some of the time. MaxiBudget will be a godsend for her. When we have some concepts she'll be an instant test audience.'

He stares at me as he walks on. 'You're a slippery son of a bitch, Ludo. Always have been.'

'Thank you, boss.' Now we're outside the meeting room.

'Right, here we go. Remember: impress this guy.'

Oscar throws open the door wearing his finest client-welcoming smile, and I see that impressing this guy – huge, lovable, anticipating my surprise and holding his giant arms out to embrace me – is the least of my worries.

Thank God I'm not still wearing his shirt.

It's at this point, in a clinch with the real Ernesto, and not the psychotic, whispering version in my head, that something shifts inside me and I know exactly who has been leaving those messages on my phone. The realisation creates a vacuum in the pit of my stomach, and the world goes black in my eyes as he finally releases me.

How could I ever have thought otherwise? No wonder the background noises of the groaning fridge, the rushing pool filter and the twittering bird are so familiar. No wonder the messages only arrive when I have a terrible hangover. I've been leaving them myself in the small hours of the morning, on the verge of passing out.

# Cafézinho

Where did it start? Was there some point of no return, before which I might have graduated to adulthood without becoming messily, morbidly bound to Melissa; one step forward into pain that I needn't have taken, without which I might have stayed safe? In fact, one moment does present itself; a scene which, as I replay it now, makes me want to scream and run into the past, waving my arms to avert disaster.

Before I followed Melissa to the city, our roles were well defined and discrete. I lived on the farm and she was its weekend visitor. That meant that I could laugh at her when she got squeamish about caterpillars or sentimental over calves, and she could allow that to happen, safe in the knowledge that her 'real' world was somewhere that might easily wrong-foot me. Now that she was my only ally in that world, and my link with the old one, the balance of power shifted, and I began to cling to her.

Zé and my mother had both made it clear that if for any reason I decided the move had been a bad idea, the process was reversible. And so after only three weeks in Angel Park I announced to Melissa that I wasn't staying.

*I am fourteen. Melissa and I are sitting on the submerged concrete stools that encircle the swimming-pool bar, drinking freshly squeezed lime juice. Melissa has taken me there to slow me down, to talk me through all the good things about the city. An electrical storm is brewing, and the palm trees sway uneasily. The sunlight, filtered through boiling smog, is the colour of mustard. This is the morning when Melissa will persuade me to relinquish my home for ever, using only a few words and one fixed blast of the eyes.*

'I'm not staying,' I said. 'I'm going back to the farm. My mother needs me and I should never have left her.'

'At least wait until you've had a chance to get used to it here.'

'I don't *want* to get used to it. Nobody seems to realise how fucked up it is.'

'They know. They've just worked out ways of living with it.'

'I already know how to live on the farm. I'm going back.'

'What about my parents? Have you thought what they might think if you go back so soon?'

I paused, swishing my legs in the water. I was wearing my old, frayed shorts from the farm, but they seemed out of place here, and I wished I'd put on the new swimming trunks that sat neatly folded in my closet at the house. I looked beyond the pool area toward the distant tower blocks of the city, which broke up the horizon like the defences of an impossible castle.

'I hadn't thought about that,' I said.

'You should. I doubt they would look at you the same way again if you went back so soon.'

My legs fell straight. I looked at her. 'What's that supposed to mean?'

'I'm just worried they might think you're . . . ungrateful.'

'Is this blackmail?'

'No. It's just . . . please don't go. Stay.'

'What difference does it make to you? You have the

"weekday me" here whenever you need him, and you can go on seeing me at weekends.'

'But now I have the *real* you,' she said, smiling. 'And I don't want to send him back. Stay with me. We'll move away from Angel Park in the end. We'll go and live in the city together, at the top of one of those towers.'

I laughed. 'Whatever you say.'

'So you'll stay?'

'I'll give it more time. So long as my mother still recognises me when I go home.'

Melissa laughed and put a hand on my bare thigh under the water. 'I knew it. You're going nowhere, city boy. Time to put one of the Pool Bar's finest toasted sandwiches on Papai's account. If that doesn't convince you to stay I don't know what will.'

We returned to the farm for the first time three weeks later, but it might as well have been a lifetime. I knew this before we'd even set off on the Friday afternoon, when Zé got home from work and took me aside. It would have been at about the time when, on the farm, Silvio was sweeping down the tennis court and clearing leaves from the water chute, whistling old Carnival tunes. I fairly shook with the excitement of returning home. I pictured myself sprinting down the helicopter steps, leaping into my mother's arms, and following her back to the kitchen to enthuse about the craziness of the city, a chipped mug of sweet coffee in my hand.

'Ludo,' said Zé, beaming as he showed me into his study. My bag stood in the hallway, ready to go, packed with gifts (a blouse for my mother, a bottle of whisky for Silvio). 'You must be excited about returning home this evening. Sit down.'

I was almost breathless with it, but I didn't want him to see that. 'Yes. Not that I'm not grateful for being here – but yes, I'm looking forward to it.'

He smiled, and cut the tip off a cigar. 'It's OK to be excited about going to see your mother, Ludo. I won't take it as a personal affront.'

'Sorry.'

'And don't apologise! You can start relaxing around here now. This is your home. Which brings me to my question. You can say whatever you like to this, do you understand? It's your decision and nobody will judge you either way.'

I nodded.

'I wanted to ask you, before we arrive back at the farm: where would you like to sleep? In the main part of the house, with the rest of us, or where you used to sleep, with your mother?'

'With my mother,' I immediately replied. 'She would be hurt if I didn't.'

'Fine. That's settled. I just wanted to know whether I should phone ahead to have a room made up for you. Now, get ready. Lift-off in half an hour.'

I left the study, still excited about going home, but no longer uncomplicatedly so, and less sure of what home was than I had been five minutes before.

As the helicopter came in to land at the *fazenda* I looked down at the heads of those in the line-up, dutifully waiting in line as I had done every week for as long as I could remember. My mother in her pinafore, Silvio in his best and only suit. They looked comical from up there. Why had nobody ever told us that? From above, that collection of coiffed heads, all being churned up by the downdraught, the way everybody shuffled and jostled in the line – it might have been designed to make us look as stupid as possible.

'Silvio's thinning out on top,' Zé remarked as we came in.

'Doesn't your mother look beautiful today,' said Rebecca, whose empathy was on a state of high alert on my behalf.

I imagined what they were thinking about down there.

Silvio would be making dirty jokes, trying to deliver his punch line as late as possible so that everyone in the line would be fighting the laughter just as the helicopter doors were thrown open. My mother would be smirking a little, but keeping it together.

And there it was, the realisation, electric: she was trying to keep a straight face for me now. Everything had already changed. No matter how sensitive anybody was to the fact that it might happen, nothing could prevent it. I felt nauseous as we hit the ground.

'Down to earth,' Zé proclaimed, as the door of our capsule popped open and the warm, leafy air of home flooded in. 'Down to earth at last.'

That first weekend was the one with the most uneasy silences, when the chasm between me and my mother seemed the widest, but everyone was desperate for this strange new arrangement to work. My mother and I took refuge in role play. I sat expansively in the kitchen, a prodigal son telling tales of the metropolis, while she proudly fussed round me, dispensing cakes. Neither posture came naturally – both involved the pretence of pride, which neither of us possessed in any quantity, and both were dropped in subsequent weeks – but something about playing the parts was a comfort to us, as the bereaved sometimes shelter under broad brushstrokes of personality to prevent close scrutiny of their pain.

'Look at my boy flown in from the big bad city,' she cried, in a flustered tone of voice completely alien to her, when we had finally disengaged from a lengthy embrace. 'Let me pour you some coffee.'

The words were a smokescreen. As so often before, my mother's true eloquence revealed itself through what she put on the table: trays of cakes, sweet pastries and savoury buns; and coffee. It felt like I had never tasted coffee as delicious as what was in the cup before me now.

Although most of the objects in my mother's kitchen were functional in the extreme, there were a few special items, brought back for her by Zé and Rebecca on trips to Europe and America, and given with the injunction that they were 'for you, not for us' and never to be used for any entertaining other than her own. As a result, they remained largely unused, except when some distant relative came to stay, or on the birthday of Silvio or one of the other farm workers. One such gift was the set of delicate Italian coffee cups that I drink from to this day. (I knew they were Italian because I found the word 'Lucca' on the bottom of each cup and saucer, and asked my mother to show me where it was in the house atlas. We got through all the Americas and most of Africa before she believed me that it might be in Europe.) As a boy I hadn't even been allowed to wash these in case I should break them. Now, they were laid out on the table for me, while Silvio, I noticed, drank from the thick, chipped mug of my childhood. I wanted to snatch it from his hand and dash my dainty cup to the floor, but I had to play along.

'Things OK in the city?' said Silvio, regarding me over the cup, the steam playing around the dark laugh-lines at his eyes. Fumes from his customary slug of brandy reached my nose. It was a smell I had known all my life.

'They're fine,' I said. 'Different.'

'You've got a nice, comfortable bed there? You're sleeping well?'

'It's pretty good.'

He took a sip of coffee, and kept his eyes on me. 'Hasn't that crazy place taught you anything yet?'

'I don't know. I haven't been there long.'

'So you can't help me answer my question?'

'I'll try. What is the question?'

He regarded me seriously. 'What did the priest say when he came home to find two whores and a monkey in his bed?'

Thank God for Silvio, especially since what had happened must have been playing havoc with his sense of feudal propriety. I was never more grateful for his jokes than now.

'While we're talking about beds,' my mother said, interrupting. 'There was an instruction to make up an extra one at the house. You'll be sleeping up there from now on?'

Silvio's laughter sent a hot spray of coffee over the plate of *empadas* in front of him. 'Looks like city boy has got himself a taste for comfy beds after all!' he shouted, before wheezing uncontrollably for several minutes.

'And he asks me why he can't be trusted with the good china,' muttered my mother, whisking the plate out of danger and fetching a cloth to clean the mess. It was too late for me to point out that I had in fact requested to stay with her.

But I did. I spent the afternoon cursing Zé for offering me the choice but not acting on my decision, and later that day, as I watched her ladling fish stock into a *moqueca* pot, I told my mother that when Zé had put the question to me, I had asked not to be moved. She stroked my cheek with her strong, tough palm.

'I'm sure you did,' she said. 'But you should sleep up there. I've been making those wonderful beds for years – one of us might as well enjoy sleeping in them.'

Somehow, time made it OK – time, and the fact that everyone wanted it to work. And in fact, the physical distance between us brought with it great benefits. Far earlier than for most, my mother became a proper friend, an equal. Now she had relinquished her pastoral responsibilities, I could complain or enthuse without moderation about my new life, in the way you might to a grandparent or an uncle, or anyone else who loves you but isn't saddled with the worry of being principally responsible.

The character of the weekends changed. Now that I was the one bounding out of the helicopter, I saw less of Melissa and the family, and spent all my time in the kitchen with my mother. I ate with her instead of with the others. And in so doing I got to know her better than I would otherwise have done.

The downside was the occasional feeling that conditions had been placed on her mother's love. From that point on, she made no attempt to hide it when she was itching to get on with whatever she had been doing when my phone call interrupted her, or when she was falling asleep after a hard day. Our worlds were moving apart.

What seemed outrageous at first became natural in no time: multiple homes, two wardrobes of clothes, staff. And now that home had stopped being home, the process of assimilation into Angel Park could gather pace.

To start with, I didn't help myself. In my third week, a guard pulled over to investigate something suspicious in one of the ornamental ponds. He feared, or hoped for, a dead body. What he found was me, floating face down and contemplating the depths, as had been my habit in the forgotten pools of the farm. The usual fray of drawn pistols and aggressive shouts ensued, before I managed to convince the man that I was a resident.

'That pond is ornamental,' said the guard, holstering his weapon as I trudged dripping up the bank. 'You can't swim in it. There are other pools for swimming in.'

'Why can't I swim in this one?' I asked.

'I told you, it's *ornamental*,' he said, as if saying the word louder would make me understand him better. 'It's not a swimming pool.' He helped me on to the bank. 'Also, some

of the sewage pipes round here don't carry so well: it's probably chock full of Angel Shit.'

'That is a reason I can relate to,' I breathed, wishing I'd
kept my mouth closed underwater, but smiling in spite of
this as my head instantly filled with Silvio's jokes about rich
turds clogging up the water chute.

School was a grand academy in extensive grounds, shielded
from the favela on its doorstep by high walls and gatehouses.
At dropping-off and picking-up time the street was impass-
able, blocked by ranks of chauffeur-driven vehicles, their
engines ticking over as they queued up to relinquish or collect
their charges as near to the door as possible. Had Melissa not
been fearless enough to leave the compound, her kidnappers
would never have succeeded. They were crazy to think they
had a chance of grabbing a pupil from that place – but the
high walls and the blacked-out cars must have told them their
prize would be worth the risk.

Although skyscrapers still towered in every direction,
behind the gates the school was a refuge of whitewashed
walls and cool corridors. Its windows had dark green shutters to keep out the light and the heat; to focus the pupils
inwards, on their learning, and not outwards at the reeking
injustice beyond the gates.

Every day, as Melissa and I were dropped off, I glimpsed
kids my own age in the favela across the street. Un-shirted,
unselfconscious, underweight, they seemed always to be
laughing. I swung between guilt at the thought that I should
be among them, and envy at their apparently simple, joyful
existence. Some days I wished I could join in – playing with
stuff they had salvaged from the rubbish, or kicking around
a rag football; others, I was grateful for the safety of the
compound, with its water-polo lessons, its basketball courts,
its chilled drinking fountains.

Melissa and Ernesto were casually indifferent to the facilities at their disposal. It had never occurred to them that an education could transform a life. And they did not, like me, feel the constant burden of how much had been sacrificed on their behalf. So I did their homework for them, and I paid attention, and I did well. I was a successful experiment – one that justified every gram of Rebecca's compassion and Zé's magnanimity – whatever effect it may have had on my relationship with my real mother, on my perception of what constituted 'home', and on my state of mind.

It took a careless joke from Zé for me to realise what was happening back on the farm, something said over dinner one Thursday, about how he wondered whether everything would be ready for the guests he had staying that weekend, or whether the 'hot young lovers' would be too distracted.

'What's that?' I asked.

'He's joking,' said Melissa, shooting her father a look.

'Am I?' said Zé, his nostrils flaring. 'Love is no joke, Meli.'

'Well, I think it's wonderful,' said Rebecca. 'They deserve to be very happy.'

'What are you talking about?' I said.

Rebecca cleared her throat. 'Zé thinks that your mother and Silvio might be having some sort of romance.'

'Is that right?' I asked.

Zé contained his smile. 'I think it might be, Ludo. But it's a good thing, isn't it? It's good that your mother might no longer be alone.'

'Of course,' I said.

'She probably hasn't told you because she's been waiting for the right time,' Rebecca said. 'And we don't know for sure. Zé is just making mischief.'

'Ok,' I said.

'From what I saw they might not have had much time yet

to speak to anyone,' Zé muttered, sniggering to himself. 'They couldn't keep their hands off each other. Silvio looked like a dog caught humping the sofa.'

Everyone laughed, including me, before I remembered at whom I was laughing. Even now it's difficult to articulate how I felt that evening.

# Sea Urchin

My life is a maze with ever-narrowing paths. It's only a matter of time before the walls hem me in so completely that I won't be able to move at all. Ernesto is the client; but of course he is. I should have known that even his self-righteous sanctimony would yield eventually to Zé's irresistible, steamrolling desire to *include*. This family – it is walled in, blind to the majority. It's how their connections stay strong. The inevitability of it all makes me weary.

Oscar stands back to watch the embrace between me and my brother-in-law, pleased with himself and the trick he's played.

'You knew about this?' I say.

'I wanted to surprise you,' he replies, and turns to his client. 'Didn't I tell you I had just the guy for you on this project?'

'You did,' says Ernesto, beaming.

After the meeting, which flies by unnoticed, Ernesto takes me aside and embraces me again.

'It's good to see you! How long has it been? Are you hungry?'

'All the time.'

'Let me take you to lunch, on me. Or rather, on Zé.'

Since Ernesto's paying I direct the taxi to one of my favourite restaurants, a Japanese place on the top floor of a new bank. Its walls are clad in clean, rustic-looking wood, as if you were eating in a rural *ryokan* and not capping off a resplendent skyscraper. Its longest wall is entirely taken up by an ice bar heaped with sea creatures, dead or dying.

And here he is. Ernesto, struggling with his table manners as usual, spilling stuff all over the place, eating like a child. I'd forgotten his enthusiasm, how he eats like a big bear with poorly coordinated paws. Watching him grapple with the chopsticks, I remember how, when Melissa and I were still living together, I used to set his place with a smaller set of cutlery when he came for dinner. Childish perhaps, but I wanted to watch his big hands fumbling around, trying to cope, to make him feel as out of proportion and awkward as possible. Forks laden with my rich sauces would clatter to the polished wood floor from his hands, and he'd mumble his apologies as he crammed his frame under the table to collect them.

How could I have blamed those phone messages on him? As well as scanning pruriently for information about how regularly he fucks his wife, I've also dipped into Ernesto's diary to see if there was any hint of negativity about me, some snobbery that was there from the beginning, which he's concealed out of respect for Melissa, and which I can use to justify deceiving him. I've found nothing. He appears to love me, and judge me only for who I am. He doesn't even call me a sell-out for what I do for a living. How I could have imagined that he had somehow changed completely and started leaving me voice-hate-mail, I do not know.

We're distracted by the range and quantity of dishes that I order – tartares of salmon and tuna, glistening heaps of roe from three different species, a mosaic of raw fish and a stack of vegetable tempura – so at first we restrict ourselves to a post-mortem on the meeting. But even down on this conversational level there's a lot going unsaid. I order a carafe of chilled sake to try and loosen him up.

'Think about it,' he says. 'The way these communities work is that everything is hijacked. Their cable TV is siphoned off everybody else's. Their electricity, their water, and even, these days, their internet access. It's all "unofficial". Their entire lives are unofficial. And what happens with their shopping isn't that different. The way to get the freshest meat is to buy a live animal and kill it yourself at home. You don't want the spoiled cut that's been hanging above the butcher's block crawling with flies for six hours. With MaxiBudget, we're going in after them – to take food to them. Affordable food. Designated food. Official food.'

'To stop them from coming and staring hungrily through the windows of our own supermarkets.'

'No!' He smiles, knowing I'm being deliberately provocative. 'To nurture their communities. To acknowledge what the government has spent years ignoring. So we can turn them away from things "unofficial" and start them down the road of becoming integrated citizens. Why is that so difficult for you, of all people, to accept?'

I slam down my cup. 'I wish people would stop saying "*You, of all people*"! Why am I supposed to know more about this than anybody else?'

There's an uncomfortable pause. I'm breathing heavily. Plates and chopsticks clink around us. Two diners look over. Then the tension is broken by the noise of a huge crab clattering off the ice bar and on to the floor. Whether it fell off because the ice is melting under it, or whether it is still alive and making a bid for freedom, I don't know. Two waiters leap over to replace it.

'Remember when you took me shooting on my first morning in Angel Park?' I ask, trying to recover my cool.

'I've grown up since then.'

'So have I.'

'I know. I'm sorry, Ludo –'

'I overreacted. But listen, fill me in, because I don't understand. How long have you been working for Zé?'

'A couple of months now.'

'Nobody told me.'

'You know how bad the family is at communicating things.'

'But I . . . I spoke to Melissa yesterday, and she didn't seem to know you were working on it. She hadn't even heard of it. Your own wife doesn't know where you work?'

'I haven't told her yet,' he says. 'I hate keeping things from her, but I haven't had the courage.'

'Why not?'

He drops a beautifully assembled piece of sushi into his dish of soy sauce, splashing flecks of brown all over his shirt, then, abandoning all pretence of eating with the chopsticks, rescues it with his hand.

'I suppose I'm ashamed,' he says. 'I spent years telling Melissa I wouldn't work for her father.'

'But it's a good cause, as you keep telling me. There's no shame in it.'

'It's not that, it's the nepotism. I've always hated the way Zé has to keep everybody pinned down. All that control-freakery. I fought off his job offers for ages, but with this project, because it's charitable, he finally found a way to get me to say yes. The trouble is that no matter how worthy it is, I feel uncomfortable. There's something almost . . . incestuous about it.'

My throat feels dry. I drain my cup of sake, too quickly, so that the alcohol overwhelms the taste, and order another carafe straight away.

'You're different,' he goes on. 'You've managed to escape it somehow. But I've married into it.'

I think about Zé threatening to take away Oscar's biggest account if he didn't give me my job, and say nothing.

There's a pause as the new sake is delivered. I top him up.

'We haven't seen much of each other lately,' he says. 'And I know it's been years now, but I don't think I have ever told you in person how sorry I was about what happened to your mother.'

'Thanks.'

Pause.

'I didn't know you were in touch with Melissa,' he says, noticing in a burst of empathy that the previous topic was unwelcome.

'We speak on the phone from time to time. She doesn't tell you?'

'To be honest, she doesn't tell me a great deal.'

Here we go.

'You've known her all your life,' he says. 'You know how difficult she can be. She closes everything down and goes into herself. And – I'm sorry, listen to me. It's been so long. I'm sure you've got problems of your own.'

'I want to hear this. Honestly.'

'All her secrecy. I think it's contagious. That's probably another reason why I haven't told her about this job. Especially because I think that her secrecy is also hypocritical. I don't think she respects my right to privacy at all.'

'What do you mean?'

'It's unfair of me to talk to you about this. You're her brother.'

'I'm your brother too. I promise I'll keep it to myself.'

'I think she's been reading my diary. It's no big deal, of course. I have nothing to hide. But the thing is, I wouldn't even know she'd read it if I hadn't noticed that sometimes the date on the file name changes, which means she must be . . . altering it as well.'

'You must be imagining that. She probably doesn't even know you keep a diary.'

He tips sake into his cup. 'She's so odd sometimes. She leaves these cryptic messages written in steam on the bathroom mirror. I have no idea what they're supposed to mean. And there's another, more worrying thing.'

'Tell me.'

'I'm probably being paranoid.'

'Tell me, and I'll tell you whether I think you're paranoid.'

'I think she might be seeing someone else. Sometimes, after I've been away, I find – strange hair in the bed. Black. Wiry. Definitely not hers or mine.' He leans across the thin wooden table, and gestures with the chopsticks that are tiny in his hands. 'But you want to know what the worst thing is?'

This is it. He's going to say, *The worst thing is that it's you she's doing it with*, and that will be that.

'What's that?' I say.

'The worst thing is that I can't even drum up any sympathy for myself, because I think I probably *deserve* all this.'

'What do you mean?'

'I mean that I'm a bad person.'

'I don't understand.'

'This job.'

'For the love of God! What's wrong with working for your father-in-law?'

'That's not what I mean.'

'How does an anthropologist come to be working for a supermarket chain, anyway?'

'He said that my studies of the favelas could help him set up his subsidised supermarkets – which are funded, incidentally, by the Uproot Foundation as well as by the companies whose products are on sale. It's basically a charitable venture.'

'But if working for a charity was your only stipulation, Zé could have got you working for him years ago.'

He sighs. 'It's not easy, helping some of these people. They're proud. They think that only someone who was born and suffered there with them is genuine. They don't trust me for a second, and they don't even know where I grew up. Can you imagine if I told them about Angel Park?'

'None of this is helping me to understand why you suddenly decided to work for Zé.'

'I wanted some muscle behind me. If you're going up against an organisation like the Shadow Command then it doesn't hurt to have Zé Generoso on your side.'

'I don't get it. "Muscle"? This doesn't sound like you at all. I thought your point was always that progress depended on trust.'

He sighs. 'You're right.'

'So what changed your mind?'

'You mean *who* changed it.'

'Ah.'

'He came to see me at the university. You know when he does that thing of phoning, and asking *Where will you be in ten minutes' time?*, and then you feel the walls vibrate?'

'I know it well.'

'The university campus isn't exactly geared up for helicopters, but you know him. He landed on the recreation ground outside my office, barged right in and said he had a proposal for me.'

'What kind of proposal?'

'You can imagine it. He can't bear anyone being too independent of him. He'd had enough of his son-in-law struggling along as a university professor, and working on these little youth projects. I don't know how much you know about what I'm going to say –'

'I told you, my lips are sealed.'

155

'For a while now, Rebecca hasn't been well. She been on antidepressants, and I think she might be drinking.'

'Really?'

'I don't know how serious it is, or how much Zé was talking up the problem to make me feel bad, but he said that Rebecca had basically given up. That the work was taking too much out of her because she cared about it so much – and that he was trying to persuade her to step back from it and hand over the running of the foundation to somebody else. "Who better than you," he said, "to take it on? You'll have free reign to take it in whichever direction you want. I know you're more than qualified. That way, Melissa needn't know what a state her mother is in, and you can amalgamate your existing projects with the work of the foundation, and put some serious money behind them – carry on your good work with a decent budget. And best of all, you're *family*. But, if none of those reasons persuades you," he said, "then do it as a favour to the father-in-law who values you greatly and believes you are the only person who is in a position to help him in this hour of need."'

'He got you through emotional blackmail?' I say. 'He's no fool.'

'True.'

'But it's not such a bad place to earn a living. And what he says about integrating it with your work is true.'

'It's true up to a point, yes. And MaxiBudget isn't such a bad idea. That part of it is fine.'

'Then I don't see the problem. Just have the humility to admit to Melissa that you've changed your mind about working for her father – that there is a reason now that you can accept. Be the *filho de papai*, and don't beat yourself up about it. You've been stupidly proud about not working for the family until now.'

'That would be fine, except . . .'

'Except what?'

'Except that it's *freaking me out,*' he says, suddenly raising his voice in a way that is very out of character.

I smirk a salmon egg down my front. Ernesto gazes out at the view, looking desolate.

'This isn't a joke. I'm in serious trouble, Ludo.'

'Sorry. I didn't mean to laugh.' I pick the orange bead off my shirt gingerly so it doesn't burst and toss it to the back of my mouth, trying to look contrite. 'Tell me about it.'

He sighs. 'You need to understand how things work in these communities. You need to understand that the idea that their lives can somehow be changed for the better by some external initiative is simply ridiculous to these people. It is laughable.'

'OK...'

'The Foundation's basic principle is that their lives can be changed – that they can be uprooted – but that concept is alien to the residents themselves. Beyond the one in a million stories of footballers playing their way to riches, or the odd politician or musician, there's no evidence to suggest that their lives can be any different, because nothing ever changes for them.'

'I am a rare exception, but we'll overlook that.'

'Rare? You're unique.'

'I know that. Go on.'

'What's more, many of them don't *want* to live outside the favelas. It's where all their friends and family are. You can live well these days, and there's a freedom from rules that is attractive.'

'That's romanticising things a little, in my opinion, but carry on.'

'The point is that every one of them has been brought up to believe that nobody is going to change his destiny but him or herself. It's what they are told, and what every experience they've ever had has taught them. The idea that someone might walk into their lives one day and offer help in exchange for nothing at all is just a fairy tale. It's not going to happen. There will be a catch.'

'OK.'

'So. Starting any kind of charitable initiative in this situation would be difficult enough, but then you hit another problem, which is that every single favela is controlled by one gang or another. They fund the municipal services. They pay the bills. And nothing happens without their say.'

'I know that.'

'But you don't realise the extent of it. If you want to do anything for these communities, whatever you do for them has to be converted into a benefit that the gangs can feel straight away. It's not enough just to offer education for their kids or to teach their people new skills. What you offer them needs to be in a currency that they can spend, otherwise the dialogue never even gets started. You're expelled, or worse, you're dead.'

'What currency are you talking about?'

'The situation is so mixed up,' he goes on, 'that there are no good and bad sides. Two weeks ago in Paraisópolis the police got so fed up with how little control they had over the community that they held up the bank. It was the *traficantes* who defended it.'

'That's very funny. But it's not entirely surprising.'

'My point is that I have spent a long time gaining the trust of the people I work with, something that Maxi-Budget and Zé just don't have the time to do. He likes to build quick alliances through grand gestures and incentives.'

'What are you saying?'

'That part of my remit for MaxiBudget involves a guarantee that I will do certain . . . extra business deals for key figures in the community, in order to ensure the security and success of the stores.'

I get it. 'They want you to sell drugs? Where?'

'Angel Park. My parents are still there, so I can get in without any problems.'

'And what?'

'Marijuana. Cocaine. I drew the line at crack. And believe me, there's no shortage of demand.'

I take a deep breath. 'Amazing. Does Zé know?'

'He knows everything that goes on in his businesses. But he would think it was . . . uncouth of me to bring it up. He would just want me to do it, discreetly, like all the nasty things I'm sure he's done over the years. And I don't think I can.'

'Don't, then.'

'It's not that simple.' He sighs, and his arms hit the table like felled trees, causing the remaining tempura vegetables to jump in their dish.

'How do you even know this is expected of you?' I ask.

'There's a guy. A gang member. Part of a gang called the Shadow Command.'

'I know them. Their tags are all over our office.'

'You and your frozen ghetto. Anyway, this guy, he's known as Jeitinho. He's not the leader, but he seems to be high up.'

'What's he like?'

'Powerful. Calm. He's younger than us – no more than twenty-two – but you can tell he's seen a lot, that there's not much he wouldn't do. And he carries a machine gun.'

'Difficult to refuse someone like that.'

'I don't think the leader is ever far away, either – my guy gets instructions from him all the time by phone.'

'And he wants you to do these deals for him?'

'Yes. It's all set up for me. All I have to do is make the drops.'

'Why can't they get someone else to do the legwork?'

'They could. They don't need me – there are hundreds of little foot soldiers they could send to do it – but it's about complicity. They want something on me, so I'm controllable.'

'And have you done it?'

'Twice,' he says, miserably. 'Please, don't say anything.' He holds up a hand. 'There's no name you can call me that I haven't already called myself.'

I know him well enough to know how much he will have been punishing himself for this. No wonder he's only just got round to noticing my hairs in his bed.

'So you're a drug dealer. This is quite something.' I can't help breaking into a smile.

'It's not funny. I could get killed. What should I do?'

'I don't know,' I say, truthfully. 'I'll have to think about it.'

I gaze out across the city, at a helicopter that flits from building to building like a mechanised bee after pollen. The rich nectar of blackmail mixes on my tongue with the salty oil of salmon roe. Finally, I've got something on him.

'You're going to think I'm being ridiculous,' he says, 'but initially I thought that I could help by doing what I've been doing. By keeping them separate. The street kids don't have to brave the security of somewhere like Angel Park, and the rich kids don't have to get shot in the favelas trying to score. I thought, the buyers and the sellers are going to find each other anyway, so why can't I just make that process as free from confrontation as possible and concentrate on solving the bigger problem?'

'Do I have to tell you what's wrong with that?'

'No,' he says. 'But thank you for not saying anything judgemental. I know what you must be thinking.'

'You might be surprised.'

I call over the waitress and ask for a portion of *uni*.

'What have you ordered?' he says. 'Nothing more for me.'

'This is special. It will calm you down. It's something so good that it can only take your mind off what you're telling me.'

'Nothing could possibly do that.'

'Wait and see. Now then, let's talk about this. You feel guilty because you're supplying the rich kids with their drugs?'

'Not particularly. They could get the stuff anywhere they wanted. But by dealing for the gangs to gain their trust I'm cancelling out all the good that trust is supposed to buy me.'

'What happens to the money you make in these deals?'

'Half of it goes straight to prison – to people you can't imagine and will never see, who run half the city from their cells. The other half goes to the *traficantes*, and from them, filters back into the community. It puts people through school. It pays doctor's bills. It covers sewers.'

'So in the end, you're helping,' I say. 'The gang leaders can choose what to do with their money just as much as the rich kids can. You should stop worrying about it.'

A dish of three sea urchins, accompanied by carefully sculpted shards of *daikon* radish, is placed before us. An involuntary sigh escapes me, they're so beautiful. The spiky blue-black shells in which they have been served resemble perfect miniature bird's nests. The gloopy yellow pods inside quiver as they are set down – jellied gold. I'm reminded of how the central cavity of a crab is known in some languages as the 'purse'.

'You're oversimplifying things,' says Ernesto, seeming not to notice what's been put before us. 'What I have been doing is weak – an easy way to win their favour so I could look as if I was doing my job when in reality all I have done is undermine it.'

'I do that every day of the week. Stop talking for a while and try this. It's *uni*, sea-urchin roe. It's delicious.'

He reaches forlornly over the carnage of his previous efforts for the dreaded chopsticks.

'Don't bother with that. Here.'

Not leaving anything to chance, I reach down, lightly holding the spiky shell, and collect one pad of roe with my chopsticks to deliver it to his lips. Nothing transforms the mouth like that delicate flavour: a taste that breaks in a creamy, briny wave over your tongue. For ten seconds, the expression on his face is blissful, as the *uni* washes through him and spirits him away to the sea.

'Amazing,' he manages, his voice coming from a different place.

'The Japanese consider it a great aphrodisiac,' I say. 'Partly because it contains high levels of naturally occurring cannabinoids.'

'Really?'

'Really. So my advice is that you stop worrying about all this, eat these urchins and get home quickly so you can bang your wife.'

I am genuinely trying to make him feel better, but by bringing up both cannabis and Melissa in the same breath I have undone the transformative good work of the sea urchin. He pays the spectacular bill mechanically, in a trance-like state brought on by all that resurgent stress.

'Send her my love,' I say as we part.

Reflecting on these developments, I take a taxi back to the office, the dull thud of too much sake behind my eyes. Ernesto the drug dealer, would you believe it. At least he's doing something real with his life, which is more than I can say for his wife, or her lover. Not that I'm technically her lover, given how infrequently we've actually consummated the relationship. As for that side of things, my adventures in

Melissa's bed will end permanently if Ernesto goes in for any more detective work. I'm just lucky that he's so well intentioned that the idea of him divining the true origin of those hairs in his bed is simply unthinkable. Not unless some-body spells it right out to him, anyway.

# Calf's Liver

I sometimes want to run away from this life to which I have been promoted , and live in a small town on the coast, where there are horses tethered on every street corner, where the dirt roads have numbers instead of names, where the local shop sells nothing but Fanta and outboard motors. But then I think of where I might be if it wasn't for Zé and Rebecca. Would I be a scavenging *catador*, running between the traffic pulling a trailer full of scrap metal? A barefoot sweet-seller, wandering the park with a tree of candyfloss? Watching over parked cars, or bagging produce at the MaxiMarket? And my mother: would she now be the hag with the caved-in mouth, setting sail through the traffic with her cart of rubbish, and sleeping in a lean-to shelter under a bridge, or behind an advertising billboard? Would we be just two more of those wrecks that rage on street corners?

Rebecca and Zé were our salvation. But am I at least allowed to wonder what might have happened if we hadn't been saved? I believe that my mother was strong enough to see us through anything the favela could have thrown at us – and that had we not been rescued, she would have made it through with her pride intact. Of all the ways in which I hurt her, I look back on my failure to snuff out my mother's conviction that she wasn't the person best qualified to raise me as the most shameful. She took the outstretched hand that was offered to her, but then she felt she owed it everything, making a mockery of her self-sufficiency. It's a pan-American story: when she had nothing but a handful of beans to her name, the tough nugget of pride at her core sustained her. Then along came Zé and Rebecca, and took away that pride, replacing it with impotent gratitude. Like the mythological pelican slashing open her breast to sustain her young, my mother fed me her blood, and she took a mortal blow for me in the process.

*'Didn't I tell you we'd go off and live in a tower together?' says Melissa. She's eating mango with a knife and fork, her coffee-cream legs topped off by the briefest pair of white shorts and a baggy old sweatshirt of her father's. I am seventeen.*

*'What?'*

*'You remember. Down at the pool, when you first moved?'*

*'What do you mean?'*

*'I'm eighteen next month.'*

*'So?'*

*'So I'm getting an apartment for my birthday, and there's no way I'll be allowed to live in it alone. You'll have to come and take care of me.'*

In this way I discovered where the next act of my life was to play itself out: the penthouse of a brand new, cylindrical block; the same penthouse that has lately become the scene of all this unbecoming cuckoldry and incest.

It was still possible at this stage to think of my time in the city as an excursion, a lengthy but finite deviation from my ultimate destiny back on the farm. I had changed a lot in three years, but life on the farm had not, and I remained convinced that I would one day return there, whatever the city was doing for my intellectual and social 'development'.

What's more, in spite of her newfound happiness with Silvio – which was genuine, and welcomed by me – my mother had started to sound frail on the telephone. I had also overheard an abruptly terminated conversation about her health between Zé and Rebecca that worried me. But once again, events were out of my hands.

It was billed as Zé's ingenious compromise solution. Melissa wanted to leave home, and Zé was concerned for her safety in the city, but he knew better than to smother her. In a plan with all the latent horror of a fairy tale, the princess would live high above the streets, and the king could drop in on her any time to make sure that all was well.

As is so often the case with Zé, the extent to which this was all calculated in advance is impossible to assess. He was so clinical with his forward planning that I could even believe he knew when he chose to adopt me that Melissa would be striking out from him before too long, and wanted to send a trained member of staff along to watch over her.

So, I wasn't always an interloper in the tower. I had a ringside seat as Melissa and Ernesto's relationship developed beyond the friendly childhood stuff, and got serious. People rationalise it now. They are even referred to as childhood sweethearts. That's bullshit. It's just what people like Zé and Rebecca and Gaspar and Olinda want to believe. It happened in the penthouse. I saw it.

From the day I arrived in the city at fourteen, the three of us grew into a powerful, close-knit group, inseparable both at school and in Angel Park. We didn't exactly shun others, but neither did we need them, and I managed to go through my entire school career without a proper friend of my own age. Then, when I still had a year to go, Melissa and Ernesto left school and enrolled at the university. It put distance between us, whether we wanted it or not. They had embarked on the next stage, Ernesto developing his anthropological interests and Melissa studying journalism, while I was left behind, and instantly rendered younger. It was only a matter of time.

*I am seventeen. Loaded with shopping bags and drenched, I clatter through the door. Above the city, the sky is iron-grey with rain. Single strands of lightning flicker on the horizon, impossibly distant. A yellow bar of light under the door to Melissa's bedroom. Loud music. Laughter. I'm unpacking the shopping when she bursts out of the room, wearing only a man's shirt.*

*'Something ridiculous is happening,' she laughs, giving me a hug. 'I think I've fallen in love with that idiot Ernesto.'*

The tower rears up in gleaming silver sections, like robotic vertebrae, and is constructed in an oval shape, which means there isn't a straight line in the place. The furniture has to be arranged in the middle of large open spaces, which gives the penthouse a permanently transient air, as if the removals men have only just left. There's a plunge pool on every balcony, and the great black disc of a helipad sits on the roof like a crown.

Zé knew when he bought the place that there were benefits for him that Melissa would overlook in her enthusiasm for independence – the principal one being that he could drop in and check up on her whenever he wanted. Sometimes he would get his pilot to hover outside the window, so Melissa or I could wave and show him it was worth his while to land. Other times, he would swoop in unannounced. Either way, you couldn't have failed to know he was coming: the walls would begin to vibrate, and the sound would roar above your head until the engines were cut, leaving the descending whine of slowing blades. Then he'd be at the door, suited and sweet-smelling, bearing cigars, or a bottle of something. When Melissa wasn't expecting him, I sometimes had to cover for her and Ernesto, frantically scrambling into their clothes next door.

'Ludo,' he would say, beaming his best business smile. 'Ludo, Ludo, Ludo.' He would gaze out of the window, puffing his big cheeks out, grinning, pretending to examine me in depth, though there was nothing in the eyes. He loves being in tall buildings and is always distracted by the view. 'My boy, it's good to see you. How are you? Studying hard?'

'Yes, sir.'

'Good for you. Enjoying the apartment?'

'Oh yes.'

'Good, good. I'm happy. That's what it's here for. Now where is Melissa, do you suppose? She can't still be in bed. These women and their showers, I will never understand it.'

'She'll be out in a minute. Can I pour you a drink while you wait?'

Those were the days. Now it is I who cower in the bed while Zé struts around outside, and Ernesto who is king of the tower. It mystifies me.

But there's no denying it. Melissa and Ernesto were a fact not long after we moved in, and Ernesto a full-time, if covert, resident. The apartment was Ernesto's escape route as much as ours. He and Melissa might have plotted the situation as carefully as Zé himself. Without me there as a chaperone, Zé would never have let her move out. With me along for the ride, she had a respectable brother–sister thing going on and the added benefit of someone who cooked and cleaned to earn his place. I felt in the way from the start.

The thing that gets me is that I *know* they're meant to be with each other. The picture of them together, it works. Ernesto, the perfect father with the worthy job, who for all his unwavering commitment would never go to work on his kids' birthdays; Melissa, his eye-poppingly beautiful wife, her inheritance supplementing Ernesto's income, her figure seeming to tighten up with every child she squeezes out. In the middle of that vision, I look like I've come to steal their television – or at least repair it.

During those years I became expert at being part of the background while discreetly adding to the foreground; of requiring nothing but being ready to supply anything. I cooked every meal. I cleaned shoes. I cultivated my herbs. I performed tasks that they took for granted to such an extent that I wonder whether they notice now how much worse everything tastes. I made sure their wine breathed; I chilled their beer to the perfect temperature. Quietly, I improved every meal, smoothed over every domestic transaction, and kept out of their way. And I might have been able to stand being that person, inheriting my mother's position and retaining for the next generation, were it not for events that made me look on them both with new eyes.

Ernesto was evolving from the slack-fleshed kid who joyrode the private streets of Angel Park into someone with a conscience. He'd started to work on case studies of life in the slums, and to feel ashamed of the easy wealth of his situation. And the distractions of this new social purpose caused him to do something unthinkable: to take Melissa for granted. He would stay away for days at a time without offering much in the way of explanation, and when he returned he would spend whole evenings lecturing us on what he'd seen.

'Do you even know how it starts, in the beginning? It starts with a single cell. Seeking shelter from the elements, a man leans a piece of plywood up against a wall. Picture it. Let's say it's the side of a packing crate. Let's say he's twenty, with no education, and only a pair of blue dungarees and a pocketknife to his name. Picture him. He cowers beneath the sheet of wood for the night. Nobody moves him on. So he stays. He improves his dwelling. One wall becomes four, then a watertight roof. Someone joins him. And if you think it's bad, what they have here in the city, you should see what they're escaping *from.*'

And so on. Melissa would never have said anything explicit about it because she believed in what he was doing, but I noticed that his self-absorption and absenteeism were beginning to affect her. Then one night, when he was away, we ended up watching a film together in her bed and falling asleep there. Somehow from then on it became the understanding that if she left her bedroom door ajar I would creep in and join her there when she was half-asleep. That way, she didn't have to face up to what she was doing, and could sigh and clamp her arm around me as I crept in beside her. I knew I was being used to provide comfort, but I saw no reason not to oblige: at this stage our relations were still strictly fraternal. This was news, of course, that did not reach my rigid body as it lay there all night unable to sleep, as tensely sprung as if the contact of Melissa's arm were passing an electric current through it.

Like my mother, I poured emotion into food. I translated my longing into culinary semaphore, using recipes to send frantic signals to Melissa over Ernesto's dumb head. I made daring, all-or-nothing declarations through meticulous cocktails, and pledged myself at full volume in elaborate, anguished sauces. Melissa and I would eat in silence, communing through the food, while Ernesto sat between us, shovelling away as if he were stoking a boiler, prattling about the needy and making inane, ill-considered compliments about the cooking.

I couldn't see how anyone could overlook Melissa. However hard your shell, she found her way in; she was like a truffle secreted in a basket of eggs, its perfume effortlessly pervasive. But not, apparently, for Ernesto.

★

One day a few months before my twenty-first birthday, I went to the shopping mall to buy clothes and run some errands. I remember the day perfectly for two reasons, and what happened at the mall is only the lesser of the two.

They had a pink dolphin captive in a huge tank that took up the space of an entire retail unit, slotted in between surf-wear boutiques, toyshops and hair salons. I found the poor creature fascinating. It swam in constant bewildered circles, sometimes bringing its high, domed head right up against the glass, and if you got in really close you could hear it making the occasional plaintive click or whistle, trying in vain to make contact with its population thousands of kilo-metres away.

The girl's name was Anabel. She came into focus in the glass of the tank, standing behind me, watching the dolphin.

'I wonder what he thinks of you,' she said.

'What do you think he makes of all this plastic?' I said, to the reflection. 'People walking around with bags. All the *retail*.'

She held my gaze in the glass. 'You shouldn't assume he's unhappy. Perhaps he doesn't mind being here at all. Maybe he just desperately wants someone to fetch him a drink from the burger bar.'

I laughed. 'You think so? All these years, and nobody got that all he wanted was a chocolate shake?'

'A chocolate shake – that's not such a bad idea,' she said. 'Are you going to buy me one?'

She was eighteen, and skinny, with long brown hair and dark eyes. She wore tight jeans, boots and a denim jacket over a pink T-shirt. Rather then lift the milkshake to her face, she kept her arms by her sides and bobbed down to reach the straw. I watched the top of her head every time she leant over. It looked fragile as an egg.

We sat overlooking the ice rink on the ground floor of the shopping mall, and as we drank our chocolate malts she asked me if I skated. I told her I never had, and she was shocked.

'There's something called an Ice Party happening tonight,' she said. 'They put disco lighting on the ice and play music. Do you want to come?'

I smiled. 'Isn't that meant to be for kids?'

'You think you're grown-up, and you've never even ice-skated?'

'OK,' I said. 'I'll come. Where shall I meet you?'

'I'll be on the ice, pirouetting gracefully in the middle,' she said. 'I'll be very conspicuous.'

I got home to find Melissa at the window. The forlorn princess, locked in her tower, gazing down at her kingdom of lights. I put down my shopping, and was about to ask her whether she'd heard of an Ice Party, and what she thought I should wear for it. Then I noticed that she had drunk one bottle of wine and opened another.

'What's wrong?' I said.

'Nothing,' she replied, without turning round.

'Tell me.'

'I don't know. I suppose it's something pathetic to do with feeling lonely. Forget it.'

'Where's Ernesto?'

'Working. It's not his fault.' She took a gulp of wine, and turned round so I could see the dark mascara deltas that held her face like fingers.

'What's really the matter?' I poured her more wine, and a glass for myself.

'I don't know. I was thinking today about when I was kidnapped. For the first time in years. Strange.'

A cloud of red and blue light shot down the avenue below us: two police cars in pursuit.

'I wasn't around to protect you back then. But now I am,' I said, looking down at her hands, and noticing the telltale rawness that came from when she had been obsessively washing them. 'I used to hate myself for not being there to stop them taking you.'

'You did protect me. You gave me a way out.'

I stared at her. 'Me?'

'You don't remember? That performance you used to do? Your way of getting out of it when we were in a fight? The rolling eyes, the chattering teeth? It was you who gave me the idea.' She smiled. 'You tried it once again, much later on, when that creepy guy Oscar tried to chase you round the garden, remember?'

I remembered. Silvio's stupid childhood routine. *'That's* what you were doing when they threw you from the car? That was where the fit came from?'

'It just came to me. You used to do it to get people to let you go, so I thought it would work for me. And it did. You see? Even though you weren't there, you were the one who saved me.'

'That makes me want to save you all over again.' I embraced her. 'What can I do to make you feel better?'

She sniffed, pulled back and wiped her eyes. 'How about something to eat?'

There was some calf's liver I'd bought on a whim. I got out my mother's old, heavy frying pan and poured in a good slug of green olive oil. When it was shimmering and the warm smell had filled the air, I took a slice of the liver and draped it across the base of the pan, watching it crawl and shrink in the hot oil. I waited for it to char a little and then turned it over with a fork. I seasoned it, then lifted it from the pan and held the fork to Melissa's lips. She took the morsel and chewed it, then she took a mouthful of wine, then she kissed me hard on the mouth, savoury and wet.

We worked our way through the liver, frying individual pieces and eating them straight from the pan, washed down with wine, and the locking of slippery lips. Oil, blood, saliva and wine were muddled together in my mouth. I wanted to press my fingertip on the metal of the pan to mark the moment, make it permanent. I thought of watching it sizzle as the hot oil erased my fingerprint and coloured the skin. What would it smell like? The burnt hair smell of a car wreck? Charred and succulent, like steak? Sweet and sickly, like plum sauce?

'Bed,' she said.

*I am twenty. The moment has arrived. Those tanned, slender legs are around me at last.*

*It is not how I imagined. She should be helpless and moaning, soaking an ellipse into the mattress, not staring rigidly over my shoulder, looking as if she were trying to banish this experience from her head, prevent it at all costs from lodging in her memory.*

*She regrets this already, but she's letting me persevere. Her mind is – God knows where. Perhaps she can't avoid the kidnap. Perhaps she is desperately trying to take her mind off this aberrant behaviour. Or perhaps she's nowhere I think she might be. Perhaps she is only thinking how good it was that she went for the most expensive spray-on tan today, so it won't rub off on the sheets.*

*Which one of us will acknowledge the failure first? Who will pull away? It is obvious that this will never work.*

To the best of my knowledge, Melissa's sexual experiences before Ernesto came along were a couple of fumbles with Angel Park boys and an affair with her tennis coach – who by virtue of hailing from a gated community near the city centre, with no private army to defend it, was the closest Melissa got to rough trade.

Not that I knew this at the time. I thought her a sexual Olympian. I'd heard her at parties: her bravado, her vocal swagger. She liked nothing better than to be overheard saying something scandalously sexual. 'A man has to have come at least twice before he's of any real use.' 'I know everyone says that size doesn't matter, but once you've had a big one, you can't go back.' Such utterances were of course no different from, or more genuine than, her manufactured persona at dinner with Ernesto's parents, or any of the other personalities she submitted for the consideration of those around her – but they had given her, for me at least, the aura of an expert.

And as for me, being in bed with Melissa was the first time I had got that close to anyone, let alone someone as dauntingly perfect as her. By the time I saw her naked for the second time in my life, twelve years had passed, and the terrain had changed considerably. I had expected things to be different, of course, but not like this. The pornography I had seen had prepared me to be polite in the face of every permutation of the untamed black bush, but this was something different, something refined and defended, and all the more intimidating for being blonde. When she lifted herself casually off the bed to peel off her jeans I was stalled by what I saw – the stark, white Y at her trunk, the tan-line crisply delineated from the milky coffee of her thighs and topped off with the thin, vertical moustache into which her pubic hair had been cropped. The whole package was so groomed that it looked as if it should be twitching above a martini, not hiding down here, coconut-scented, haughtily inviting me to handle it if I was qualified.

Afterwards, when it had been silently acknowledged that this was a one-off, a write-off, she thanked me for the food, and the comfort, and went to sleep.

I sometimes thought of Anabel when I went back to the shopping mall and saw the deranged dolphin in its murky tank. I wondered how long she had waited, and whether she went skating regardless, pirouetting with abandon, looking out for me amid the flashing disco lights.

The next day I stormed off to the lunchtime special at a Por Kilo restaurant on the Marginal, where they weigh your plate after every sally to the buffet and charge you accordingly. I went in hard, not wasting time at the salad bar other than to pick up a couple of spoonfuls of quail's eggs, some palm hearts, and two dollops of crabsticks in Marie Rose sauce. For hours I sat there, with the concentration of a gaucho at his *chá mate*, mechanically devouring steaks, sausages, chicken, pizza, beans, rice, sushi, pasta, trying to work out what had gone wrong the night before. The next day, as I pulverised myself in the university gymnasium, still trying to understand, I felt no better.

Helplessly, I graduated to full obsession. I lay awake thinking of her chest rising and falling in the next room, of the pulse in her neck, the blonde hairs on her thighs. I craved the hot grip of her cunt. I checked the drawer where they kept their contraceptives, and started to sift through the bathroom bin for evidence that she was menstruating so that I could know for sure when he wasn't going to have her. I became a filthy bathroom scavenger, grubbing for clues as to the health of their sex life.

And thus began our habit of kissing to pass the time. The attempt at sex was not repeated, and never spoken of, but the adolescent petting and the bed sharing went on – when she wanted it. The one time I presumed to lean in myself, I was rebuffed, and called a 'freak'. I was a passenger, a blow-up doll, a practice model. While watching television, chopping vegetables – though generally after she'd had plenty to drink and Ernesto had pissed her off somehow – it might happen. Thus we grew into each other, like twisted trees planted too close together. To separate us, one would have to be hacked to pieces. And only the finest specimen would be salvaged.

One evening, over a year after our doomed bed-venture, when I thought the two of us were alone, I found Zé standing with Melissa at the window. I'd been in my room, and somehow hadn't even noticed the throbbing walls as he landed. I walked in just as he was enfolding her in an extended bear hug. He closed his eyes and exhaled slowly, his daughter protectively clasped to him, then opened his eyes and affected to have only just seen me enter.

'Ludo – how are you, my boy?' He detached himself from Melissa, and strode across the room to shake my hand.

By the time I had come over from the kitchen island with a tray of drinks and canapés, Melissa and her father were deep in conversation, and made no effort to include me. This wasn't unusual, so I retreated and got to work on a risotto. It was obvious that tense remarks had been exchanged, and as their conversation got more heated they made less of an effort to disguise the topic under discussion.

'You have to get in the corporate game, like I did, before you can have any clout in the political one,' Zé was saying. His voice dropped to a more conciliatory tone. 'I'm not asking you to betray your beliefs. I'm asking you to cherish them – to safeguard them until you can act on them.'

'You mean bury them,' said Melissa, in a flat voice. 'You mean forget them.'

'I have done something wonderful for you,' said Zé. 'Don't you see?'

'I don't want what you have done for me. However kind it is.'

'Do you know how valuable a place at this school is? It's one of the best business schools in the United States. And that means in the world. Do you know what it would do for you to go there?'

'I don't want it, Pai.'

'But it's the opportunity of a lifetime.'

'So give it to him instead,' she said, pointing over at me.

Zé turned round so that now they were both looking straight

in my direction. It was as if the characters in a *telenovela* had suddenly turned in my direction and started referring to me. My wide-eyed stare showed that I'd been eavesdropping on every word they said. I dropped my head back down towards the risotto pot and began stirring intently.

'I mean, I'm sure he would appreciate your offer,' Melissa went on, trying to smile.

Zé turned back to Melissa without a word to me. She might as well have been gesticulating at a piece of furniture.

'Why does it take Ludo to understand how lucky you are?' he said. 'Why will he appreciate my offer when you will not?'

'Maybe because Ludo is better suited to this life you want me to lead.'

'No, Meli, that's the wrong answer. The reason why Ludo would jump at the chance to take up this offer is because Ludo hasn't always had the luck you've had. He wasn't born in a golden cradle like you. He knows that it's every man for himself in this world, and that not to take the opportunities you're given is insane. These people you want to help – these people Ernesto is devoting his life to – you think they would have your attitude if you gave them the opportunities you've had?'

'Even if that were true, does that mean they shouldn't be helped?'

Zé's voice dropped. 'Don't just stay here with Ernesto. You're so young.'

'This is about Ernesto more than me, isn't it? Let me tell you: Ernesto is worth it. He's doing something worthwhile. The sort of thing you talk about but never actually do.'

'He's naïve. I want to change things for the better too. But you have to *be* somewhere to do that.'

'It doesn't work like that any more. You know that.'

Zé stood up, and whirled to face the window. 'Bullshit,

Melissa. That's bullshit. Take it from me. Take it from Ludo. You think he'd be attending university now if we hadn't taken him in? You think he'd be doing so well? Of course he wouldn't. He'd be living in the gutter and holding up gas stations. Ask him yourself.'

'I'm sorry about this,' said Melissa to me. This doesn't have to involve you.'

I said nothing, and kept stirring. Building a risotto is an exercise in patience. The butter, the fat, the stock – eventually all are absorbed by those initially recalcitrant little grains, which look as if they will never soften, but ultimately, after the right amount of persuasion, become fondant and loaded with flavour. I had been thinking of Melissa as I stirred, reasoning that if I took things slowly but insistently, I could soften her in the same way.

But the discussion was not over, and Zé was in pursuit. 'Why won't you do this, Melissa?'

'Because I want to stay here with Ernesto. Give this opportunity to Ludo. He is your son, you know.'

'Very well. Since you are so stubborn. Ludo, stop cooking. Come here.'

'The risotto will burn.'

'So turn down the heat.'

I did as he suggested, crossed the room and sat down.

'Ludo, I would like to offer you the chance to study business in the United States. I have spent a lot of money to secure this place. It should be easy enough to change the arrangement so that they are expecting a son instead of a daughter.'

'I don't know what to say,' I said.

'There's no need to say anything. Just be grateful. Something of which your sister seems incapable.'

'What about my university course here?'

'You can finish it later.'

For one thing, I didn't want to study business; I was enjoying my degree at the university, and I was doing well at it. For another, the idea of leaving Melissa was unthinkable. But turning down this chance would be a far more complicated undertaking for me than it had been for her. As with every opportunity the family provided, refusal was not an option. It felt like yet another wall of the prison that had been rising up to contain me since I was born.

Zé was preparing to leave. He got to his feet, took a phone from his inside breast pocket, and called his pilot. 'Leaving in five minutes. Start the engines please.'

If I said nothing now, Zé would take my silence as assent. It would be a done deal. Melissa had suggested I take the place, but she couldn't have meant it. I was back at the stove now, resuming work on the risotto, but I was preparing to say something, anything, to lodge my objection.

The helicopter started to whine into life above us. Zé drained his glass, and made for the door.

'I'm glad you have some sense, Ludo,' he said. 'If she is too spoilt to take advantage of this opportunity, then I shall make it available to you, who appreciates it. She can stay here with her loser.'

*She never sees her loser*, I thought. *And the loser can't be trusted. She needs me to stay here and look after her, to make sure she's OK.*

'For your information, I'm marrying my loser,' she blurted out.

'What are you talking about?' Zé said, freezing at the door. 'You can't get married. You're too young.'

'I'm old enough to be pregnant.'

I stared, my hand stilled, as the rice in the bottom of the pan began to blacken and burn.

# Beirut Sandwich

'So the problem is . . . what? You can't stop thinking about her? You're addicted?' asks Flávia.

We're at the *lanchonete*, drinking milkshakes and eating steak and melted cheese 'Beirut' sandwiches. Flávia slipped her cutlery from its plastic bag as soon as the food arrived and is now cutting up her sandwich into neat morsels, which are disappearing into her one by one at speed. I haven't started mine. A lot has happened this morning, and I am unashamedly offloading it on to her. She looks bored.

'Perhaps I am addicted. I don't know. I left the country for a year once, and being away from her definitely helped.'

She swallows carefully and wipes her mouth before speaking. 'There's one solution for you to start with: try not seeing her. She is your sister. And she's married.'

'She's not my real sister, remember?'

Flávia shrugs. 'Whatever you say.'

The phone ringing in my office this morning was so unexpected that I momentarily felt a surge of adrenalin, imagining that I was about to catch my nuisance caller in the act – then I remembered that his cover had been blown for some time. The one voice I did not expect to hear was Melissa's.

She got straight to the point. 'Ernesto knows.'

'What?'

'OK – he doesn't know, but he suspects.'

'I could have told you that. I had lunch with him yesterday.'

This stalled her. 'How come?'

'He's a client of mine. You should take more of an interest in his work. He changed jobs without even telling you. He works for your father now.'

'Yes, he told me that too.' She sighed into the phone. 'This is all too much for me.'

'It's OK,' I said. 'He doesn't know that it's me who comes to stay. He's not even sure that anyone does. You just have to reassure him.'

'We can do better than that. I called to tell you that you're never coming round here again.'

'Don't be hasty.'

'This is the opposite of hasty. You should have stopped a long time ago. When I'm alone, at least. I think we both know it's a little weird.'

'You called *me* last night, remember?'

'It doesn't matter who called who. It's messed up, Ludo. Ernesto mentioned a couple of other things – stuff about messages on the bathroom mirror, and someone reading his diary – so unless you want to talk about those as well, I suggest that we leave the conversation there and agree that we won't see one another like that any more.'

'Wait.'

'And if you ever come over here uninvited again I'll tell Ernesto exactly who creeps into my bed while he's gone. Understand?'

My second attempt to say 'Wait' met with a dull telephonic full stop.

I charged out of my office, intending to find her and remonstrate with her in person, but ran into Oscar in the corridor. He gave me a punch on the arm that was meant to seem playful, but felt like he was trying to cause me pain.

'I bet that gave you a shock, didn't it?' he said. 'Finding out the MaxiBudget client is actually your own brother-in-law?'

'It did. But I guess I shouldn't have been too surprised – Zé likes to keep things in the family.'

'It should be fun, anyway, all of us working together. How was your lunch?'

'Very instructive.'

'Excellent. Now, to business. Just because the client is family doesn't mean that I don't want an incredible piece of work from you on this. You don't want Dennis showing you up, do you?'

'What?'

'He may only be here temporarily, and he may be half-foreign, but he's good. He's already come up with some insightful stuff. It would be embarrassing for you if we went with one of his ideas over yours, wouldn't it?'

'Very.'

'So get working. That reminds me. Have you got another of your focus groups with the cleaner lined up?'

'I can organise one.'

'I told Dennis you'd run his concepts past a real slum-dwelling lady. Just stop by his office and pick up some copies of his work next time you're seeing her, will you? See what she makes of them.'

'No problem.'

'See you at the meeting.' He was already halfway across the office floor, his retreating form framed by an enormous red, womb-like oval on the wall, so that he resembled a cartoon character walking off into the sunset at the end of the feature.

I went to find Dennis, who took me aside and told me he was worried he might have caught something from the prostitute.

I was in no mood to console him. 'You didn't take precautions? Even with that bulging bag of prophylactics? Perhaps you should get yourself tested. Go see the company doctor.'

'Thanks,' he said, looking only momentarily confused by how well I knew the contents of his wash bag. 'Let me know what you think.'

I left his concepts in my office. Deflated, trying to overlook the fact that no matter how bad they were, I had come up with nothing, I headed upstairs to the bathroom that used to be Flávia's kitchen for a think. Which is where she found me.

On finding out that her shift was ending, I dragged her out immediately with the promise of sandwiches and milkshakes. She protested that she had shopping to do first, so I herded her at speed around the small local supermarket until she had collected the groceries she wanted. This morning's events were weighing on my mind so much that it was only when I saw Flávia counting out her coins at the checkout that I thought I should probably have offered to buy her shopping. Now we are back at the *lanchonete* I can make up for that.

She has finished her sandwich and is distractedly rubbing a red string bracelet up and down her wrist. It catches and tangles but she smoothes it back. She is trying but failing to look interested. I guess she thinks that her listening to my moaning is the price I'm asking for the parade of shakes and snacks I am bankrolling on her behalf.

'Anyway,' I go on. 'Not seeing Melissa is out of the question. She's my *sister*. We spend family weekends together.'

Flávia sighs. She hasn't got time for my soap operas, but her compassion functions all the same, and makes her want to help me in spite of the fact that mostly she despises me.

'So what are you going to do?' she says.

'I don't know. Judging by this morning's conversation things might be out of my hands.'

The end of her straw gurgles and hisses as it seeks around in the base of the glass, craving more sugary, milky fuel.

'What you think I should do?' I ask.

She laughs. 'Dear Lord! How do I know what you should do? Aren't you rich enough to afford a real shrink?'

'I care what you think.'

'Why do you care what I think? I'm just the woman who cleans the toilets.'

'You're the only real person in my life.'

'Why? Is this a fairy tale? Are you so poisoned by the people in your life that you can only have a real conversation with a poor old toilet scraper like me?'

'I'm not saying that. I'm saying that somehow I have lost sight of myself.'

'What?'

'I don't know how to express it. My opportunities have blinded me.'

She curses, and spits, and stands up, assembling herself in sections. She might not make it – bits totter and teeter – but she pulls herself together.

'I think you should stop buying me milkshakes. Right now, I want to punch you in the mouth, and I don't think that's going to change any time soon.'

'What's wrong with asking you –'

'You're a brat! I'm sick of your whining. Some of us have real things to worry about. Like sons recovering from gunshot wounds.'

'How is he?'

'Go to hell.'

The valediction is emphatic, but her departure is not. It takes her a full minute of muttering to collect up her shopping and shuffle to the door. After she's finally gone, I sit toying with the greaseproof paper my sandwich came in. Then I throw a wad of damp money down on to the bar, and rush after her.

*I am fourteen. Yesterday I ate my first club sandwich. Today it's Rebecca's turn to have me for the day, to keep me occupied before school starts. We're welcomed at the door of a small, clean building not far from an immense out-of-town favela, which Rebecca has explained to me is one of the orphanages she oversees. As the lady at the door shows us in we are swamped by a tide of children, a tsunami of uncomplicated love. Rebecca steps to one side, but I am caught. They climb my legs, and clamber on my shoulders, and hang from my neck. Rebecca addresses each child by name, and introduces me. As one boy goes politely to shake my hand she sees me flinch at the sight of the outbreak of pink warts that stands out from the dark skin of his hand.*

*'Shake it, now,' she mutters, deadly serious. 'This could have been you.'*

'I don't want to talk to you.' Flávia is motoring along the pavement at what is probably approaching her top speed.

'I didn't mean to offend you,' I say, orbiting her like a satellite.

'Leave me. Get out of my life. Why do I waste my time listening to this playboy?'

I drop away and follow her from a distance. Her staccato, angry stomp eventually settles into a graceful lope that must be her long distance pace, her cruising speed. She's still exclaiming loudly, taking her outrage and indignation round the block, scolding herself for the time she has squandered on me and my problems.

We double back past the office, and she carries on walking, towards the favela. I follow. I don't notice the frontier – there isn't one – but I can tell when we're on the other side. All the buildings we pass are both 'unofficial' and precarious, or else reclaimed, and on their second or third use. Kids kick a bald football around a rubbish-fretted clay pitch. Radios blast loud funk and hip hop from holes in the honeycomb. One boy in a yellow T-shirt flies a small, multicoloured kite that zips and veers over the players. I know that kites are used as warning signals, to let *traficantes* know when the police are coming, and I wonder whether this boy is merely playing, or earning a wage. At one end of the pitch, three men in coloured vests stand around a rusty car chassis holding tools and arguing, looking like they're trying to reassemble the vehicle from scratch. Only a street or two from the office, this is a different world, where the sterility of progress is held off by something that is all the more vital for being so precarious.

The main body of the community is fringed by fragile wooden homes, the defences these afford broken up by narrow alleys. Ancient political posters and advertisements peel on every flat surface – I notice what could be Zé's faded, peeling eye, bleaching to monochrome, one step from oblivion. Faces look out from behind the hoardings: those who have set up home under the shelter of advertising. I recognise the remains of one poster as an idea of mine from a year ago, a brand of sports shoe whose slogan is *Deserve the Best*. A skeletal horse is tethered to one end. The squat behind of a rusty Volkswagen Fusca protrudes from the other.

We pass a butcher's – a small shack with two or three large hunks of dripping meat hanging from hooks outside, and live goats and chickens up on the roof. It is unlikely the animals will see ground level alive again. Meanwhile Flávia ploughs on, as if daring me to get closer. I keep my distance, on the opposite side of the road, on the crunchy concrete of a half-finished pavement. I'm looking around me at a dilapidated apartment block, at the football pitch's broken streetlights, at tyre shops whose owners loiter in overalls at the front of their shacks amid piles of chrome and rubber. When I glance back, she has disappeared. I have no choice but to turn down what I assume to be the alley she took.

The heat is gone immediately, replaced by a cool, shadowy atmosphere – the smell of damp brick dust with a sweet under-note of decaying rubbish and the sour tang of human waste. The steps before me are incredibly steep, as if they were built for a taller race of people. In fact they are just pragmatic. Taking the shallow, leisurely route isn't an option here: space is at too much of a premium.

And then the concentration of it starts in earnest: the crawling, hotching humanity of it. Improvised half-doors salvaged from building sites are set into low walls, whose concrete is broken up by decorative mosaics of smashed floor tiles and bottle glass. Reclaimed staircases crammed into new contexts lead to cubbyhole houses filled with people, packed in together like larvae in seedpods. I'm standing there wide-eyed, staring up at the improbably narrow thoroughfares, at the thick canopy of wires and pipes that shades them, and taking in the smells of food bubbling on stoves, of bleach, of rotting vegetables, when I hear her voice, close to me.

'You shouldn't be here. You'll run into trouble.'

'Just let me talk to you,' I say, seeing her round face floating at a corner.

'Not in the street. Come to my house.'

She sighs as she climbs the steps. I go to carry her plastic bag for her but she snatches it out of my grasp, saying nothing. I walk tentatively behind her, trying to take everything in, working out how it measures up to my expectations. The surreal quality of the knowledge that I come from somewhere like this, even somewhere worse than this, is overwhelming. It is as alien a place as any I have ever been in, yet somehow it is not discomfiting. There's something in the human proximity that is intimate, almost soothing. I wouldn't be so crass as to suggest it's like a homecoming, but for the first time it doesn't feel humiliating that this is the world that people like Oscar use to define me by.

I bathe in the friendly normality of it, pleasantly surprised by the fact that I am not caught in a vicious gunfight, by the familiar shouts that greet Flávia as we progress up the alley, by the sight of house-proud ladies sweeping the streets and watering the pot plants that flank their almost-doorways. I feel ashamed of these thoughts almost as I have them, and then spare an angry thought for Melissa, who would probably be terrified of this place, yet wouldn't notice if you upgraded her sofas in the night.

'Is your son here?' I ask, sensing we might be close.

'I told him to leave the city for a few days. He's gone to stay out of town, with my father.'

'Sounds like a good idea.' I'm short of breath.

Flávia ducks off through a low, flimsy door in the wall, with a gate in front fashioned from an old piece of wrought-iron garden furniture. The stairs take us down sharply, through three other dwellings: two boys watching TV, a teenage girl washing her hair in a plastic bowl, a man in a vest smoking as he stirs a pan of rice on a gas ring. These last two both greet Flávia and regard me with polite interest. I share Oscar's surprise at the fact that they all have televisions and fridges, but then I'd probably have been equally amazed if they didn't.

Only when Flávia puts down her bag do I conclude that we have arrived, that this is her space: a red-painted waxed floor with a small kitchen area and two beds separated by a blanket strung from a clothes line.

'Your son sleeps in there?'

She nods.

'Do you mind if I look?'

'There isn't much to see.'

I hook a finger round the partitioning blanket and pull it to one side. It could be the room of any boy, if it qualified as a room. The space is scarcely larger than the bed it contains. Two old football posters adorn the walls, and there's a bench at the end of the bed with a padlocked box on it that I assume contains the boy's valuables.

Flávia is bustling around, unpacking her shopping and stowing it in a small fridge and an old cupboard that serves as her kitchen unit. I notice a framed photograph of her and a younger Milton at a party, him wearing a clean white shirt, her holding up a bottle of beer to the camera, laughing.

'Where the hell is my kitchen knife?' she mutters. 'Nothing stays put around here. There's no respect for personal property.'

I know where the knife is – it's in police custody, having been prised out of a dusty palm tree and taken away as evidence. I don't suppose Flávia would be pleased to hear that.

The girl who was washing her hair next door comes in with a Polaroid camera.

'Stand together!' she says, without asking who I am.

Flávia has been sweating as she climbed the steps. She smells spicy, almost horsey, giving me a brief sensory memory of the hot, enclosed air of the farm stables. I'm sure I don't smell too good either.

The *pow* of the flash. It's like a weapon. Momentarily, it shocks every blemish on the wall into revealing itself. One of Flávia's purchases, a box of rice, the smallest you can buy, moves on the counter. I glimpse the retreating back of a cockroach, and realise how minimal the lighting is down here, how much it keeps hidden.

Holding the camera at arm's length with one hand, the girl flicks her hair distractedly with the other to dry it, and looks at me, indicating for the first time that she might be interested to know who I am.

'My name is Ludo,' I say.

She smiles. 'Funny name.' She pulls the Polaroid from the camera and waves it around in the air before handing it to me.

I look ill. Flávia looks tired. But there's spontaneity in it. We're both cracking a smile, and the smiles are real. A trick of the light, something reflective caught by the flash, means that there's a white ghost between me and Flávia in the picture, like the spirit of her son, materialised to keep us apart.

'I like it,' says Flávia, taking it from me. 'I'll pin it to my wall to remind me of the strange man who sleeps on toilet floors. Now go. I've had enough for today. I'll talk to you tomorrow. Don't turn left into the alley if you want to make it back to work.'

'Good bye, "strange man",' says the girl. Her smile. It's a shaft of light. She follows me back through Flávia's door to her own place.

'Aren't you going to tell me your name?' I ask her, on my way out.

'No.' She laughs.

'How about a photo of the two of us?'

'Those things cost money, you know! Anyway, I've run out of film.'

'Bye, then.'

I wonder why I worried about setting foot in this place. I feel relaxed, relieved. By the time I have found my way back out to the football pitch, I'm almost grinning openly.

A proper game has started since I walked past before. I stand there for a minute or two, watching these lean, bare-foot dancers in the dust, admiring their skill, until I am noticed.

'What are you looking at, my friend? Unless you're scouting for Corinthians, you can keep moving,' shouts one of the older players.

He makes a grabbing gesture at his groin that could just be an insult or could be my first and only warning that there's a gun in his waistband. Not taking the chance, I turn immediately, and walk in the opposite direction, and don't react to the volley of catcalls that follows. My composure has left me, and my guts are turning like clothes in a spinner.

'That's right, playboy! Turn, and walk, baby.'

'Be glad we're playing an important game so we don't need to come and empty the pockets of that nice jacket.'

'Keep walking.'

'Bang.'

I jump. They see the involuntary flinch in my shoulders and their shouts dissolve into laughter. I don't turn around.

Instead of heading back towards the office, I walk away from the favela in the other direction, and end up crossing a patch of waste ground encircling two dead apartment blocks – each one not unlike what our office must have been before Oscar stepped in to fix everything. These blocks have had their backs broken; their floors sag like slumped shoulders. I enter one of them through a lobby dripping with water. It smells of urine, and is ominously quiet. I climb the stairs slowly, noticing the same gangland tags on the walls that we have enshrined in plastic resin at the office. The Shadow Command must have been in control of this area for some time.

Melissa had a toy, on the farm – I think it was called *Laberinto*. You had to steer a steel marble through a maze by twisting knobs on a box that tipped the floor in different directions, avoiding holes. That's what it's like in this building; I feel like a ball-bearing in somebody's game of *Laberinto*. The floors move as I walk on them. I have to jump gaps in the concrete. As I climb the staircase I hear the metal straining to bear my weight. This place has decayed beyond squalor. Even the squatters have moved on to better-appointed wrecks. It ought to be scary, but it isn't. It's almost exciting that the floors might concertina sharply downwards at any time. I picture what Oscar would do with this building. He'd fix the floors into one position with metal struts, setting things for ever in one random state, cancelling the building's capacity for variation and killing its personality.

The door to an apartment on the second floor is open. The windows are shattered, and the apartment is empty but for one three-legged orange plastic chair, peppered with burn marks. I balance on the chair, testing to see if it will hold my weight, then I sit, awkwardly enthroned, watching the sunset through shattered windows and a gap in the wall, imagining some democratising fire sweeping the city, consuming every community, gated and improvised alike.

# Watermelon Pips

*I am twenty-one. Ernesto and I sit in a damp side chapel behind the altar, where a flickering CCTV monitor has been set up so we can watch footage of the guests as they arrive. Under the water of the wobbling, blue-washed screen, they resemble anthropomorphised sea creatures attending a plush undersea ball. Here are crabs and lobsters. Here are taut-skinned puffer fish with surprised eyes, and sly, menacing sharks.*

*'Who are these people? I don't recognise any of them,' Ernesto says, blinking into the monitor, tugging at the stiff collar of his new shirt. He's nervous, and his hair has been slicked back with wax, giving him the louche appearance of a telenovela villain.*

*He's right. It's a gallery of strangers, but for the odd regular from the Angel Park pool bar, and one or two faces I half-remember from photographs, or glimpses through letter-box apertures in tinted car windows.*

*'It's everyone,' I say. 'Everyone who matters. Isn't it?'*

*'Is your mother here? I would love to meet her.'*

Of course she was there. She was at the centre of the event. She was its throbbing heart. Her whole existence since Rebecca brought her out of the favela had led up to this moment, and she was on high alert. To make matters more fraught, a busload of deputies had been sent from the city to assist her, and this would not make for a relaxed working atmosphere. She could not produce dinner for 400 people on her own, but the extra staff made her nervous, even though they had been recruited to Zé's specifications and well understood his requirements, and even though she insisted on spending a full week drilling them on their duties in the run-up to the event.

Once he'd got over the shock of Melissa's pregnancy, Zé had warmed to the idea of her marriage to Ernesto. He was a known quantity, and his parents were on many of the same residents' committees. Zé (I suspect) foresaw that Ernesto was someone he would win over in the end, just as he had every other obstacle in his life. But any acquiescence on his part to the *idea* of Ernesto would never transmute into a desire to make him feel at ease and comfortable. Once Zé had got over the shock of the fact that he was not to be the architect of this pivotal change in his daughter's life, he reasserted his authority in every other way he could.

There was no discussion over where the wedding would take place; if there was ever a location geared up for this kind of celebration, it was Zé's pleasure farm. And so much the better if, away from his home turf, Ernesto felt awkward and out of his depth. It would weaken him nicely; leave the stage free for Zé and the wonderful speech everyone expected of him.

Besides, there was no time for lengthy debate. Even though Zé and Rebecca insisted that the pregnancy was not an embarrassment, the wedding was hastily put together. Melissa's state was never alluded to, and steps were taken to disguise any hint of a bump. It would have been a brave man who brought up that topic on the day.

We both knew that my role had been devised and approved by Zé, but Ernesto still made a pretence of asking me to be his best man, just to make me feel better.

'Melissa is the best thing that has ever happened to me,' he said. 'And you're closer to her than anyone else, apart from me. That means you're closer to me than any of the other idiots I grew up with.'

He had a point, of course. He never connected with the Angel Park kids, and that is not surprising. They had too much money, and were so afraid of leaving the compound that they terrorised everyone until they finally plucked up courage at the age of seventeen to take their first baby steps beyond the razor wire. So what he said was a perfectly reasonable argument for his picking me over them.

If only he hadn't included those words, *apart from me*.

The *fazenda* had never known anything like it. Silvio and his men deforested an area the size of a football pitch to create an accommodation plateau for wedding guests, which Zé referred to as 'the parade ground'. Temporary shelter was assembled here in the form of huts and teepees. The way they sprang up overnight was almost military – and sure enough, I found out that Zé had bought the magnificent bivouac dormitories in bulk from a humanitarian aid supplier. They were refugee huts, assembled, upgraded with bathrooms and decorated in the theme colours of the wedding.

The invitations were hand-sewn with multicoloured ribbons and flawlessly addressed by calligraphers. Every employee of the farm was set to work pruning, trimming and beautifying – erecting tents, stringing lights from trees, replanting flowerbeds. Every lamp post between the church and the entrance to the farm was draped with a huge banner bearing the entwined initials of the bride and groom, which mystified the local residents, who thought they were either part of a campaign on the part of a political party they hadn't been told about, or an advertisement for some life-altering new product. Neither assumption would have displeased Zé.

The nearest church to the farm – a damp, chalky adjunct to the nearby plantation, whose best days had ended around the same time as slavery – was given a facelift. Zé and his family had occasionally graced it with their presence at the weekends, but no amount of casual patronage could have prepared the building for this. Its flaking plaster was replaced, its gilt polished, its whitewash renewed. Where any decorative features had deteriorated or vanished they were plundered from similar churches or bought at auction. The place was virtually rebuilt.

When the day came, a troupe of orchestral musicians from Amazonas, along with a stripped-down ensemble selected from the cream of the Manaus Opera House choir, were flown down by jet along with the wedding flowers, the centrepiece of which was a splash of jungle orchids that had been quietly growing in the rainforest only a day before. The church hummed with them, with their indignation.

When the congregation was seated there followed a parade of principal players – the traditional pairs of *padrinhos de casamento*, selected old family friends from the city, all smoothing the way for the main attraction. When my turn came I was told to walk slowly to my seat, following the rhythm of the processional march struck up by the musicians, and Ernesto's parents did likewise. They entered slowly, like royalty, smiling in every direction, determined to make the most of this moment in the spotlight.

Then Zé and Rebecca pounded down the aisle. Zé wore his usual 'nothing to see here' grin in spite of the carefully rehearsed orchestral crescendo that accompanied their entrance, while Rebecca managed to look as serene as usual even at the speed at which she was being propelled by her husband. Both beamed and kept their heads down in a mockery of bashfulness, and did a fantastic job in the process of making themselves look like the main attraction. They were past masters at drawing the gaze of others in their direction by pretending they thought nobody was looking at them.

Melissa came in alone. As she walked down the aisle, I stared ahead at a candle dripping hot wax on to the flowers, ready to step in if needed. That way, I didn't have to watch her approach, and risk picturing the alternative scenario, the dream scenario. Better not to look at all – although the shape my eager imagination assembled from my peripheral vision and the quiet gasps of the congregation was unbearable enough.

I'd smelt the rain coming as we went into the church. Inhaling damp air, I had looked down the valley and seen it approaching, in a bright, rolling cloud whose hard edges stood out against the lush green of the trees. As if on cue, it arrived during the vows, the darkness rendering the candle-light suddenly more atmospheric. You could hear the water beating up the hill; time it to the second as it broke over the church roof.

The wind rang the bells too early in the tower. A panicked bat flitted from one end of the church to the other. Rain pounded on the metal roof during the prayers. Gold glinted. Incense burned. Candles guttered. Ernesto smiled nervously. Stomach turning, I watched the spray of rain from outside spurt under the church door and on to the stone as the promises were exchanged.

By the time it was over, so was the storm, leaving behind fresh air, dripping leaves, and roads that gushed in the evening sunlight with milky orange water. As usual, the rain brought hordes of frogs out on to the driveway, croaking and belching and slipping about in the mud. The guests' roaring cavalcade of off-road vehicles smashed them all in a euphoric blare of car horns and klaxons as it sped back to the farm. Their burst bodies lay there crisping for days afterwards.

Silvio's ingenuity was tested to the full – and not just because of the strain this party was to put on his emergency back-up generator, or the number of vehicles he had to extricate from the avalanching mud. His water chute had been cleaned and re-sprayed and lined with coloured lights, so that guests could shoot themselves through the darkened woodland at speed, as if through a magical night kingdom, the bats and owls of the farm crossing over their heads. Silk lanterns that hung from the trees like ghosts became objects of fascination for all the humming, buzzing animal life. It felt like a betrayal. I felt disappointed in the creatures for not carrying on as normal, for adding to the atmosphere in that way, buying into and acknowledging the event.

And then there was the food.

A theme had been devised, of classics fused with contemporary national influences – meaty river fish, powerful jungle herbs and unexpected rainforest fruits – but that was just the beginning. A wok station and a sushi bar operated all night. Seafood bars carved from solid ice were deposited round the swimming pool, piled high with crab claws and lobster tails, with oysters and clams. Racks of dripping quail spun slowly in gleaming rotisserie machines. Silvio erected a device that he called the Carousel – a spinning wrought-iron cage that ensured that the meat encased within it had constant distribution over the coals beneath and created a downdraught that coaxed from them an even, generous heat. The spinning cuts flew around like colours on a child's top. It wasn't the only contribution Silvio made to cooking apparatus. Also flown down from the forest were twenty peacock bass and a *pirarucú* fish the size of a man, which he entombed in a ditch of glowing coals for the day, roasting it whole. And for the main event, a miracle, engineered by my mother: 400 perfectly cooked fillets of beef, with a delicate truffle sauce.

By the time the guests had got stuck into all the other food available at the buffet, drunk their fill from the caipirinha bar, and snuffed up whatever else they had brought along to enhance their evening, their appetites had died. In many cases plates were left untouched, as guests were lured to the dance floor by a favourite song. As the music struck up, I swept away the debris of the meal, collecting the intact steaks and pocketing them, munching on them like apples, getting the meat down even when it hurt my throat to swallow, devouring it so it wouldn't go to waste, trying to get round the tables and clear as many of them as possible so that my mother wouldn't see them coming back. I carried on for as long as I could, with tears in my eyes at the injustice of it, with mounting pain from all the meat I was dry-swallowing and from the swelling in my stomach.

'Tidying up, Ludo?' said Zé, clapping a hand on my back. 'You have better things to do – like enjoy yourself.'

'Are you enjoying yourself?'

He sighed. 'How could I not? Look around you. It is what this place was built for. I suppose I had better give my speech before everyone is completely insensible. Perhaps after something sweet. Come and sit with me.'

As I was talking to him, one of the desserts appeared – piles of slices of watermelon heaped with homemade ice cream. We found an empty table, Zé scanning the area before he sat down to see if there was anyone more important in the vicinity. Realising that I needed to eat quickly so he could be on his way, I began removing the pips from my slice of watermelon with a fork before taking a bite;

my mother had taught me that this was more polite than spitting them out.

'I wouldn't do that!' said Zé, staying the back of my hand with a cool palm and a mischievous smile. 'Try one.'

'One what?'

'A pip. You might be surprised.'

I did. Solid, dark chocolate.

'They're French. We had them made especially.'

'Someone had a boring job putting those in,' I said.

'I can't imagine it,' Zé agreed. 'Whoever did it must have the patience of a saint. Now, I think I ought to give my speech before conditions deteriorate further.'

He was right. Looking up I could see two guests tearing down a string of red and yellow paper lanterns and chucking it in the pool. If he didn't speak now he would lose his audience.

During the speech – a sparkling number, with plenty of proprietorial references to 'my Melissa', a couple to her new husband, and one mention of me – things continued to fall apart. Several girls were thrown into the pool fully clothed, one of them glancing her head on the side. Two men tried to play football with a ball they had doused in petrol and set on fire. Others lit handheld fireworks that spurted hot wax as they detonated low over the heads of fellow revellers. The water chute, overrun with those eager to discard their outfits, and others who didn't bother, was suddenly running beyond its capacity. The plunge pool at its base seethed with bodies. The playground had been overrun by contenders, with high expectations, and never had so much been asked of it. The only thing more shocking than the abundance of it all was the manifest indifference of those it was meant to impress.

After I had congratulated Zé on his speech, I tried to warn him about what was going on. 'There are people trying to walk across the lily pads. They're smashing them to pieces.'

'Are they?' he said, grinning. 'I've always wanted to do that. You shouldn't worry so much. This place can take it.'

I found Ernesto devouring a slice of watermelon and fretting about his father-in-law.

'He hasn't spoken to me,' he said. 'And he barely mentioned me in his speech.'

'I'm sure that wasn't deliberate.'

'It was. And I know why.'

'What do you mean?'

'He offered me a job yesterday, and I turned it down.'

'You turned down a job with him?' I said. 'That must have paid a fortune.'

'He wanted me to give up my studies, and take a business course so I could work for him. But that's not me. I want to work for myself.'

'He's just sulking because you refused him. He doesn't like it when things don't go his way.'

'And have you seen him and my parents? They're best friends all of a sudden.'

Whatever Zé's initial misgivings about their son, he knew Gaspar and Olinda well. They were his kind of people. He had entrusted the well-being of his daughter to them and their beach house many times. They were on fine terms, and working the event as a pack.

'It's a disaster,' Ernesto went on, 'I've annoyed him before the marriage even starts.'

'I think you did that before today, when you got her pregnant.'

'Shut up, will you? We're not talking about that.'

'How is anybody going to explain where this baby came from when it appears? The truth will come out eventually.'

'Well, it's not coming out now. If there was one thing I

could do that would piss Zé off more, it would be to release that little bit of information.'

'Stop worrying about it. You're family now. He has to like you.'

'I guess you're right. Have you seen my wife?' he said, looking around him.

'I'll go and look for her.'

I had no intention of finding his wife – at least not for Ernesto – and I needed to see my mother. I feared that she was being taken for granted as much as the place. Never had she been treated so conspicuously as a servant, and I hated it, so much so that I was angry with her for putting up with it.

'Look at my son all dressed up,' she said, sweeping a speck from the shoulder of my jacket. 'You look so perfect – anyone would think this was your wedding. Where have you been all this time?'

'Busy. Not as busy as you though. The food is incredible. Everyone is saying so.'

'I'm glad you came to see me. I have been wondering how you are.'

'I'm fine. I didn't even have to make a speech.'

'I don't mean that,' she said, wiping her hands on her apron. 'I mean, how are you about Melissa getting married?'

'What do you mean?'

'Ludo. Who do you think you're talking to here?'

'She's my sister.'

'We both know she's more than your sister.'

'That's an unhelpful thing to say.'

'She's pregnant, isn't she?'

'Mamãe. Lower your voice.'

'You can't hide that sort of thing from me.'

'Just keep quiet about it.'

'And you can't bear it, can you? That's why you're running off to the United States.'

'I thought you of all people would find the idea of my turning down the opportunity to go to the United States unthinkable.'

'Of course. So long as you are doing it for the right reasons.'

I paused, suppressing a shout. 'Thank you for your advice. You should get back to work now.'

I wanted to go back, to say sorry immediately. I got as far as the kitchen door. Then I saw her shrug sadly, grab an icing squeezer from a waitress, and start putting the finishing touches to a mountain of cakes. The look of concentration on her face rekindled an old instinct – I knew she was not to be disturbed. I turned to go again. My last sight of her that evening was a glimpse down a long corridor stacked high with shiny aluminium pots, her forehead beaded with sweat, setting out *petits fours*, and I never did apologise.

Tramping out from the kitchen and down to the pool area, I saw the tree house ladder hanging from the foliage of the fig tree. I bolted up there, a wounded animal retreating to a trusted refuge.

My blood fizzing with regret at what I had said, and the vestiges of the anger that precipitated it, I sat breathing heavily, my legs crossed and my eyes tightly shut, inhaling the woody aromas of the tree house, hoping to be spirited away by them to simpler times.

Feeling the lumpen shapes of three or four steaks in my pocket, I took one out, rotated it in my hand, and bit into it. The outer crust of charred flesh and cracked peppercorns made black marks on my palm. I closed my eyes, and chewed, concentrating on the black, bloody flavours, hoping if not to be taken away to childhood then at least to be transported by the meat.

The band had started playing. Called Funkcetera, they were a successful outfit at the time, specialising in wacky outfits and polished, anodyne music. Looking down, I could see the dance floor near the pool undulating with multi-coloured, disco-lit revellers. I relaxed, enjoying my place of safety, and decided to stay there hovering over the reception like a ghost for the rest of the evening.

A distant pop sounded, and the music went dead, along with the lights. Suddenly the farm was a flickering darkness of lanterns and scandalised laughter. It was Silvio's worst nightmare. The power grid, unable to cope with the demands of the party on top of the storm, had given out. At least it had happened after most of the food had been served.

There was warmth in the unforeseen darkness, in my comfortable hiding place in the dripping trees. The smell of wet forest was suddenly sharper in the air, and the sounds of the night rose to a higher pitch, as if this reassertion of nature over man and his pleasures was that apparent, that physical. And with no town nearby to light up the skies, the darkness away from the feeble light of candles and lanterns was almost total.

I knew exactly how long it would take to get the power back. Silvio would be careening down the hill to the back-up generator with his torch. He'd have to get down there, hope the generator room wasn't flooded, possibly refuel the machine and spend a few minutes getting it started up. We had about half an hour of this lamplit magic.

I could hear Ernesto's voice as he searched the party for his wife. There were roars of laughter and volleys of sarcastic remarks.

'Good start, Nesto! You've lost her already!'

'She couldn't face it! She's run away into the night!'

A slithering sound in the darkness. Someone hoisting herself up the ladder. Who else could it be?

'Shh.' A whispered giggle. Her teeth glinting in the darkness, she planted a big kiss on my mouth, tasting of vodka and lime juice. I licked my lips, delighting in her proximity, in the coconut warmth of her skin.

'Drink?' she said, handing me a cold glass, clinking with ice.

'You're drinking? You shouldn't –'

'Oh, shut up. It's my wedding day.'

I took a gulp of the drink. It was powerful, delicious.

'You're supposed to be congratulating me,' she said. 'Not hiding up here.'

'You should be careful of your dress,' I said. 'It's not meant for tree climbing.'

'It's done its work,' she said. 'It concealed my bump. It got me married. I can destroy it now. Before my husband rips it off.'

I paused, swallowing. 'I was just enjoying being above it all for a second.'

'I knew you were here. I saw you disappearing.'

I allowed myself a glance at what I could see of her face in the dark. 'You look –'

'Shut up. You don't need to say anything like that.'

'But you do.'

Her hair. The child's plastic watch.

'You smell amazing too.'

'You smell of dinner. How many steaks have you eaten?'

'Too many.'

She laughed and took another swallow, and we sat side by side, staring down into her wedding, listening to the shouts and giggles of guests as they stumbled around in the gloom.

'Why didn't you look at me in the church?'

'Sorry. There was a candle. It looked like it was about to set fire to the flowers. I didn't want the place to burn down.'

I shifted awkwardly, suddenly aware of how long I had

been sitting cross-legged, and feeling the onset of cramp. 'I should get down to Silvio at the generator. He's probably knee-deep in mud.'

'In the absence of my husband, his best man has to look after me. I think you'd better stay here.'

'I expect Silvio could do with my help.'

'I'm serious. Stay with me.'

'We can't stay up here. You have to get back to your wedding.'

'Not now. I mean don't go to the United States. Stay with me.'

'You're going to have a family now. I couldn't stay living with you even if I wasn't going away.'

'Are you telling me you haven't thought it?'

'Thought what?'

'That it could be *our* family?'

'Unless the gestation period for a human baby has gone up by over a year, I think that is very unlikely.'

She laughed.

'Don't say stuff like that,' I said.

'Sorry.' Her hand found mine in the dark. 'So, you're really abandoning me.' Her damp lips brushed the back of my knuckles in a half kiss.

The lights came back on. A microphone whined feedback from the stage. A huge cheer went up. Reality kicked back in like the accelerating drone of a new cine-reel kicking into action. A voice from the stage through the microphone. *Sorry for the technical hitch, everyone! Now for the second part of tonight's show!*

'Maybe you should go,' she said. 'Perhaps it will be good for you. I'm going back to work. You can finish the drink.'

Crawling across the floor to the ladder, she left the glass on the wooden floor of the tree house, the smells of vodka and limes in the air, droplets of condensation sliding down the outside. If I could live for ever in a single moment of time, this might be it, looking at that half-full glass she left behind for me – that tiny, longed-for pulse of goodwill in my direction – still ice-cold, her handprint glazing over on its surface.

The rain and the blackout had sent everyone to a higher pitch of excitement. Something about the calm of the power cut (how many furtive moments were stolen during that half hour?) meant that when the electricity came back on, the guests felt the need to compensate, and began a more violent process of destruction. We were in for a long night.

I drank the rest of the vodka, too fast, so the alcohol made me reel, and the cold brought on a headache. Then I came down the tree house and made my way down the hill towards the generator, so that I could show Silvio I had at least intended to help him fix the problem.

I ran into him on the way up, his suit spattered with mud. He looked old, and his breath came out in a wheeze.

'Looking good,' I said.

'It'll brush off when it dries. I'm still respectable enough, aren't I?'

'I was coming to see if you needed any help.'

'You've got more important things to do than help an old man start an engine.'

'I haven't. Sorry not to be here sooner.'

'I wasn't expecting you.' He put an arm round me fondly. 'Come on, let's go and have a strong drink. The worst that could happen has happened, so there's no reason for me to stay sober. And your mother and I have hardly seen you.'

'I'll meet you up there in ten minutes,' I said.

'Where are you going?'

'Quick walk,' I said, carrying on past him down the hill. 'Pour me a strong one. I'll be right there.'

'Don't think too much,' he called after me. 'You'll hurt your head.'

I couldn't be sure I had found the right spot, but when I guessed that I was close to where Melissa and I had made our jungle hideaway fourteen years before, I sat down at the foot of a tree in the rain, watching leaves dancing in the drops. I grimaced, and stretched out my arms, and begged any forest spirits who might be listening to bring her back to me, whatever the cost.

# Poor Man's Pudding

It's the day of the big MaxiBudget meeting: Ludo versus Dennis, with Oscar and Ernesto looking on. I have done nothing. Since yesterday my visit to the favela has been replaying itself on a loop in my head. I even found myself in a photographic shop this morning, buying five packets of instant camera film – and I don't know the girl's name.

Oscar is on high alert, as always when new work is being presented. He gives a jumpy, enthusiastic preamble on how revolutionary an idea MaxiBudget is; how much good it will do; how the fact that it benefits us and our clients is a beautiful added bonus, and nothing to be ashamed of. The speech is for Ernesto's benefit, to show him how excited we are about the job, but rather than reacting generously to Oscar's bluster, as I would expect – however little he buys into it – our client sits hunched over his coffee, failing to look engaged. Ernesto has always lacked guile. His feelings show as plainly as if they were tattooed on his forehead, and knowing him as well as I do, I can tell that something is wrong, and that it has nothing to do with the meeting.

Dennis is trying to be modest, but is keen to make an impression. He thinks his ideas are something special, and eventually his moment arrives.

'All feedback welcome, of course,' he says, standing to unveil a series of large boards. 'They're just concepts really.' He retreats further into the silence. 'A starting point, at least.'

The images before us are of happy, well-fed children of all races standing by piles of food waste – rotting fruit, flyblown meat, ripped plastic bags – and looking up with smiles on their faces into the beaming light of the MaxiBudget logo, from which bursts fresh produce of every variety, along with the names of some of the big brands whose products will be available in the stores. There's a choice of two different lines printed in large yellow letters over the images. One reads *MaxiBudget: On Your Side*. The other reads *MaxiBudget: Now It's Your Turn*.

'I was trying to play around with this benefit we're offering – that with MaxiBudget you'll have access to the quality brands you couldn't afford before. That you aren't alone. MaxiBudget as your ally, if you like.'

A couple of people round the table murmur noncommittal compliments, waiting to judge the mood of the room. Everyone looks expectantly at Ernesto.

'I think we've got something interesting here,' says Oscar, in the gap left by Ernesto's silence. 'It's simple, and clear, and it would work across all the different media. I don't see these as final strap lines, but as a starting point for the tone of the launch I think they are promising.'

'OK,' says Ernesto, knowing he's expected to respond.

'It's only a start,' says Dennis. 'But I think it could set us in the right direction.'

Ernesto turns to me. 'Ludo, what do you make of this?'

'Honestly?' I say, not looking in the direction of Oscar or Dennis.

'Of course.'

'I think it's patronising.'

Oscar's eyes widen. His urge to leap for my throat is

tempered only by the presence of an important client.

'It implies they're already at rock bottom,' I continue. 'It implies that they want the same things we have brainwashed the rich into wanting – and that the summit of their ambition is to be consumers like us.'

There's an audible intake of breath. If Oscar wasn't conscious of my family link to Ernesto then I would be dead by now. Yet again my connections are my safety net.

'These people aren't beneath us,' I say. 'They're just unlucky. They deserve nothing but respect. Everything is against them, but they hold on. They are humanity at its most tenacious. Can you imagine living like that? If your house is washed down the hill, you have no choice but to regroup and start another. It's a state of near-anarchy. But somehow, the system works. Ingenuity prevails. Walls are built from scrap and rubbish; materials are reclaimed and recycled. People struggle on.'

Dennis tries to talk over me, but I hold up a hand to stop his voice.

'One day we may all have to live like this. And then they'll have the last laugh. Answer me honestly: who around this table would know how to build their own house? Who would even know where to *start*? These people are the advance guard. They're trained-up and ready. They are insured. I don't think we can speak to them like this. They won't listen. They'll laugh in our faces.'

Everyone's looking at me.

'So what would you do, Ludo?' says Ernesto, with interest. Thank God he's not a real client. If I spoke like this to someone who actually cared about his business I'd be thrown out of the window.

'I don't know. Something that's more of a tribute to their powers of survival than a lesson in how to graduate to a consumer lifestyle.'

'And how exactly is that going to launch a chain of supermarkets?' says Oscar, keeping his rage in check for now. 'This is a business. We have a commercial responsibility, not a social one.'

'But even looking at it purely from an advertising point of view, this campaign won't work. Of course these people have aspirations, and of course they want a better life, but they are also proud of the communities they have made. Don't try and tell them that we have what they've been waiting for, and that it's a scaled-down version of what's available to the affluent. They won't want to hear it.'

I sit down again, shrugging my shoulders as if to say *Take it or leave it*. Dennis wants to weigh in to defend his idea, but Oscar is shrewd; he holds back to see how Ernesto reacts.

'I agree with Ludo,' Ernesto says, quietly. 'The last thing we should do is be patronising.' He is barely in the room – just staring off into space – but it's the steer Oscar was waiting for.

'Well done, Ludo. Those focus groups of yours are obviously paying off,' he says. 'But what should we do instead?'

'I'm not sure,' I say. 'I have a nasty feeling that the whole idea of the MaxiBudget chain is suspect.'

'Could I talk to you alone for a moment?' says Oscar.

When we're out of earshot of the meeting room, he pulls me into an alcove that's painted with a huge, cartooned grim reaper, his scythe menacingly poised over Oscar's head.

'Brother-in-law or no brother-in-law, this is starting to piss me off. You're putting an important piece of business in jeopardy. I don't care what this is all about – maybe you're in love with that cleaner of yours – but whatever it is, don't ever undermine one of our ideas in front of a client again.'

When we return to the meeting, Oscar says, 'I think we

should take a short break, and come back with some fresh thoughts.'

Everyone files out, leaving Ernesto staring down at a pad on the table, making listless notes.

'That was very unlike you,' he says, looking up. 'I enjoyed it.'

'Good. Now are you going to tell me what's wrong with you?'

'Can we talk somewhere?'

'Let's go for a walk. Get some street food.'

I take him to a place I found yesterday on my way back from the favela: a ramshackle kiosk near a news-stand on a dusty street corner, manned by a jovial guy in a filthy apron who is probably one of Flávia's neighbours. We order salt cod *bolinhos* and cheese pasties, and stand at the counter eating and talking, while the man behind the counter makes fresh sugar cane juice, forcing the long, fibrous stalks into a giant pulping machine and collecting the sweet green liquid in beakers at the other end.

'I wouldn't have pictured you here,' says Ernesto. 'I thought you were only interested in the finest restaurants the city had to offer.'

'I'm only a snob about quality.'

'Hear that?' says Ernesto, transmitting my compliment to the proprietor. 'You should be delighted – this man is hard to please.'

Setting down our juice, the owner smiles appreciatively, and flexes his bicep for us, like it's an indicator of his culinary prowess. As we're about to walk off with our food, he holds out a plastic pot of individually wrapped wooden toothpicks.

'For after your meal,' he says. 'The poor man's pudding.'

'Poor man's pudding, exactly,' Ernesto says, smiling at him.

We stroll back in the direction of the office.

'So what's the matter?' I say. 'Let me guess. Your wife?'

He nods. 'I talked to her about the stuff we were discussing the other day.'

'You did? How was it?'

'It could have been better. I came clean with her about working for her father. She told me off for being secretive. And that annoyed me. So I just brought it up.'

'Brought what up?'

'My suspicions. I didn't mean to. It just came out.'

'And what did she say?' I ask. My food is instantly inedible.

'That I was right. That she had been seeing someone else.'

Interesting.

'Some guy from her office,' he goes on. 'It's over now, apparently, and it only happened twice.'

'Shit, man. I'm sorry to hear that.'

*What fucking guy from the office?*

'How are you feeling about it?' I continue.

'I'm glad, in a way. It means I'm not going mad – that there was something happening when I was away.'

'What else did she say?'

'Actually she told me to come and talk to you about it. She said you'd know what to say. Sisterly love, huh?'

I smile. 'That was good of her.'

*What fucking guy from the office?*

During the second half of the meeting, my legs quiver. The urge to overturn the table and sprint out of the room is so strong that I want to hit myself into submission. Dennis stands with a marker pen while everyone else calls out words that describe how it would feel to live in a favela. I have said nothing, but words like *angry* and *hungry* and *impotent* are accumulating fast on the whiteboard. Knowing that I will have to RIP OFF MY SKIN if I am made to stay in this room for a moment longer, I get to my feet.

'Ludo? You're leaving us?' says Oscar.

'Bathroom.'

'Come back with an idea, will you?'

I take a deep breath as the bathroom door closes behind me. Flávia has been here recently – the smell of her eucalyptus cleaning fluid and a hint of her sweat linger on the air. Already though, the floor round the urinals is tacky. Oscar, no doubt, idly hosing all over the place while his mind lingered on something unpleasant. To think that Flávia has to deal with this every day, cleaning up after people who imagine themselves too busy to take proper aim.

I need time to think. I can't deal with Oscar staring me in the face waiting for an idea when Melissa and her 'guy from the office' are on my mind. What does it mean? Is it a signal from her, a warning shot? And what is this other feeling – this crippling guilt towards Ernesto? Suddenly, the sight of his big, desolate face across that meeting-room table is more than I can bear.

After staring at myself in the mirror for a minute and splashing water on my face, I quietly re-enter the airless, mindless room.

'We had an idea while you were away,' says Dennis, impossibly smug.

'Tell him,' says Oscar.

'I'm sure you have a point about the strategy being wrong,' says Dennis. 'I don't know enough about it yet. And those ideas were just a starting point. Perhaps I should spend some time in a favela to see it for myself.'

'That might help.'

'In the meantime, I had another thought that might be interesting.'

'This is great, Ludo, listen to it,' says Oscar.

'I thought we could organise a launch night for MaxiBudget here in the building. Invite everyone from the favela round the corner and announce our intentions – to make sure they understand where we're coming from.'

'Isn't it a cute idea?' says Oscar. 'A launch party where we invite all those kids right on our doorstep to come in, explain the plan to them, and get feedback on how we should position it. Like a big community brainstorming event. You say we haven't got it right, Ludo – well, let's *ask* them. Let's throw open our doors and show them a good time.'

'You could even, if you liked, only serve the brands we represent, seeing as those companies will all be present,' says Dennis.

'Better still, have themed courses, sponsored by different clients. That way everyone can be involved – even the detergent people,' I say, not entirely seriously.

'Now you're getting it!' Oscar claps me on the shoulder with a damp palm. 'And your job, Ludo, is to use the contacts you have in the favela to get the word out. Explain to them what's going on and get them all to come over here. I think we should do this soon. At the end of the week, if we can. Let's aim for Friday night.' He turns to Ernesto. 'Happy?'

Ernesto nods miserably.

'Excellent. Perhaps we could even see if our friend Zé Generoso is available to attend,' says Oscar. 'If we all ask him at once, he might be persuaded to make the time.'

'OK,' Ernesto says.

'You're a genius,' says Oscar to Dennis, who smiles awkwardly in his spotlight. 'This guy. What would we do without him? I swear if he was a woman, my next love child would be quarter Australian.'

After the meeting, Ernesto and I go to my office.

'What do you think I should do?' he says, collapsing on to the sofa.

'I don't know what to say. I can't believe she's been so stupid. I'm furious with her myself.'

'Please don't say anything to her. I don't want her to think I'm being indiscreet by talking about this stuff with you.'

'As you wish.'

His last words as we say goodbye in reception are, 'I just don't know where I went wrong.'

When he's gone, I rush back upstairs and call Melissa at work.

'What's this about a guy at the office?'

'Educated people usually begin telephone conversations with some form of greeting.'

'Tell me. What's his name?'

She sighs. 'For a genius, you can be very stupid at times.'

I pause, trying to catch up. 'There is no guy at the office?'

'Of course there isn't. I did you a favour, though I can't imagine why. The guy from the office is *you*. And as I told my husband, I'm not seeing him any more. Haven't we already had this conversation?'

'You . . . you did it for me?'

'I didn't see any reason to endanger his friendship with you as well as his marriage to me.'

I blink twice and stare at the graffiti on my office wall. The word FREEDOM, painted in giant yellow letters, swims before my eyes.

'Ludo? Are you still there?'

'I'm here.'

'How is he?' she asks, tentatively.

'Not great. I think you're right – it has to stop. For good.'

'I'm glad you agree.'

'Thank you for not saying it was me.'

'You're still my brother, though. You're not ducking out of that one.'

I sit at my desk, head in hands. There is no guy at the

office. The information should make me feel better, but it doesn't. Because of me, Ernesto thinks his wife has been cheating on him, and the simple fact is that she hasn't – at least, not in the way he thinks she has. Her mind slams the door on me whenever we are together, and keeps it firmly shut. It isn't right that Melissa should be protecting me like this. Nor is it right that Ernesto should be imagining something worse than the truth.

I pick up the phone again.

'What's so urgent that we have to meet now? I have a lot of work to do and I need to get home to see Melissa. This thing is eating me up.'

'I have to talk to you first.'

We're in a bar halfway between my apartment and the penthouse, a comfortable, unpretentious place we liked during our student days, with sawdust on the floor and little wire cages on the tables for salt, pepper, toothpicks, Tabasco. The Bohemia beer pump on the bar is so chilled that a thick carapace of solid ice has formed around it, and our glasses of very cold beer are refilled automatically by the waiter as we talk. A spirited game of dominoes is taking place at the table behind us, and there's a pleasant, after-work vibe which would make this meeting agreeable, were it not for the conversation Ernesto and I are about to have.

'Well – what is it?' He tosses a palmful of peanuts to the back of his mouth, and holds up his beer glass, which is slick with condensation. 'Your health.'

'There are a couple of things I need to say to you. The first is that I think I might be able to help you with your other problem.'

'What other problem?'

'The one you told me about, to do with the Shadow

Command. I think there might be a way I can get them to leave you alone.'

'Are you sure?'

'No, but I can try. What was the guy's name again?'

'I only know him as Jeitinho.'

'And you don't know which favela he lives in?'

'Not exactly, but I think it's not far from your office. What are you going to do?'

'Leave it to me, will you? I want to sort this out for you.'

'Ludo, this is incredibly dangerous. You should stay out of it.'

'Believe me, I should be the one doing this for you.'

'Why?'

I look him in the eye. 'You aren't going to like it.'

Something firms up in his expression, and now I have his full attention. 'OK.'

'Melissa is lying to you. There is no guy at the office.'

'How do you know?'

'Just listen for a second. She's lying to you. But you can trust her. Because she's only lying to protect me.'

His beer glass stops halfway to his mouth. 'To protect you? What do you mean?'

'It's me who's been sleeping in your bed. I go over there sometimes when you're away. She hates being on her own.'

'You?'

'Yes, me.'

'But just like a brother–sister thing.'

I pause, keeping his eye. 'Not always, no.'

He exhales slowly, painfully, riding the wave of this revelation.

'But as far as where our heads were, *always* a brother–sister thing,' I say. 'And nothing more.'

'This is difficult.'

'I don't expect you to like it, or to like me for it. But I

wanted to tell you so that you knew the size of the problem. And believe me, it's tiny. It's nothing. Because she is devoted to you.'

Telling him was the right thing to do. His mind is no longer blitzing him with the worst it can muster. But it isn't going to make my life any easier. Now, he has the tough gristle of this fact to focus on, and work over.

He looks at me, aghast. 'What am I supposed to do with this information? I don't want to have to start hating you.'

'You don't have to do anything. I'm the one who has things to do. You should go home and see Melissa. Call me if you want to shout at me, or make an appointment to beat me up.'

'What do you have to do?'

'A lot, as I am beginning to realise.'

The promise I have made to Ernesto is crazy. Attempting to enter the favela, track down the *dono* of a drug gang, and persuade him to sacrifice some of his business is suicide. It's more than that; it's violent torture, then suicide. And there is a ticking time bomb waiting for me in the shape of Flávia's son. But something has changed – I want to face up to these things. I want to put myself in harm's way. Inexplicably, this realisation and my confession to Ernesto combine to give me one of the best night's sleep I can remember.

*Angel Park. I am fourteen, and Rebecca has come to wish me good-night. By my bed stands the photograph I have always known, taken on the day she came to rescue us: my mother and Rebecca with their bowls of beans, sharing their flashlit black and white smile over my infant form. The look between them in the picture is so trusting and complicit that it is hard to believe they have only just met.*

*'Are you settling in OK?' Rebecca asks, sitting on the bed. 'Is there anything you need?'*

'No, thank you.'

'You aren't missing home too much?'

'A little. But I'm excited to be here.'

She picks up the photograph, which is leaning on my bedside light, and smiles at it. 'It's a long time since this was taken. Look at you, sweet little baby.'

'Do you think my father was there then? On the day you came to find us?'

'What do you mean?'

'I sometimes wonder whether he was living in the same favela as us at this time – or whether he'd already run off.'

'I don't understand.'

'You know – if the camera had been nudged at the time the picture was taken you might have seen part of his arm, or something. Looking at this, he could be just at the edge of the photo, in the background.'

'He wasn't,' Rebecca said, standing up abruptly. 'Take it from me. I was there. Goodnight.'

The set, slightly flushed expression on her face as she leaves the room is puzzling. If I didn't know better I would think I had angered her. It takes me hours to get to sleep, and I resolve to steer clear of the topic of my father in future. No good ever comes of it.

Driving past the office gatehouse, under the shady mantle of the avocado tree, I wave at the guard behind his bullet-proof screen, and he waves back to signal that he is letting me in. The twin red and amber lights above the entrance to the underground car park blink their ambivalent message as the metal gate slides sideways on rusty hinges. Bright sunlight is extinguished as I drive down the ramp with a squeal of tyres, and I remove my sunglasses to accustom my eyes to the gloom. The cosy, rubbery smell of subterranean safety and the echoing rattle of the closing gate tell me that nothing can come for me now. As I lock my car and walk to the lift I wonder how Melissa's and Ernesto's evening ended last night. Even if she is furious with me for exposing the fact that she lied to him, I still think I did the right thing.

At the ground floor the lift doors open on Dennis, looking worried, standing by a potted cactus. He gives me a hesitant look before stepping inside, so I conclude he must be brooding because I laid into his work. But I am well rested and feeling optimistic, and I greet him warmly.

'About yesterday,' I say. 'I hope you weren't too upset by what I said about your ideas. They just got me thinking.'

'I'm not precious. You spoke your mind.'

'Good. I wouldn't like you to think –'

'I've been doing this a long time. Don't give it another thought.'

'OK.'

'But listen, I spoke to Oscar. He said that in the absence of any better ideas we should at least run mine past a test audience. He mentioned one of the cleaners here – someone you know?'

'He said that, did he?'

'She works in the building, right? So we could do it this morning.'

*In the absence of any better ideas.* By the time the lift doors unleash me on the second floor, that good mood has evaporated completely.

I scour the building, trying not to look as if I am listening outside the door of every toilet – which I am – before I hear the shrill blast of her waistband radio.

'Get out of here. You know this is the Ladies?' she says shooing me away from the door of a fourth floor facility painted bright green.

'I need to talk to you.'

'I'm working. I don't want to listen to your crap today.'

'This is work too. I need you to come to one of the meeting rooms.'

Our intimacy was so hard earned and so fragile that this remark destroys it completely. 'What's the matter? Is the room dirty?' The sudden formality in her voice is hateful.

'No, we just need to ask your advice about something.'

I try to make conversation during the walk to the room but her retreat away from me is complete, and she barely responds. *At least Oscar isn't going to be there as well*, I think. But I have reckoned without Dennis's enthusiasm.

'Good morning, Senhora. It's a pleasure to meet you. Ludo tells me that you work in our building,' says Oscar from the doorway, somehow managing to smuggle through this ridiculous slight in a gush of charm. He must have walked past her a thousand times.

'Pleased to meet you, Senhor,' she says, quietly.

'We wondered if you could help us by looking at some work in progress, and telling us what you think of it.'

'OK.'

'These posters are very early ideas, so please say whatever you like about them. We would greatly value your opinion.' He speaks slowly, in a voice so patronising I want to punch him.

The Australian lays out the boards he presented in yesterday's meeting. *MaxiBudget: On Your Side. MaxiBudget: Now It's Your Turn.* He and Oscar stand back to watch Flávia as she looks at them.

'I'm sorry, Senhor. I don't understand.'

'Just tell us what you feel when you see them, please.'

'You want me to say what I feel?'

'Yes please. Anything at all.'

My stomach lurches. What if she can't read?

'*Now It's Your Turn*,' she says. 'I don't like the sound of that. My turn to do what?'

Oscar and Dennis laugh indulgently, as if she's making a joke.

'Your friend Ludo thinks that positioning MaxiBudget in this way is wrong, because it's talking down to people. But don't you think having an ally like this in your life would be a good thing?' says Dennis.

Oscar jumps in quickly. 'I think what we're asking is a much more simple question. Would you be tempted to shop at this supermarket?'

'What supermarket?' says Flávia.

'You didn't know this advertisement was for a super-market?'

'No, Senhor. How was I meant to know that?'

'From the food in the pictures. And the logo.'

'But the pictures are mostly of children. And the food is all rotten.'

Oscar is losing his patience. 'You really didn't know it was for a supermarket?'

'Sorry, Senhor. No,' she says, quietly.

'But I thought Ludo had been doing research with you into your feelings about budget supermarkets.'

She looks at me, bewildered, then back at him. 'I don't understand.'

'I see. You can go now. Thanks for your help.'

Oscar's words pursue me as I slip out of the room to follow her. 'You're a fucking liar, Ludo.'

Flávia has collected her rubbish sack from the bathroom she was cleaning before I interrupted her, and is dragging it slowly up the stairs to the next floor when I intercept her.

'I'm sorry about that,' I say, trying to sound friendly. 'Shall we have lunch?'

She turns on me quickly. 'Please don't ever speak to me again, unless you're asking for more toilet paper.'

'What do you mean?'

She stops on the stair, breathing heavily. 'These supermarkets. How cheap are they?'

'I think they are going to be very cheap.'

'Give me examples. How much is a kilo of rice at this supermarket? How much is a piece of salt pork? How much is a papaya?'

'I don't know,' I say.

'Then I will give you some advice, and it won't cost you one damn milkshake. Don't tell me that *It's My Turn*. If you want me to shop at your supermarket then tell me that I can feed my son for a handful of coins, and then I might think about it.'

I stare at her. 'Why are you being like this? I wasn't the one asking you those questions.'

'Yes you were. If you want me to be your guinea pig, then tell me that's what's going on. But don't ever pretend to be my friend again.'

It is darker today, and without Flávia the favela feels different. Loud, jarring music plays from unseen windows, and the air feels charged. As I pass the tattered fragments stuck to the billboards on the outskirts, I hear an argument raging behind a door, and pass it quickly, afraid that I might bring the anger down on my head. The intimacy that pleasantly surprised me before – the noise, the lack of space, the sweet smells of rotting garbage – all this seems oppressive today. But I can't afford to be nervous. I stopped wondering whether coming here was a good idea some time during Oscar's screaming fit in his office. I decided it was better just to do it.

*I don't care who you are. I don't care who your father is. Start taking this seriously or there will be no job. Why do you always have to let me down like this? Why do you have to disappoint me?*

This time I think he means it. But Oscar could shout all

day and it wouldn't make a difference, because at work nothing stands to change for me whatever I do. That is not the case where I am now.

I think I've lost my way, and feel a squirt of panic in my stomach. Then somehow I manage to find the steps to the low door that leads to Flávia's home. Unsure of what is polite, I knock on each door and surface that I can find, quietly announcing myself between each home. I make my way through, clutching my gift of Polaroid film.

The old man is out, and I know Flávia isn't here either. She's still pacing the corridors at work, furious with me.

'Come in,' says the girl.

She's doing homework. I have time to notice that the exercise book she is writing in is one that I designed two years ago as part of a Books In Schools campaign.

'Hi,' I say.

'What are you doing here?' Something is wrong. The look on her face is very different from before. She looks almost scared to see me.

'I brought you these.' I hand her the packets of Polaroid film. 'You said you had run out.'

'You came all the way back here just to bring me camera film?'

'It's not far.' I shift awkwardly in the low, cramped doorway. 'I work nearby.'

'That's kind. Thank you. But now you have to leave.'

'Why?'

'Because you're in danger here. I mean it. Get out.'

'Why?'

'My brother is about to come back. And I swear he will kill you if he finds you.'

'Your brother?'

'Milton. Flávia's son.'

Shit.

'He's your brother?'

'Half. Same father.'

'Shit.'

'What did you *do* to him? You should have seen what happened when he came home this morning and found the photograph of you and Flávia pinned to the wall. I've never seen anyone flip out like that before.'

I try to keep calm. 'I want to see him. It's part of the reason I came here. I need to explain what happened between us.'

'I don't think you should do that. He is not in a good mood, he's been drinking since this morning, and he has a terrible temper. Did you think you could just come in here and talk to him?'

'Sister, sister,' says a voice from the street. And then the curtain parts, and in he comes: quick, athletic, etched with intent.

He looks older than I remember. There are heavy bags under his eyes, though he seems to have put on weight in the last couple of days. He's probably been fed restorative meals while out of town. He's also washed his hair and put on a decent T-shirt. Were it not for the fact that I was expecting him or for the sling that hangs across his arm, I might not even have recognised him. But there isn't a chance in hell that he will fail to recognise me.

At first he's incredulous. He thinks he's dreaming. Then he weighs in, screaming and pushing. He wants to get started before I even have the chance to say anything.

'What is this, man? What are you trying to do to me?'

'Let me explain.'

'There is no explain!' he roars. 'You got me shot in the street.'

'It wasn't my fault. I tried to stop it happening. You didn't have to try and mug that guard.'

'And now you're in my *house*?'

'Listen to me for a minute.'

'There is no listen. And I'll tell you why.' He rips aside the curtain and ducks into Flávia's room, emerging immediately with the photo in his hand, the drawing pin still stuck through it from where he plucked it off the wall. 'This is why. I don't care what this is. All I know is I don't ever want to see you again.'

'Listen –'

'No you listen, you son of a bitch. You are not safe. Understand me? You could disappear in here if I wanted it. So get out while you have the chance. Final warning.'

'If you'll just let me talk to you for a moment –'

'You don't get it, do you? I'm trying to control myself. But this . . . *photographic evidence*, man. It's enough to drive me crazy.'

He's waving the picture in my face, and as I'm staring at it, at those saturated Polaroid colours, at Flávia's smile and mine, at the ghost shape between us, something shifts in my mind. Something enormous.

I feel as if I might pass out.

*Photographic evidence.*

'OK, I'm going,' I say. 'Let me just tell you that I regret what happened. OK?'

'Get the fuck out of here.'

My head is still spinning by the time I reach the alley. I break into a run down the steep hill, trying to remember the way out, but I take a wrong turning. I follow a drainage ditch choked with plastic bags, assuming for some reason that following the sewer will flush me away from danger. Looking up though chaotic bundles of electric wire, I see shadows against the sky – the shape of someone running across the rooftops, hurdling the aerials and satellite dishes and bright blue water tanks, tracking me. I hear the metallic squawk of voices spoken through a walkie-talkie, and the panting of athletic bodies on the move.

He only kicked me out so he could hunt me down – so that his sister wouldn't see what's about to happen.

I start running faster. The low doors and rusty staircases and the music from the open windows close in on me. I no longer know which way I'm going. I'm just running. When I emerge panting into a tiny courtyard that I haven't seen before, I know for sure that I'm lost. A fat dog in a doorway lifts his head to look at me. I return his gaze. And the sack comes down over my head.

# Cake

*I am twenty-two. My new friends look on as I perform my signature trick of drinking tequila from the cavity of the stuffed caiman I keep on a shelf in my apartment. The guests have gorged themselves on a four-course meal, and spirits are high.*

*A roar of approval crashes round the room as I swallow the final dregs and hold the desiccated, laminated creature mouth-side down to show that it's empty.*

*Things will get worse before they get better.*

Stepping on to the campus was like entering a film set. I felt I had lived through this cold autumn before, with its fallen leaves, its spotless pavements, and its cast of effortlessly entitled characters. Which does not mean that I felt at home.

My English was good when I arrived, but not fluent – and my character changed as a result. This is the personality transplant of a language barrier. Severed from your mother tongue, you resort to slapstick and other clownish behaviour to make friends. My classmates were generally rich, older than me, and supremely confident of getting what they felt they deserved out of life, which was nothing more or less than inheriting the universe – or at least the helm of a multinational company.

I had nothing in common with them at all, and yet I found

myself wanting to impress them. So I turned myself into a sideshow. It was I who drunkenly ate live goldfish for a bet, I who took reckless quantities of drugs for the diversion of the others, I who won money for sticking my fingers in plug sockets.

But I learnt, and capitalised on the opportunity in a way that Melissa never would have. My English improved. I honed my cooking skills. I participated eagerly in all the mindless group team-building exercises. I read voraciously. I learned a little about the workings of corporations. I bought popularity with flamboyant meals and raucous parties. Even so, it was a lonely time. The people around you define you. And if you spend enough time alone you forget who you are.

I spoke to my mother every week, happily supplying what she wanted to hear: tales of the magic of the United States and the transformative effect my time there was having on me. I listed the books I was reading, wowed her with half-learned facts, and let her picture me in collegiate, first-world splendour, never letting on how out of place I was. And she told me to wrap up warm and be sure to eat well, and kept me up to date with what was happening with the family – from whom I heard little.

I had written Zé a long, formal letter shortly after arriving. It sought to thank him for all he had done for me. 'I will never be able to repay the debt I owe to you, for this, and for every other opportunity you have given me,' it read. 'But I hope at least to make you feel that in choosing me, you made a wise investment.' Something about the finality of the tone might perhaps have made him think that this was the end of our transaction – that he had sent me off into the world to succeed. For whatever reason, the fact is that after I sent the letter I heard nothing from Zé or Rebecca for almost four months.

When I spoke to Melissa she was breezy, spilling over with some new comment on pregnancy or marriage, and apparently perfectly happy. I spoke to Ernesto too, when he answered the phone, and he always sounded delighted to hear from me. They sent me joint letters, some of which contained photographs, so I could see how big she was getting, and watch from afar her growth into a radiant mother-to-be.

Something about the distance was healing. Now that I did not see Melissa, and our contact was restricted to platitudes exchanged over thousands of kilometres, I realised how much of my life she had dominated, and what I stood to reclaim. It was for that reason that I let the frequency of our calls drop off, and started to feel self-sufficient for the first time in my life. As a result I only found out from my mother two weeks after the event that Melissa had gone into labour early, and that her baby had been stillborn.

'Are you OK?' I said into the phone. I had been calling every couple of minutes for three hours since hearing the news.

Her voice was cracked and tired. 'It wasn't very nice. I wouldn't recommend it.'

'I'm sorry I'm not there.'

'Looks like I could have done the business degree after all,' she said. 'Is it worth it?'

'I'll let you know.'

After that we resumed our regular conversations. I knew that what had happened had affected her, but felt that it was not my role to console her. Another three months passed. Deposits of cash arrived in my bank account every month, but they were not generous enough that I could have afforded a flight home. And still there was nothing but silence from my adoptive parents. I was not invited back for the holidays, so I assumed that I was to stay put.

When, just as I was about to start my third semester, I answered the phone and heard Zé's voice at the other end, I jumped.

'Ludinho, my boy.'

'It's *you*,' I said, absurdly.

'We never hear from you. You went completely silent after writing that sweet letter. We've been wondering how you are getting along. How is your English? Are you ready to come and run my business yet?'

'I am having a wonderful year, Senhor,' I said, resorting to formality, at once pleased and nervous that he'd called. 'I don't know how I can repay you.'

'Good, good,' he said. 'Now, Ludo –'

There was a pause. His sigh broke over the long distance line like a crackling, static wave.

'Ludo, Ludo, Ludo.'

'What is it?' I said.

My first thought was of Melissa. There had been further complications. She was hurt. She had been taken again. Because I had abandoned her, she had lacked protection, and someone, or something, had pounced.

'I regret that I am phoning with bad news.'

*Here it comes*, I thought.

But Melissa was perfectly safe.

It started with an accident in the forest. Silvio was away visiting relatives in the northeast, but you can't blame him for what happened. There were dozens of people on the farm who could have helped if she had been the kind of person to ask.

It was a Sunday; almost a year to the day after Melissa and Ernesto were married. A sudden storm came, and just as before, the power cut out. Zé and Rebecca had not come for the weekend, so there had been no guests to cook for, and no Silvio to feed either. I see her preparing for the week ahead, doing what can be done in advance, planning how she will feed the workers in the coming days. I see her settling

234

down in front of the television when the power goes down. I see her curse as the lights flicker out, then head down the hill to start the emergency generator, surprised as she steps outside by the intensity of the wind and the hot rain.

She slipped, landing on a sharp, protruding branch of a fallen tree and slashing open her thigh. Unable to stand, she crawled the remaining distance to the generator house, which was flooded with water as usual during heavy rains. By the time she was found the next morning she had contracted pneumonia.

But this was my mother. She could have survived anything, I tell myself. And I am right. She could have shrugged all of it off, were it not – and here is the fact that makes me want to scream at the sky and beat my chest, because how can this be true, how can a world exist where this can happen – were it not for the fact that she had *not been eating properly*. With nobody to cook for, she had simply forgotten to feed herself. She was too weak after her night bleeding in the generator house to fight off the pneumonia, and she died three days after the fall.

It is a simple enough fact: the forest, which always threatened to step forward and reclaim some of its territory, finally did so, and took my mother when nobody else was around. But the fact is also that the spot where she fell was only metres from where Melissa and I had made our jungle camp all those years before – and only metres, therefore, from the spot where a year before to the day I had promised the forest anything if it would bring Melissa and me back together.

When I flew home, the family were already out at the farm, so I took the bus there for the first time. During the six-hour journey, I imagined my mother's first trip out here, on these very roads, to take up her employment. I pictured myself lying in her arms, and imagined her nervousness as the bus left the city behind and headed into the wild. I had heard the story enough times for it to have acquired the feeling of a legend – something that had happened to somebody else.

By the time I reached the town nearest to the *fazenda* and alighted from the bus, my satanic pact with the forest had become an incontrovertible truth. I sat with my luggage under a concrete bus shelter shaped like a question mark, waiting for Silvio to collect me, staring at the bright red earth of the road and the dark green foliage behind it, wondering how I would ever atone for having killed her, and resolving never again to speak to the person who was my motive.

*I am twenty-three. No extreme weather has blown in to lend drama to this occasion. It's simply a beautiful day: strong hazy sunshine, the noise of crickets and birds, my mother's body in a coffin.*

*I feel Melissa's presence in the cool church, but I do not look around. Melissa is not what I should be thinking about.*

*Melissa is what brought us here.*

*I must never look at her again.*

I avoided her afterwards, too, circulating away whenever I perceived her dark suit making its way towards me through the wake. Luckily there were farm folk queuing up to offer me their condolences, and Silvio to talk to at length.

We stood around the pool during the muted party, eating bowls of a *moqueca* that my mother had prepared before she died. The farm workers and other locals who were present probably had no idea, but I could tell it was hers, and tried to chew every mouthful of the sumptuous, spicy fish as slowly as I could, to draw the experience out as long as possible. Zé gave a dignified, warm address. I was offered the chance to speak but remained silent. I had nothing to say. Silvio chose not to speak either, but paid tribute by constructing a bonfire from the wood of the tree that had wounded her. It might as well have been her pyre, so painful was it to watch the flames.

Somehow, through trying so assiduously to avoid Melissa, I ended up alone with her father, standing on the lip of the hill, not far from my mother's kitchen, gazing down the valley towards the river. I held an untouched glass of wine. He had just finished eating a short, stubby banana, and now he was drinking a caipirinha and smoking a cigar.

'I shall miss her so much,' he said. 'It feels like the spirit of this place has been taken away.'

'I know what you mean.'

'I hope this isn't too painful a day for you, Ludo. If there is anything I can do . . .'

'It's odd,' I said, truthfully. 'I hadn't seen her properly for so long, even before I went away. I hadn't been living as her son for years.'

Zé coughed gently on his cigar, and chewed ruminatively. 'I know that we took you away from her, but she was always your mother. You know that, don't you?'

I nodded.

'I don't know how we will ever replace her,' he went on.

'Replace her?'

'Or even whether we should. It's a terrible thing to admit, but often your mother's delicious food went to waste here. She was cooking like crazy seven days a week, and we were hardly ever here more than two days a week to eat it.'

I pictured her, sweating in the kitchen, working, as she saw it, for her life. I thought of the mountains of cakes she must have made over the years, the oceans of soup. I tried to calculate how many animals had been raised and murdered to fuel this entertaining machine.

'Naturally we were delighted to take her on,' Zé went on.

'To have given her employment out here. And a safe place to raise you. But that doesn't mean that it is necessarily cost-effective to replace her.' He took a large swig of his caipirinha and crunched on the ice, like a horse chewing sugar cubes.

'And it wouldn't be the same,' I offered.

'No, it wouldn't be the same,' Zé agreed, swallowing. 'Your mother should not – could not – be replaced.'

He pulled on the cigar. 'It was extravagant in any case to have *two* cooks. And now that you young people don't get out here as often as you used to . . . I think that what we will do instead is to start travelling with Claudia, from the city. She can just come with us when we go away for the weekend. She knows all the recipes.'

'Good.'

I could see him looking sideways at me, working out how long he needed to pause before changing the subject.

'The other question,' he said eventually, 'is what *you* want to do. You may not want to talk about this now, but you ought to think about whether you actually want to go back to the United States after this.'

'I can tell you what I think now.'

'And?'

'I want to stay here. Will you mind if I don't go back?'

He gazed down the valley. 'No, I won't mind. What do you want to do instead?'

I paused. 'Maybe I could stay here, on the farm. I could help Silvio. Take over from him when he retires. What do you think about that?'

His laugh echoed off walls and caused mourners to look over from the fire.

'You don't want to be stuck out here for the rest of your life! We can find you something better than that. In the city. Something with prospects.'

'What do you have in mind?'

'I have already thought about it. Do you remember a man called Oscar Cascavel? He used to come and stay here regularly, for a time.'

'I remember. You used to play tennis with him.'

'I still do. He's a big shot in the world of marketing now. Runs his own agency. I could probably get you a job working for him.'

'Zé. You overwhelm me.'

'Let's give it a try. See if you like it. Then maybe you can come and work for me later on. Be my marketing director.'

He flung the crushed lime halves from his empty tumbler into the bushes with a casual flick of the wrist and ground his cigar into the earth, where it mingled with bracken and leaf litter. Individually, either one of these actions would have signalled the end of the conversation – together, they buried it.

'Thank you, Zé – yet again,' I said. 'Now if you don't mind, I'd like to spend some time in the kitchen.'

'Of course. Take all the time you want. We won't be clearing it out for a day or two.' He shook his shoe, one of a pair in soft Italian leather, to shake off the natural debris he'd picked up in stubbing out the cigar, and then turned to head back to the party. 'I'm going to see if any of the boys would be interested in kicking a football around. I think it might be a welcome distraction, don't you?'

'I'm sure it's what my mother would have wanted.'

Something was already different about the kitchen: the door was closed. It had never been closed in my life. Security wasn't an issue out here, and my mother never took holidays. I wondered whether she had left the farm at all in the twenty-two years she had worked there. She had been tied to it by her gratitude, by the obligation, by the gift with conditions.

The songbirds still twittered under the eaves outside. I walked down the line of cages, opening each one, and watching as each bird found the courage to flit out to nearby tree branches. Only one, the fat monk parakeet, stayed in his cage, even though I left it open all afternoon, so when I left I shut his door and took him back to the city, where he lives with me still.

It was dark inside, pleasantly cool. The fire in the hearth had burned out. I found a piece of stray cardboard, propped it up, and put a match to it. It curled and flared briefly, then died to a glimmer. The table, planed down and built up again so many times by Silvio, was piled high with cakes and sweets ordered from a flash city patisserie. They were nothing next to what my mother would have produced. I looked inside the ancient gas-powered fridge that is now my own: remains and leftovers, in plastic containers and porcelain bowls. These last swirls of sauce and morsels of meat had suddenly become very important. Pulling out a half-eaten roasted chicken, I stuck my thumb deep into what remained of the breast and gouged myself a big chunk. Nobody was around to tell me off for not carving a neat slice.

Still chewing, I opened the freezer compartment. It was filled with meticulously labelled tubs: stews, *moquecas,* soups. These were commodities whose value had shot up in the last twenty-four hours. Once, the contents of these tubs had been commonplace. Now they were finite, priceless. I began working out how I would get them back to the city without thawing them – I would not leave one portion here to be forgotten or discarded.

The door was pushed open with a creak. Melissa stood in the entrance, dust around her hair, the light at a high pitch.

She looked older. Those legs of hers were more intimidating than ever. But she wore the same white, plastic watch.

'Shall I leave you alone?' she said.

'No.'

'You've been avoiding me.'

'Yes,' I admitted.

She stepped inside. I inhaled slowly, pulling the warm earth and tree bark of the outside through Melissa's perfume and into the homely smoke of the hearth. The bone-warm air of the farm, so different from the liquid heat of the city.

'It's good to see you,' I said. 'How's married life?'

'Truthfully? It's a little lonely.'

This room that signified my mother, now empty of her, felt different. There was a need to fill the space with some-thing – to reoccupy it.

'Ernesto isn't here?'

She shook her head. 'He heard it was a small, family thing. And he's working. But he asked me to give you a hug from him.'

And then came the embrace, that became a soft kiss on the cheek.

'I've missed you,' she said.

'I wanted to come home before – after what happened to you.'

'It was painful. But Ernesto was wonderful. It shouldn't be a big deal any more.'

'But it is?'

She nodded.

And now, as on no occasion before or since, things grad-uated smoothly, logically. After several botched attempts, the only meaningful time Melissa and I made love took place on the kitchen table, dutifully planed down by Silvio, amid the cakes ordered for my mother's funeral.

★

And that's where it should end, with the two of us gloriously fucking there, smearing food all over ourselves, giggling, finally able to be with one another in the way I had known we could be. The forest, delivering my reward.

But it doesn't end there. Because all she was doing on that table was snaring me, pulling me further on to the hook. And we have this vulgar postscript, tacked on to the story proper, which now threatens to dwarf it, like a tumour grown larger than its host. Because for nearly three years since then I have lived this half-life, hiding in my one-room apartment, with my caged bird, and my one plate, my one knife and my one fork. And the only thing I have in my life which I value is the withdrawn version of Melissa I sleep with today, and Ernesto deceived, and Oscar down my throat, and no way out of any of it.

It does not seem like a fair deal, the one that I struck with the forest. If I had the Melissa of that day, the one on the kitchen table, the one who missed me and wanted me and needed me, then I might be happy.

But the deal does not work.

I do not feel adequately remunerated.

# Mango

Slanting light cross-hatched by sackcloth threads. The inside of the bag smells of must, food and urine. There's the feeling of insects, too, though that could be my skin creeping at the texture, with the fear. A door slams, and I am thrown to the floor.

'Did you think you were getting away that easily?'

A spiteful kick to my stomach makes a reply impossible. I double up, curling away from the unseen foot. My hands grope across a textured, humid floor.

We are somewhere in the favela, and Milton has found some friends – at least two good, strong pairs of arms brought me here. The process of disorientation was deliberate, they marched me down so many tight alleys and round so many corners that it was like stumbling round a never-ending Escher staircase. I am smothered by dirty heat, maddened by this crawling skin and by the buzzing of flies. Escape is out of the question.

I wonder if I still have it in me to pull all those facial contortions I did as a child – rolling my eyes back in my head, teeth chattering, as if performing a *Macumba* ritual – the performance that saved Melissa. The one that might save me now.

'Please – give me some air,' I say, taking laboured, rasping breaths. 'I think I may be about to have an epileptic fit. Take off the bag.'

There is laughter. 'Having a fit, are you? Shame.' Milton brings his mouth in close to my ear so that I can feel his breath even through the bag. 'You don't fool me, brother. I'm the conman, don't you *rem-mem . . . ber*? So be sensible, and stop the theatrical shit. If you try anything like that again you'll make things much worse.'

He pulls away, and raises his voice. He wants to appear in charge, to assert his ownership of the situation, and of me, to the others – whoever they are. 'Now. This flimsy little guy is on trial.'

'You don't need to do this,' I say. 'I came here to apologise.'

'And bring my sister little love gifts. And pose for pictures with my mother.'

'I didn't know she was your sister,' I manage, fighting nausea, trying to get my breath back.

'Half-sister. And I'm very protective of her. Which means that you, my friend, are in trouble.' His friends laugh.

'You can't be serious. Just because I brought her some camera film –'

'I'm very fucking serious, playboy. If you speak to her again, I'll cut off your tongue. And if you try to see her, I'll poke out your eyes. Understand?'

'You always were a tough talker. Take this bag off so I can see your face.'

Another kick, this one to my ribs. The pain explodes in my chest. I scream.

'Keep making jokes and see what happens. No, friend, the bag stays on, so you can't see how terrifying we are to look at. So you can imagine the worst thing in the world, and then double it, and then shit your pants. Stand up.'

'If you want me to shit my pants I would rather stay seated.'

'Do you want another kick? Because I'll do it. I'm all ready to hurt you, brother. Just like you hurt me. You should be impressed. Even with this busted collarbone I can still kick you round the floor like a rag football.'

'Don't. I can't move as it is.'

I am still rolling on the floor from the second kick. Inside the bag, I am drooling, and I can taste the salt-rust tang of blood. My chest is on fire. Two pairs of hands grab me by the arms, haul me to my feet, guide me backwards and push me down into what feels like a flimsy plastic chair.

I feel as if I have been duped, as if the girl were nothing but bait, a juicy decoy left hanging for me inside the gaping jaws of a flytrap. It isn't like that, of course. The boy is not nearly as in control as he pretends. He is scared and confused. He is also, as I am beginning to realise, extremely paranoid.

I can make him out through the sack – a heavy-breathing, anxious shape. He wants to start hurting me properly, but if he does he might never find out how I came to be here, paying visits to his sister, and how there came to be a photograph of me with my arm around his mother on the wall of his kitchen. I tell myself, *These are just children. They're boys. Don't be afraid.*

Milton is certainly afraid of me. He can't imagine how I infiltrated his life like this. I mustn't let him know that it happened entirely by accident. If I demystify myself he will remember nothing more than that I got him shot, and I will end up dead.

'What shall we call you? We'll call you bag, seeing as that's what you are. You are just a bag, right?'

'Right,' I say, settling in the chair, trying not to topple over.

'Just a bag that we can use how we like, right? For example, we could fill the bag with shit and chuck it in the street. We could piss in the bag. Couldn't we?'

For the first time, I hear a voice other than Milton's. 'Why are we doing this? Why don't we just rob him and get out of here?'

'Because I found a picture of him with my *mother*.'

I speak quickly. 'I can explain that. We work in the same building.'

'Did I tell you that you could speak, bag?'

'About the photograph. It's very simple. I work with your mother, and we became friends. That's it.'

'You work in that building? The Beehive?'

'Yes. Check my wallet if you don't believe me.'

'We'll be taking that anyway, my friend. You needn't worry about that.'

A set of hands pats down my pockets roughly until they find my wallet, and remove it.

'Do you see? Please, just take off the bag, and let's talk. For God's sake, I'm like you. I come from somewhere just like this.'

'You are not like us. Look at you. Look at your clothes. Someone like you is never going to be friends with my mother.'

'I swear I am. I was born in Heliópolis.'

There is much laughter at this, which enables me to guess how many there are in the room. Three, maybe four.

'Born in Heliópolis?' says Milton. 'I don't think so.'

'I was adopted. By this guy. He owns supermarkets. You know MaxiMarket? He owns them *all*. Understand? So he has plenty of money. Whatever you want, he will pay it.'

Pause. They smirk. They start laughing again.

'I can't believe you're jumping in offering a ransom. You rich guys – you think we just kidnap people all the time? That kidnapping is just what we *do*?'

A third voice chips in. 'I don't need your money, brother. I got all the money I need. I got the latest Nikes. I got enough to snort. I got enough to smoke. We're doing this for *personal* reasons, understand?'

'There's no point in doing this,' says the second voice. The one belonging to the guy who just wanted to rob me and have done with it. 'This fool would say anything to get out of here. He's no playboy. I say we kick him down the hill. Or leave him here to die.'

'No!' I say. 'If you don't believe me then look it up. I bet one of you can get to a computer. Find out about Zé Fischer Carnicelli. He's my adoptive father. He'd pay all the money you want.'

A pause. I can sense them looking at each other, thinking, *What the hell?* In my terror of being hurt, I've turned this into a kidnap situation. Ingenious.

'You better be right about this.' My arms are lashed.crudely to the plastic chair at the elbows with what feels like electric wire. A door opens, and I hear retreating footsteps.

'Wait!' I say. 'Can you bring me some water?'

'Don't bet on it, bag,' says the last of the retreating voices.

I am alone, tied to the chair with a bag over my head, with nothing but the sound of a lively Carnival classic from a distant, tinny radio: *Mamãe eu quero. Mamãe eu quero. Mamãe eu quero, mama . . .*

*Saturday night on the farm. I am eleven.*

*Unusually, there are no weekend guests, and in their absence Zé is even more relaxed than usual. He played water polo with Melissa and me this afternoon, and is embarking on his fourth caipirinha of the evening.*

*'Tell me a story,' he says, leaning back in a huge white armchair. 'I wish to be entertained.'*

*'What would you like it to be about?' Rebecca says, a glass of wine in her hand. She is relaxed, too, and enjoying her drunk husband.*

*'How about the story of when you came and found me and my mother in the favela?' I ask, emboldened by the intimacy of the atmosphere.*

'Found you?' Zé says, not thinking, staring at the ceiling. 'You found us, more like.'

Rebecca jumps in, cutting off his sentence. 'That's enough from you. I'll tell you a good story if you shut up.' She speaks so quickly I almost don't have time to register what he said.

But I do register it. And the flash of panic in her eyes.


The bag, the solitude, the pain – it's all taking my head to unfrequented places. I don't know how long I have been here, alone with my mind. But it is dawning on me that I may be here for some time. And because I'm me, the fear has made me hungry. So hungry that my groaning, coiling stomach feels like it might digest itself.

I can tell it's getting dark. Not just because of the change in the light – the atmosphere is changing, too. We are probably in a quiet corner of the favela, but I can hear activity, and voices, as workers return home, and food is prepared, and drinks are poured, and cigarettes lit.

A thin strip of flesh, salty with blood, hangs from inside my cheek where I have bitten myself during the struggle. I work my teeth around it, chewing the tiny morsel a little before swallowing.

Suddenly, they are back. I can smell *cachaça* fumes, and one of them is smoking a joint.

'Water,' says a voice, and a plastic bottle is held to my lips. It barely contains a mouthful, but I try to swill it round as much as possible and swallow gratefully.

'So, bag. We did some research. This father of yours is a pretty important guy. So we're going to feed you up. Got to keep you in good condition if we're going to get a nice, fat ransom. I got you something special.'

There is pressure on my head. I can feel them tying a bandanna round my eyes. It cuts out the light altogether. Then they lift up the lower part of the sack and fold it up and over the blindfold, so that my mouth and nose are exposed, though I can see even less than before.

An object is wafted under my nose. The smell is ripe and tropical, sweet yet spiked with something more fundamentally delicious. It's mango. Luscious mango. The smell of childhood. The smell of freedom. Saliva springs in my mouth.

'Like the smell of that, do you?' says Milton. 'Want me to cut you a piece, "Ludwig"?' They have been looking through my wallet.

'Ludo. People call me Ludo. Yes please,' I say, trying not to gasp it.

'Get ready, because here it comes.'

'Are you ready?'

'Yes,' I say.

'Open your mouth then.'

Something passes between my lips. Something wet and fibrous. Something that is not mango. The taste of putrefying, rotten meat blossoms in my mouth and too late the stench reaches my nose. I spit and retch simultaneously, and a bitter jet of vomit shoots down my shirt.

They laugh. I moan, trying to expel images from my head of what it might have been. My imagination is running wild though I am desperately trying to suppress it. Who knows what it was: flesh, a decaying creature.

'What was that?' I manage, after another dry heave.

'I'll tell you what that was,' says Milton. 'That was a lesson in trust. You lied to us. You abused our trust. So we fucked with yours. And that's the way life is.'

'What do you mean?'

'I mean that we looked up your Zé Carnicelli – and there's nothing about you anywhere. It says he has a daughter called Melinda, and doesn't say anything about you.'

'Melissa. She's called Melissa.'

'And the name in your wallet is dos Santos – and so I think

your little scheme has fucked up, "Ludo". What are you going to do now? Now that we know you are worthless. Now that we know you are nobody.'

'Believe me, it's true. They made me keep my name for protection. So that kidnappers wouldn't know about the connection.'

'Is that right?' More laugher. 'I have to hand it to you,' Milton says, 'you improvise well. But I seem to remember you being somewhat rude about the story I told you when we first met. Remember that?'

'I remember.'

'So I won't trust you either. That seems fair. I don't think you were born in Heliópolis, and I don't think you have any connections with this Zé guy. I think you are nothing at all. You're just a bag. A dirty bag covered in puke that we need to hose down and throw away.'

I hear a zip being undone and even though I don't want to, I know what's coming next. A thin stream of liquid hits my chest as the boy urinates on me, not much, no more than a token effort – something symbolic.

'And now we're going to make you wish your nerves were dead.'

A kick to the jaw, so hard I see a flash inside the bag. My head snaps back. The pain is a bomb in my face.

And now the fear is real. These people wouldn't care if they killed me. Why should they? I am fighting for my life.

'Jeitinho,' I say, through a bubbling mouthful of blood. Even saying the word sends a jolt of agony through my jaw. 'Jeitinho.'

'What?'

'Jeitinho, from the Shadow Command. I know him.'

'What did you say?'

'A friend of mine – my brother-in-law – does business with

him. So you have to stop this now. He won't be happy. His name is Jeitinho. Do you know him?'

A hot, anxious, heavy-breathing silence ensues.

'How do you know that name?'

'That's what you should be asking yourself. How do I know that name?' I speak quickly, through the pain, through the blood.

I can understand his confusion. 'One minute you tell us you are from a favela. The next that you are so wealthy that we could ask for any amount of ransom money for you. Now you're saying you're best friends with a Shadow Command *traficante*. Just who exactly are you?'

'It's all true. The first two things might not matter to you, but this one does. Are you prepared to take the risk that I might be telling the truth? Is Jeitinho the kind of guy you want to piss off?'

'You mean it?' His voice has changed completely. 'He's a foot soldier. He wouldn't fool around with you like us. He'll kill you. He'll quarter you and burn the pieces in a ditch so the cops have to rake through the ashes to identify you from bits of bone. He's done it before. I'm serious, man. You don't want us to get him.'

'I think you're afraid to get him. In case I'm right,' I say. Panicking. Bleeding. 'And he finds out you pissed on me, and hurt me. And decides to put one in your head.'

That dangerous pride of his again. 'You're killing yourself here – you know that? Calling someone like him to the room changes everything.'

'So get him,' I say, breathing hard, heart thumping. 'And mention MaxiMarket.'

The door opens and closes, and the steps retreat again. And I suspect that this might be the last time I hear from them. Or from anybody else.

★

I sit lashed to the flimsy chair, trying to avoid the pungent smells and cloying sensations of vomit and urine cooling on my front, and to come to terms with the fact that I am about to die. I struggle pointlessly against the greasy, chafing electrical wire on my wrists, and try to make the chair legs buckle in the hope that this might somehow help to free me.

The vacuum in my stomach begins to shout louder, especially now I have been sick. With every move I make, I am squandering priceless energy and fuelling further pangs of hunger. Food parades before me when I close my eyes: legs of roast pork dancing in theatrical chorus lines; cobs of corn spinning like the dials of a fruit machine; collapsing kaleidoscopic polygons of chops and steaks. At first I encourage the visions, but then I stop, because they're making things worse. I imagine I can hear my mother's voice through the radio that booms somewhere nearby, saying, 'Avoid your favourite foods. There will be a time when you can't have them – and the more you eat them now, the more you will yearn for them then.'

And then, because I'm trying so hard not to think about food, all I can think of is sex. Visions of Melissa's deep red nipples, of those succulent nuts and berries, of my thumbs shaping the slope of her back as she sleeps, of her warm, scented skin. I find myself wondering whether in spite of the restraints I could contrive to masturbate. Then I fear that if I did I might lose vital minerals and vitamins. I used to be afraid to do it. My mother told me when I was very young that my father's ghost would be watching if I so much as looked at myself. It was a near-perfect deterrent. Even now, as I contemplate the idea, and feel tingling constriction in my underpants, his spectre rises before me. His face is in shadow, as always, but I sense the leering expression, and his hands are reaching towards me out of the darkness, proffering dollar bills in my direction as he urges me on like a pervert in a lap-dancing club.

An insect has bitten or stung my leg in several places, and there are two or three inflamed knots in the muscle of my calf where the venom is travelling, as if my captors had cut my skin and slipped peanuts into the gaps. Reaching down behind my back, pulling hard against the tightening, cutting plastic wire, I can just reach the bites. They itch maddeningly but pierce with pain when I touch them. Contorted in the chair, I play with them idly, enjoying the extremity of the sensation, rubbing sweat into the inflamed areas and vaguely imagining that by working the venom into my system in this way, I am making some kind of *roux*, a poison sauce. The pain should provide enough of a distraction to banish the thought of sex, but something about the inflammation, the concentrated blood, means that it has the opposite effect.

My thoughts about Melissa expand to encompass the whole family. Why did they have to *adopt* me? To own me in that way, without even declaring it to the world? From where I am sitting now, the answer is clear. Zé took me in to use me as a decoy, to protect his darling daughter, and stop her from being taken ever again – and here I am, in her place. That insurance policy they bought has finally paid out.

'Insurance policy,' I say out loud, and for some reason it makes me laugh.

And still the hunger shouts. Louder and louder. The churning in my stomach becomes so acute that I imagine myself capable of an equal kind of force. So I waste more energy struggling uselessly against the electric wire.

They had better leave me here to die, or kill me themselves.

They had better do that for Melissa's sake.

I thrash about, wrestling these indelicate thoughts. I want to cry out, but fear it might attract the wrong kind of attention. So I try biting the sackcloth and edging it up my face to get back my eyes. But the blindfold is too tight, and gravity is against me. I need a free hand to wrench away this rank cloth from my face. The anticipation of that moment of freedom gives me the impetus to suppress any fears of harming myself and I start rocking the chair from side to side until one plastic leg buckles and I fall sideways. With no sight and no arms to stop it happening, I crack my shoulder hard against the ground. I curl on the floor in the shape of my chair-prison, lashed in a right angle; a shape convulsing with belts of hot pain.

Coming to terms with the floor takes time. There are new smells (that mango is still lying around somewhere, along with whatever they replaced it with), and new sensations to contend with. The shoulder pain cools after much cursing, and some crying, but the dull throb in my jaw persists. Movement of that arm must be kept to a minimum, but I have to get the restraints off somehow. I kick around the floor in a circle, pulling at the wire in every direction, and gasping when the shoulder is touched, but with no success. Eventually I force myself to relax and close my eyes, and I lie with one cheek to the floor, trying to calm down.

Bang.

What sounded like a pistol shot brings me round with a start. Somehow, I fell asleep. I try to return to consciousness slowly, willing my pounding heart to slow down. The shot sounded close, but I hear nothing else.

I stare into the darkness and my mind wanders. It lingers on those two words, spoken by Milton.

*Photographic evidence.*

That photograph of me, newborn, with my mother and Rebecca is part of the furniture I grew up with. The mythology of Rebecca's visit to Heliópolis is so hard-wired into me that I have never thought to question it. But now, lying on the floor, lashed to a chair with electrical wire, the picture appears before my eyes. I look at it properly for once, in my head – at the black and white smile that I have understood to be the defining moment in my life for as long as I can remember. And suddenly I know that I have to get out of here somehow. Because I recognise the background to the picture. I know the room where it was taken.

And it is not in a favela.

I begin to calculate how to get to my feet, so I can circle the room with the chair still attached and try to find a way out. But just as I start to move I hear a sound from the opposing corner of my prison; a scratching, shuffling sound, too loud for an insect, too soft for anything bigger than a rat. If I can get it to come over here, perhaps coat some of the wires in blood to get it to gnaw through them, I could get out, I could get this bag off my head and scratch my scalp and scream and see and plunge my head into clean water. But how do you entice a rat to cross a stinking floor and gnaw wire from your wrists when ripe mango and rotten mango substitute and God knows what else already litter the place? The wire will not appeal, but my flesh might. I begin rubbing my wrists against the grit of the floor, to try and break the skin, to get some smell going for the rat to follow.

'Come on, boy,' I say, still cartwheeling in the dirt. 'Get over here. Who wants mango when you could have wrist-flesh? I'll let you chew on my skin like sun-dried beef. Come on, rat. Eat me, rat.'

'Are you talking to me?' says a voice. The girl. The sound was no animal, but her quietly opening the door. 'Because I don't like being called rat.'

At the sound of the voice I sob, and relief buckles my body. 'Help me.'

'My God. What have they done to you? I could tell it was something bad by how much they were laughing. You *stink*.'

I hear her crossing the room.

'Get this thing off my head. Get it off now or I might go mad.'

'Stay still.'

I feel her hands grabbing the sack where it bunches tight, at my ears. A wave of her scent – a clean, feminine smell. The hands grasp, and pull upwards, and my head is stripped clear, and the world returns. Light streams into my eyes. Morning light. Have I been here all night? My mouth snatches at cool air. I grind my hair into the grit of the floor, imagining lice, insects, maggots, wanting to mince them all, to lather my scalp with gravel.

'OK, OK,' she says, cutting off my scream of relief. 'You're OK now.'

'What time is it?'

'Nearly eight.'

I look around at my cell, which is not nearly as squalid as I imagined, with its red floor, its clean, concrete walls, its small glassless window. I catch sight of the piece of mango on the floor, and stop looking around. I don't want to know what the second object was.

'Can you get up?' she says, and I look at her face for the first time.

'Don't cry,' I say. 'I'm not that badly hurt.'

She slaps me, sending a shot of agony through my jaw. 'I'm not crying for you, you idiot. Some *traficante* pistol-whipped my brother. He came back a couple of hours ago with a massive cut and bruise under his eye. And on top of that Flávia went crazy at him for hanging out with those people. Like he needs that after what he's been through.'

'Are you serious?'

'You must have some pretty important friends,' she says, with contempt. 'Milton told me you were here, and that I should let you go straight away.'

'Why didn't he come himself?'

'Does it surprise you to hear that he doesn't want to see you?'

'Does Flávia know I'm here?'

'She doesn't know anything. And you're not to tell her. That boy has had enough trouble without her beating him up over you as well. Sweet Mary, the smell of you.'

I look into her face, the black pools of her eyes, and smile, swaying, the pain in my shattered shoulder and my jaw, the bites on my leg – all forgotten.

'Not in a million years,' she says. 'And certainly not today. Get out of here.'

Stumbling, I follow her through the twisting maze of alleys, breathing sweet morning air, blinking in the light, and feeling the sun on my face. She says nothing, and drops back behind me. When I turn to thank her at the outskirts of the favela, she has gone.

I stagger, reborn, on to the street.

*I am twenty-seven. For once I am early for work. Hugging my arms around my battered body, I walk past the clay football pitch, staring dully at the rubbish heap behind the ramshackle goal posts.*

*On a wall, pasted over innumerable faded old images, is a poster advertising a party tonight to celebrate the launch of MaxiBudget – to take place at the Beehive, round the corner.*

*My shoulder is bleeding, my chest hurts with every breath I take, I have lost a shoe, and I am covered in urine and vomit.*

*I feel OK.*

★

I should go home, but the office is closer. Never have I been so glad to see the restored block, the security gates that encircle it, or the avocado tree behind the gates, its branches sprawling like splayed tentacles over the road. I feel automatically in my pocket for my entry pass.

'May I help you, Senhor?' The guard's voice is metallic through the microphone that enables him to remain safely behind bulletproof glass. Unless you're a cleaner, arriving on foot is suspicious. The guards let me into the car park every day, but they don't know me – they only know my car.

'Good morning, er . . . who is this? I can't see you.'

'Can I help you?' the voice repeats. 'The party isn't until tonight. Come back later. Good day.'

'I work here. But as you can see, I've had an accident. I have been mugged, and held hostage. My name is Ludo dos Santos – you can check it on the register.'

A small aperture in the window shoots open, enough for me to see the guard's face. He's someone I haven't seen before, possibly a new employee. Though I'm not sure I'd even recognise one of the regulars – I drive past and wave at the glass each morning without seeing the person behind it.

'If you haven't got a pass I can't let you through.'

'I know how I look, but I'm an employee of this company.'

'I am paid to let people in when they have a security pass. And not to let them in when they do not. If I may say so, you don't even look fit to clean the building. And you stink,' he adds, helpfully.

'If you call my boss, Oscar Cascavel, he'll tell you that I work here.'

'I'm not calling anyone.'

'Please! I have been kidnapped.'

'Come on, Senhor, you're going to have to do better than that. I've been a doorman for years. There's no story you can tell me that I haven't heard before.'

'Just let me in.'

'No way. Now you need to leave before I get my gun out, OK?'

'You're going to get your gun out?'

'If I have to.'

'You're going to get your gun out.'

'There. What did I tell you?'

I'm staring down the barrel of an automatic pistol, which is poking through a tiny aperture in the security glass.

'Please leave now,' he says. 'I don't want to have to shoot you.'

I stumble through the morning air, noting the song of starlings and the bright green flash of a parakeet above my head, until I somehow manage to blag a payphone token from a person in the street. Huddling under the shelter of the phone's giant ear, I dial Oscar's office number.

'Ludo dos Santos. This is early in the morning for you. You haven't been to bed, have you? Where the hell have you been? Getting fucked up again?'

'I was kidnapped. In the favela. They tied me up.'

He laughs. 'That's the best one yet. Now get in here, you can explain it to me later. We've got lots on. The party is happening tonight, and your family are all coming.'

'You'll have to send someone down to let me in. The guard wouldn't because I lost my pass.'

'Good for him. They're under strict instructions not to let anyone in without one.'

'As I told you – I got mugged. They took my wallet. I don't look very good.'

Oscar sighs. 'You really are hopeless, Ludo. If it wasn't for your father . . . I'll send someone down.'

The guy waiting behind the gates – one of Oscar's minions, an up and coming executive – is smirking before I even reach the door.

'Good morning Ludo – the boss told me you had a heavy night last night, but my God! You look as bad as I've ever seen you. Is that vomit? What happened to your face?'

'Thank you,' I murmur, tripping on the step as I am buzzed in through the gates.

My glare is met with silence from behind the smoked glass.

The receptionist looks up in alarm, ready to press her panic button, until she recognises me.

'Wow, Ludo. I can't wait to hear about this one,' she says. 'Did you get into a fight?'

'I'll tell you all about it as soon as I've had a shower.'

I had hoped to make it through the corridors relatively unscathed, but obviously Oscar has been doing the rounds, and the route to my office is lined with people who have come out to witness this supposedly catastrophic hangover – there are even cheers and applause as I walk towards my office door.

The building seems lighter than usual, the graffiti art more vivid than ever. The wave of good humour and hilarity slumps as I pass by and those thronging the corridors are able to smell me. I get through as quickly as I can, and close the door on a crowd whose mood is rapidly curdling from one of amusement to one of quiet disgust.

The message light is flashing on my phone.

I push the button, and listen as I peel off my stiff, congealed shirt, bunch it and throw it in the bin.

Message One: Oscar, yesterday. *Where the fuck are you? Listen, this party's happening. We've got all the food and drink lined up and we've leafleted the whole favela. I think it could be good, and I want you to throw yourself into it. Come and find me the second you get this.*

Message Two: Melissa, today. *Good morning! I wanted to get you nice and early so that I could be the first to say: Happy Birthday!*

*Call me. I'm going to be seeing you at this party tonight. As it's Ernesto's job as well as my parents' shining new project, not to mention your office, I suppose I'm going to have to be there several times over.*

*Also, listen: I know you told Ernesto the truth about . . . things. And I wanted to tell you that it was brave of you to do that. And that it helped. I think we're going to be fine.*

*Anyway, call me. I love you.*

Christ. It's my birthday.

# Party Food

*I am twenty-seven.*
  *No, I am twenty-eight.*
  *My God, has it been that long?*

I take a long shower, then I hide in my office for an hour, licking my wounds. Finally I venture outside, naked from the waist up, to buy a cold Coke. The vending machine sits in an alcove that, beneath its fixing resin, bears the blood spray of a heroin injection administered during the building's previous existence. I collect a fresh shirt from the company stockpile and return to my office, then pour Coke in a glass and dilute it with *cachaça*, drinking enough to take myself one step back from recent experience. Barring what was fed to me in the favela I haven't eaten since yesterday lunchtime, but for some reason my hunger has died. I remove the foul shirt from its plastic wrapping and put it on, and after some more drink and a couple of strong painkillers I start to feel better. Even with my attendance record I would be justified in taking the afternoon off today, but there's no point in going home only to have to come back again later.

Tonight is the night. The agency is buzzing with it.

We often hold parties in celebration of the acquisition of new pieces of business, but this one is different. We have never opened our doors like this. Tonight, everyone comes together, those who will work on the project, those who have developed it, and those who will benefit from it.

I am looking over some concepts Oscar has left in my office, getting to grips with the work and squirming against the office shirt, when Flávia's head appears in my doorway. She's not wearing her shapeless smock, but a cream-coloured dress that must be her Sunday best. Mindful of our last conversation, I steel myself for a frosty encounter, but her mind seems to be elsewhere. She looks exhausted – which is not surprising given what happened in her home last night.

'You look smart,' I say.

'You look terrible,' she says. 'I thought I had a bad night.'

'What happened to you?'

'You don't want to know. My useless, good-for-nothing son. His first night home after the shooting, and he gets into a fight with some bad-boy gang member. He can't help it. It's like he wants to destroy himself, just like his father. What happened to you?'

'Nothing I didn't deserve.'

As I'm speaking, she plucks my rubbish bin from the floor to empty it into her sack, and stares in horror at the solid lump of shirt it contains.

'Lord Almighty. This is not what I'm paid to clean up. Didn't I tell you to stop drinking? This is just the sort of crap that killed my husband.'

'I haven't been drinking. I got attacked.'

'You have to be so careful in this city,' she says, shaking the bin several times until the shirt drops like concrete into her sack. 'It's a war zone out there. Who did this to you?'

'Don't be too hard on your boy,' I say, wincing with the pain in my chest as I lean back in my chair. 'These situations happen without anybody wanting them to. You can't control it. You get drawn in.'

'Then you have to fight to get away!' she says, raising her voice and gesticulating with the bin. 'Swim against the tide, rather than letting it take you. Don't be lazy. That's what I say to Milton, not that it makes any difference.'

'It's good advice. I'm sure he will heed it one day.'

She makes a face that is both disgusted, and very sad. 'I don't want to talk about him. Stupid boy. I want to look forward to my party. I haven't been to a party in ages.'

Amazingly, in spite of what has happened, she still seems to be in a good mood, animated at the prospect of attending an office event for once rather than cleaning up after it.

'That girl I met when I came to the favela. She's your daughter?'

'No. She has the same father as Milton, but a different mother. I take care of her.' She pauses in the middle of setting the bin back down, and looks at me. 'Why do you ask?'

'No reason. Just interested.'

'It's not more survey stuff? I warned you about that.'

'Of course not. It's just friendly interest.'

'OK then. See you at the party. If you're lucky I might even dance with you.'

She giggles at her own remark in a way that makes me beam at her big, retreating back. My jaw hurts.

It's Friday night. A beautiful pollution sunset bathes the city in pinks and reds and oranges that glint in shards off the skyscraper glass. Helicopters take to the air like fat flies, shuttling the rich to their weekend homes. But one helicopter won't be heading out of town tonight, not yet, at least. It has a social obligation first, here in the city. Tonight, my twenty-eighth birthday will be celebrated at a party launching a new subsidised supermarket scheme for the poor. Zé Generoso, its architect, will be there, as will its inspiration, his wife Rebecca. Flávia will be there, representing the grass-roots of the project, its target. There is every possibility that her son Milton will also be in attendance. Oscar will be there, trying to impress Zé. Ernesto will be there, fretting about any one of twenty things. Melissa will be there.

Lighting rigs and a backlit stage lend shallow glitz to the reception area, which has also been decked out with the preliminary executions of the new campaign printed on large plastic boards. Our aeroplane-wing reception desk has been decorated to resemble a chrome supermarket shelf, doubling as part of a long buffet bar. Women totter on heels and men preen in suits, waiting to put on a show. Zé Generoso himself is coming. And as usual, his generosity will know no bounds. Anyone from the local favela is invited to come in and have a drink and something to eat, so that they can be briefed about this thing that is coming to change their lives.

People have taken me aside over the course of the afternoon and told me that they think this will be 'an emotional occasion'. What are they expecting? Starving children and humble women and their meek, respectful husbands, so bowled over by the generosity of this marginally cheaper supermarket that they weep quietly as a mark of their gratitude? However it has happened, the mood is charged. Oscar probably sent round a memo of motivation, demanding gravitas. But who are we fooling? It's going to be a social occasion, with a few impoverished chancers bussed in to make everybody else feel better, and themselves just hoping for a decent meal and a good time. It will be undignified. It will be voyeuristic. It will be embarrassing.

I had thought the dinner would somehow reflect the kind of food available in store, but instead, someone has taken on my half-joking suggestion that our largest clients should each sponsor a course. A printed menu is tacked to the wall. Tonight's starter of beef rump with papaya salsa is brought to us by Limpia detergent. The main course of salt cod with its reduction of black beans comes courtesy of UltraBanco. There follows a cleansing sorbet of rainforest fruits, offered by MaxiMarket itself, and a dessert of hot *tiramisu* in association with the BonBon chocolate company. Each course will be served buffet-style from the wing of the bomber while Oscar gives a brief audio-visual presentation outlining the campaign.

Initially, it looks like nobody's going to turn up. Excited agency people circle round one another in party dresses and pressed shirts, making half-hearted attempts to mingle with the members of the cleaning and security staff who congregate to the side in an uneasy group. I recognise the guard who denied me entry earlier in the day and raise a glass to him across the lobby. He raises his in return, looking nervous. I imagine most of them are wondering what the hell they are doing here. I wonder who's supposed to be protecting the place if they're all in here drinking with the rest of us. Then I remember that Zé is coming. Arrangements will have been made.

And then I spot them – my adoptive parents. Zé is surrounded by a group of eager young acolytes, nodding and beaming with Rebecca to his side. He looks as tanned and healthy as ever, exuding control and good humour. Rebecca does not look so good. The halogen lighting of the office does not flatter her china complexion. Zé spots me and charges over, dragging his wife with him.

'My boy,' he says, embracing me. 'I'm genuinely pleased to see you. It feels like an age. How are you keeping? I hear from Oscar that you're doing well. And Melissa tells me that you two keep in touch.'

'It's wonderful to see you both,' I say.

'You look tired, Ludo,' says Rebecca, who looks shattered. 'And your chin – is that a bruise? Are you taking care of yourself?' She kisses me on both cheeks, and I feel a brief flicker of childish comfort, remembering how she would emerge from the helicopter on Friday evenings, her arms outstretched, and envelop me in scent.

'I'm fine,' I say. 'How are you?'

'I'm better than I have been,' she says. 'Ernesto is doing a wonderful job of easing some of my burden with the Foundation. He seems to be taking to it well.'

'Glad to hear it. Well! This!' I say, gesturing round at the lobby. 'It's a tremendous new direction. Bringing both of your worlds together. It's very exciting.'

'You don't know how delighted I am to hear you say that,' says Zé. 'I've been having trouble persuading her that we're doing it for anything other than profit. It is, as I keep saying, an *evolution*. It makes sense.'

He looks triumphantly at me and back to his wife, who shrugs through a cloud of medication. She looks as though she's finally given in to him, and I can't say I blame her. It's impossible to resist him for ever.

'Of course,' Zé continues, 'not everybody sees it that way.'

'What do you mean?'

'Oscar tells me there could be violence tonight. Have you heard about this?'

'No.'

'The police went into a favela near here last night, and shot someone. Retaliating for something – I don't even know what. But the mood is not good. We were even advised to call off the event, can you believe it? I refused point blank. We're not the police. We're here to help them. They shouldn't blame whatever happened on us.'

'What does Oscar think about this?'

Zé laughs. 'He's nervous about letting some of these kids run loose in his building, but I told him to just shut up and do it. He's always been something of an old woman.'

'That's an absurd worry, given the history of this place.'

'True – but you never know with these people. I've tried to make my peace with them, but they can be . . . volatile.'

'How have you tried to make peace with them?'

He gives me a conspiratorial smile. 'You know how it is. You can't get anything done in these communities without engaging with the gangs in some way.'

'So what did you do?' I ask.

'You've heard of this outfit, the Shadow Command?'

'What about them?'

He takes a big gulp of the drink in his hand. 'I offered them a percentage point of every sale we make in the MaxiBudget supermarkets.'

'Seriously?'

'Of course. Nothing would get done otherwise. Think of it as ground rent. You can't own land in these places anyway, so this is the alternative – it means we shouldn't get our windows shot out in the first week. In fact, I wouldn't be surprised if the Shadow Command responded very violently to anyone jeopardising this project. It's like having your own police force – but better!'

'You've thought of everything,' I say.

'You *have* to,' he says, putting an arm around my shoulder, which makes me wince with pain, though I try not to show it. 'You have to be prepared. That's why we've got tremendous security here tonight; rented from Angel Park. Just in case. I've even got a couple of snipers installed. If anyone starts causing trouble they can be taken out in seconds.'

I stare at him. 'Snipers? What sort of trouble are you expecting?'

'None – although you can't throw open the doors to everyone without a few unsavoury characters getting through. But I sincerely doubt there'll be a problem after the deal I've struck. And Ernesto has been taking steps to keep everyone sweet.'

'Very thorough.'

'You know, that boy has come on tremendously in the last few years. I'm proud to have him as a son-in-law.'

'He's a good friend of mine, as you know.'

'And I'm very proud of you too, Ludo. I hope you know that. You've turned into a fine young man. I can see you running all of this one day.'

'Thank you.'

At this point Oscar dives into the conversation, surrounded by snapping shoals of colleagues who all want a dose of the Zé Generoso charm. I take it as my opportunity to move away before Zé has the chance to attempt further awkward compliments.

Dennis is crossing the lobby with a beer in his hand. 'What do you think?' he says, gesturing around him.

'Very impressive,' I say. 'Especially given how little time you had to put it together.'

'And how little help I had,' he says, pointedly.

'I'm sorry about that. I've had an odd couple of days.'

'I'm sure you have,' he says, pausing and looking me in the eye. 'Do you know what I did today? I finally got up the courage to ask the concierge at the Windsor Hotel if I'd had a call girl up to the room since I'd been in residence. He said the only person who'd been up there the whole time was you.'

'You have to admire their discretion, don't you? That kind of old-fashioned service is hard to come by these days.'

'I guess it is,' he says, looking puzzled.

'Now, I don't know about you, but I need a drink. Again – well done. It's great to have you on the team.'

I leave him as quickly as I can, and approach the bar. Tonight it will be vodka on the rocks. Vodka is what reminds me of Melissa – of that glass beading with condensation in the tree house on her wedding night. It conjures her.

I turn away from the bar with my drink, and as if on cue, there they are, arriving, having just got past the front-door security. It has been years since I saw them together, and I expected the sight to fill me with bile, but it doesn't. Of course it doesn't. These are my friends, and they fit each other perfectly.

They both smile and approach, and I embrace the two of them at once – Melissa, warm and loving; Ernesto, his great bear arm around my neck, forgiving me.

'Are we going to be OK?' I say to him.

'We're going to be fine. What the hell happened to you?'

'Nothing. It's nothing. So long as I'm forgiven.'

'You're forgiven,' he says.

I wonder what Melissa has been telling him about how screwed up I am that I should earn such swift absolution. Whatever it is, I'll take it.

'Happy birthday,' they both say.

They have brought me a gift, which I open. It's a gold watch, with my initials engraved on the back.

'I have never owned a watch.' I realise this for the first time as the words come out.

'We noticed,' says Melissa.

'I don't know what to say.'

'Don't say anything. Just put it on.'


The lobby starts to fill up with guests, all of whom have in common the fact that they are wondering how to behave. The smartly dressed are eating the food and chatting, but looking uneasy at the increasing swell of people they wouldn't normally see except when they're having their windscreen washed at the traffic lights. And these people, tentative at first, begin to dominate the event, drinking and eating, dancing to the music, until eventually they are enjoying it without reservation. The building seems to be evolving yet again, right before my eyes.

Then the lights dim, the screen lights up, and the audio-visual presentation begins. Deep, sad string music plays against a scene of street poverty. Children cry and wail. The camera focuses in on a pathetic mound of rotting fruit peel topping off a rubbish heap buzzing with insects. We pan back on a dried-up river bed, clotted with plastic bags. Then, appearing like a sun over the horizon, the beaming contours of the MaxiBudget logo come into view, and the mournful strings are replaced by uptempo electronic music, and the children's faces break into smiles as they find themselves in a Garden Of Eden. Fresh fruit and vegetables are piled in abundant heaps. Calves and piglets run around green fields. And, in bold, coloured lettering, we are asked: *MaxiBudget – What Have You Got To Lose?*

Oscar takes to the stage, his squat form lit by the final, joyous images of the presentation, a smug grin smeared on his face like the evidence of something eaten in secret.

'Ladies and gentlemen, welcome! This is a special night – but it is only the beginning. So I won't speak for long. I just want to welcome our esteemed guests this evening, in particular our patrons, Senhor Zé Fischer Carnicelli and his beautiful wife Rebecca, who are the architects of the MaxiBudget project, and to whom we are so grateful for the opportunity to communicate its benefits. It's wonderful to have you here.'

Looking around I notice that the majority of the guests are mystified by Oscar's speech – they have no idea what this evening is for. All they know is that it's a free party, with free food. After some initial interest, they start to talk over Oscar, but I can hear him.

'I also want to thank Ludo dos Santos, whose unique insight into the issues facing the inhabitants of these communities, helped in part through his in-depth research with another of our employees,' (he checks his piece of paper) 'Flávia Pereira de Souza, have helped us to crack this project. Thanks to them, we have really got under the skin of our future consumers.'

Hardly anyone is listening. The crowd is talking away, and the tide of people in the room seems to be getting larger and larger. A crush is developing at the door.

'This venture,' he goes on, lowering his voice to a hushed, reverential tone, 'will break down walls. Will bring us closer together. Please – keep your voices down for a moment. Just for a moment, ladies and gentlemen!' I see a flash in the darkness behind him as one of the snipers on the balcony adjusts the grip on his weapon.

'And finally,' says Oscar, 'I wouldn't normally advertise this, but I thought I would tell you, since nobody else will, that I am sixty years old today. So here's to me.' Laughter rolls around the room and into a smooth wave of applause. 'Enjoy the evening,' he says. 'Eat! Drink!'

The room, the crowd, the noise – all recede from my consciousness, as if I have taken a step backwards, into myself. I stand, staring at the empty stage, my hand frozen in front of me holding my drink, and I hear Ernesto's and Melissa's comments as if they are being phoned in from another world.

('I never liked that guy,' says Melissa. 'Didn't he use to try and feel up your mother back on the farm?'

'He didn't even mention me, the little worm,' says Ernesto. 'Did you know his birthday was the same as yours?')

A terrible realisation is taking root, and as much as I want to ignore it, the thought is growing fast, choking my brain like a weed. And though I am screaming in my head, telling my mind to STOP WORKING, it's too late. The idea exists.

It is expanding, feeding on the supporting evidence, gaining shape and substance.

I see Oscar, a young man, in desperation, coming to his friend, the young and promising Zé Generoso, already a player even now, in his thirties . . .

*I have messed up, my friend.*

*What's the matter? says Zé.*

*A girl. She says I knocked her up. What am I going to do?*

*You idiot. You fool. OK – we'll think of something. We'll work it out. Don't panic. Can she cook, this girl?*

*Yes, she can cook. She cooks like a dream.*

*OK. That's good. We need someone on the farm. She can have the baby and come and live with us out there. We'll take her on.*

*You mean it?*

*Of course. That way you can see the child when you like – make sure it's doing well.*

*Zé. I will owe you for ever.*

As easy as that, I see it happening. Zé Generoso lives up to his name once more – and Oscar is in debt to him for life. He will work for nothing on every one of Zé's projects, whatever it may be – even if it's a grand, misguided venture designed to show his wife that he has a heart.

And although Oscar will be so ashamed from then on that he hates me every time he looks at me, he will keep on looking.

There was a reason that my mother panicked after she told me that I shared the same birthday as my father.

That reason is that I might one day discover his identity.

Because I know him. Because he's the man I found with his hands on her in the kitchen.

The news is blinding.

Zé wasn't the one keeping me in my job after all. It was

my reluctant father. The one to whom I was smoothly passed on as soon as my mother had died, without even realising it.

Oscar, who tells me to make him proud at the end of every meeting.

Oscar, whose look of frustration when I fail him goes far beyond the disappointment of a boss.

Oscar. Filthy, small-minded, foul-minded Oscar.

No wonder I recognised the background to that photograph – it was taken in the kitchen on the farm. Not in any favela.

With Oscar's words, all the exotic fathers in my head, patient teachers whose love was transmitted to me through my mother over the years, wither and curl to nothing like photographs on a fire.

I can picture the conversation that led to my adoption, too:

*I am worried, Zé. The boy's brain is turning to mush out here. He struggles to answer even basic questions. He gibbers like an idiot. What can I do about it?*

*Let me talk to Rebecca. We might be able to come up with something.*

*Zé Generoso. Once again, I am speechless.*

What other secret conversations and agreements did I miss? What pacts did Oscar make with my mother? What threats over her? How did they meet? Whatever mundane, disappointing truth lies here, I don't want to know it yet.

The sleight of hand of it: all of them in collusion, to lead me here, and for what? To shield me from the fact that I'm related to that poor little man? The fact that I was unintended, not born of love?

Milton. Dennis. I've been lashing out at alternative versions of myself wherever I found them – but this is the only person I was ever going to be. I've been home all along. It's like being a piece on a chessboard with only one square.

'I have to go,' I say, hearing the protests of Melissa and Ernesto like muffled sounds from another room.

I cross the lobby in a daze, vaguely aware that the mood is becoming more frenetic, that a scuffle has broken out at the door. A couple of kids in basketball vests and shorts have taken the microphone from the stage and are expertly rapping over the music. Suddenly, against all the odds, it feels like a real party. I see Oscar trying to make conversation with some boys and being physically joshed around. He's trying to make light of it but I can tell he's nervous.

I have to get home.

When I finally make it through the crush at the door and out on to the street, I can hardly believe what I see. A riot is breaking out at the front of the building. So many people are trying to get in that it looks like a Carnival procession. A sound system has been set up on the pavement, and one enterprising man has set up a grill on which he is cooking enormous red sausages. The branches of the avocado tree are being shaken. Some people are dancing on cars. Two police vans are parked at the end of the street, warily surveying events. Already I can see that things will turn ugly.

I walk away down the street, far enough that the noise begins to die down, and look back. The crowd at the front of the building surges back and forth like a storming battalion. Smoke rises from the hotdog stand. A huge bang rings out as someone lets off a firework, which lights up the bright green foliage of the avocado tree from inside as it detonates.

I walk away, and keep walking for twenty minutes, past shabby condominiums and a dusty park until I reach a freeway, where after several attempts I manage to persuade a taxi to stop, and brave the furious horns of the slowing cars behind him, and take me home. The flyover seems to rise so high that I might get vertigo.

When I enter my apartment I realise straight away that something is wrong, but it takes me a minute to work out what it is: the silence. The place is quieter than it has ever been. The gas-powered fridge I inherited from my mother, whose whining and groaning has provided the backdrop to life in this place ever since I moved in, has finally died. The amount of relief I feel that the noise has finally stopped surprises me.

It means the freezer is also out. And that means that the time has come to eat the last of my mother's leftovers. Of the tubs I brought back from the farm after she died, one remains. It is unlabelled, but whatever it contains is bound to be delicious. I have never been able to bring myself to open it. I suppose I have been waiting for a push like this.

I take out the tub and leave it in hot water to thaw. Leaving the lights off, I take a candle and a bottle of beer outside to sit under my canopy of plants. I inhale deeply. The air is full of feather-light particles that could be water or dust or pollution.

I run my hands over my skull, feeling its knobs and protuberances. My blood is heavy. My limbs feel as if they were lined with lead. Reaching up to the birdcage, I flick open the door and try once more to entice my fat little parakeet to fly away. The stupid thing won't move. He flits away from my reach to cringe on the other side of his cage.

I will consume my mother's last meal out here. I will dine with her one last time, before I ask Zé for the truth tomorrow. Then we'll see where we are.

My phone rings. I do not answer.

When the message comes through I hit the speakerphone,

and let Melissa's voice ring out over the darkened balcony. She's having to shout, almost to scream, to be heard over the jarring, thumping background music.

'Ludo, I don't know whether you're still here, but we're leaving. This thing is getting out of hand. We have the helicopter waiting on the roof and my father told me to find you . . . My God! Did you hear that? I think someone just fired a gun. If you are here, get to the roof if you want to come with us. Papai says it's going to be like the Saigon airlift.'

I stop the message before it comes to an end.

There will be a last encounter with a treasured friend. A last swallow of your favourite food. A last kiss from the love of your life. Most of the time you won't know when it's the last time. But tonight I do – so I can make sure it's done right. It will be a singular sensation, tasting my mother's love for the final time just when I am questioning it the most. On one hand, I have found out that she lied to me for all of my life. On the other, I know that she was only part of a grander plan, of which she was never the principal architect.

I go to the kitchen area and open the carton. The smell of congealed fat rises from inside. Something offally and unpleasant. What was I expecting? This thing has been frozen for years. It's inedible. I will have to find something else to eat.

I drink my beer, which has warmed up in the dead fridge. A newscaster's voice drowns in the janitor's radio downstairs – I can just make out something about violence at the opening of a new charity initiative.

Everything will be different tomorrow. From tomorrow I cease to be a passenger. I'm going to talk to Oscar, and hand in my resignation. And if he confirms that I'm his son then I'm going to resign from that position too.

I sit, watching yet more weekend helicopters vectoring

smoothly overhead: their casual straight lines; the simplicity of their existence. I imagine a stinger missile shooting up out of the favela, bringing one down. I picture the machine, mortally wounded, spinning out of the sky with crippled rotors.

There's plenty to think about. But for now, there are simple pleasures to enjoy. My beer. These plants. A grilled bird, sticky in my fingers. The hot, sweet air, full of fumes and hope. The beauty of this vast city at night, and all the possibility it contains.

# Acknowledgements

The author gratefully acknowledges the invaluable advice and encouragement of Clare Alexander, Nick Armstrong, Jean-Paul Burge, Louise East, Sam Gilpin, James Gurbutt, Oliver Harris, Henry Hitchings, Carolyn Lindsay, Margaret Stead, Ellie Steel and Jonathan Wise.